# THE GOLDEN ROAD

## RICHARD RYAN

RICHARD RYAN

# THE GOLDEN ROAD

**NO EXIT PRESS**

This edition published in 2002 by No Exit Press
18 Coleswood Road, Harpenden, Herts, AL5 1EQ

www.noexit.co.uk

A CIP catalogue record for this book is available from the British Library.

ISBN 1-84243-045-9 The Golden Road

2 4 6 8 10 9 7 5 3 1

Printed by Omnia, Glasgow.

Typography by Able Solutions (UK) Ltd, Birmingham.

# One

**I WOKE UP** just as the bearded trainman was dragging me across the boxcar. He wore a dark cap with the black and red emblem of the Chicago and Northwestern Railroad.

"Fucking bum," he said as he pulled my arms.

I was dazed and still waking up. I wanted to tell him that he should clean up his language. I meant to say something about the damage he was doing to my designer expedition boots, but the open door of the boxcar was suddenly before me. He was holding me by the front of my shirt, his pock-marked face inches away from mine. I tried to wiggle free of him and couldn't. He grinned as he pushed me out of the car, and I could see the glitter from a gold tooth. The airstream of the speeding train caught me and spun me around toward the cascading rush of colors.

This shouldn't have been happening to me, I said to myself, and I tried to swim through the air to safety. Then I got slammed, as if someone hit my entire body with a board. I heard the air go out of my lungs.

I gasped for breath, and everything went dark.

I woke up scared. It was still dark, and somehow I thought the dark might go away, and the movie run backward, taking me into the daylight and the rush of colors and then to the train and the grinning brakeman waiting like death itself. I grabbed a rock beside me to keep from swirling backward into the light. I held onto that rock as if it were my best girl friend. The drone of cicadas finally convinced me that this was merely night and that I was alive and perhaps safe. I sat up slowly. I hurt everywhere. My skin felt as though it were on fire. But I didn't have any big pains. Beginning with my toes and fingers, I made little movements up and down my body. Cautiously I stood up.

"Bloodied but unbowed," I said to the bugs and the trees.

It was a literary remark, and I couldn't remember the source. I knew I was all right.

I patted my shirt pockets for my pad and pencil. The man in the sporting goods shop had been right. No one opened these pockets but their owner. I could feel the shape of my notebook inside. In the morning I wanted to write down a summary of the boxcar episode, just as I had written down everything else since I left Louisiana.

It just didn't seem possible to be having an adventure in the middle of the United States. At least not in the 1970s. Ours was the wrong time for adventure. Writing it all down somehow made it convincing.

I was ready to sit back against a tree and think about what had gone on since I walked out of my apartment and into the rather improbable life of a treasure hunter. Then I remembered the gold.

I reached inside my shirt and felt for the straps that held the leather pouch. I groped around the way I had once reached for the chain that held my gold cross when I was religious. I couldn't find anything but my dirty flesh I took off my shirt and felt more slowly, rubbing across my chest in patterns. I moved calmly and slowly, the way a person who's trying to lower his blood pressure breathes.

But there wasn't any strap or any leather bag of gold. I fumbled my pants off and shook them. I struck a match and squatted on the ground. No bag. No glitters from any coins responded to the flickering light of my matches. I patted the ground in widening circles. The match burned my thumb and index finger. I shook it away.

The dark seemed a lot deeper then. The sound of the cicadas got louder, like a chorus pronouncing a moral. Smart people got paid for their adventures, but like the absent-minded fool I was, I'd lost my pay. All those people had died, and their money was gone. I snapped my shirt pocket open and tossed my pad into the brush. Notes—what a joke. I wanted to stand up and scream my name to the stars, but the night was overcast.

When I woke up the next morning, I felt dry and dusty. I had slept under some bushes not twenty feet from the railroad tracks. I was still in my undershorts and had used my pants for a pillow. God, but I felt awful. Jason's survival training had prepared me for discomfort, but at least he had showers. It had been—what?—three days since I'd bathed. I glanced at my watch, but the crystal was smashed.

I tried to go over events; I began by counting out days on my fingers so that I might know how much time had elapsed since the meeting on July 22, 1979. But I got lost in the days. There was Mr. Johnson explaining the price of gold, and then here was Howard telling me this, and

6

Sylvie Mae telling me that. Then both of them were gone.

I stood up to get dressed and saw a movement in the brush.

I took a step and was about to run away. For the first time since I'd left St. Louis, I was scared.

I didn't want something bad to happen, and I especially didn't want something bad to happen when I didn't have most of my clothes on. It was embarrassing to be attacked in the nude.

I saw the movement again, though it wasn't so much a movement as a flash.

Of course.

Artie Hokum's leather bag of gold lay open in the brush like something you might find at the end of the rainbow. Krugerrands were scattered around. When the sunlight hit them, they flashed and glittered like a scene from fairyland. I counted them out. There were ninety-nine Krugerrands. Gold was around $300 an ounce. I had about $30,000, and things looked a trifle better.

One coin was missing, but who cared? I hoped that it would be found by someone down on his luck. I had thirty grand. Thirty big ones. I had fleeced the gold from the golden fleecer.

Half naked, I did a rough pirouette and bowed to the brush and the railroad tracks and the absent figure of Jason Rotbart.

"I won, you son of a bitch. I won," I yelled to the brush and the bright day.

I put the coins back in the leather pouch. Though the fall had opened the case, it and its straps were still intact, and I took that as an omen. I hung one strap over my neck and pulled the other tight and buckled it so that the bag felt snug against my chest. I put on my shirt over the small leather pack and got dressed in the rest of my clothes. I found my notebook and snapped it back in my shirt pocket.

I looked around for the sights and sounds of civilization, but the railroad tracks seemed to be in the middle of nothing but farm fields. I couldn't see any roads or towns, so I walked along the tracks, figuring that they would bring me to something.

As the day warmed up, I started to feel good for the first time in weeks. Beginning with the waist-high thistles at the edge of the railroad bed and extending out to the grid of the cornfields and the hazy blue

7

beyond, the scene was predictable and comforting. A mile in front of me, a grain elevator stood like a grey abstraction of a church. It had a sign advertising Old Timer's Pigfeed.

*Three, zero, zero, zero, zero* I said over and over to myself. The numbers coincided with my steps; and soon each step became a coin, and each coin took me $300 from my past life.

# Two

**MY STORY BEGAN** with the ad in the Personals section of the Sunday paper. It was a rainy Sunday. I was bored and, for no particular reason, reading the entire paper.

> *EXPEDITION—Men of QUALITY sought.*
>
> *After numerous EXPEDITIONS in SEARCH of GOLD and precious METALS in the UNEXPLORED UPPER AMAZON BASIN, my last Expedition ISOLATED A PROMISING Andes Mountain Region that I Believe could provide enormous OPPORTUNITIES for GOOD MEN willing to WORK HARD and COURT DANGER.*
>
> *UNPREDICTABLE NATIVES make it Imperative that I Select only FELLOW COUNTRYMEN that I can DEPEND on to WREST our Fortunes from the Dangerous and Bloody earth.*
>
> *OUR ENDEAVORS in this remote, difficult, but FABULOUSLY PROMISING REGION will require a COMMITMENT of one year. My MEN will be PARTNERS in this VENTURE with me. This is an OPPORTUNITY to become RICH beyond your WILDEST dreams.*
>
> *My PARTNERS will be required to pay expenses and travel costs in exchange for a lifetime of my EXPERIENCE and KNOWLEDGE.*
>
> *INFORMATION will be available at a PUBLIC MEETING to be held at the PARADISE MOTEL. It will begin PROMPTLY at 21:00 hours, 22 JULY.*

There wasn't an address, as if to say that adventurers who couldn't find the Paradise Motel weren't worthy of a cause printed in italics and capital letters.

It would have been easy to make fun of the ad. What an amusing story to tell at a cocktail party. But I was tired of feeling superior to everything. The ironic after awhile is as boring as the enthusiastic.

Look, I was an actor in St. Louis. That says it all, doesn't it? I was equally far from Hollywood and New York, and equally unlikely to get a job in either city.

What's more, I was in the troupe of what the *Post-Dispatch* said was (I think I remember the quote exactly) "arguably the third-best acting company in the city."

Really. Third best in a third-best city. And I wasn't even at the top of this very small heap. I wasn't even Polonius for someone else's Hamlet or even, for that matter, Rosencrantz or Guildenstern. I was Osric maybe. Most often I was a Gentleman, a Gentleman that would enter, stand silently while the play went on and then, in brackets, exit. I played people who didn't quite matter in an acting company that mattered even less. In college, we called actors like me Spears. Which is what we held as we stood behind the hero.

"Owen," one of my friends told me. "You're in several kinds of trouble. The first is your name. You can't turn *Owen* into a nickname of any kind. Second, your hair looks too good. It's too thick; you make all the men who are going bald nervous. And that's like making over half the male population nervous. Third, you've got a pompous voice. Every time somebody hears you, they'll think you're about ready to discuss hemorrhoids or dental floss."

"I sound like I ought to be a president," I said.

"No," he said, "more like a presidential candidate. A presidential candidate who doesn't make it through the primaries."

Well, how would you feel?

I hadn't started out to be mediocre, God knows. I mean, who does? Even Millard Fillmore must've aimed higher than he ended up.

I had good grades in high school and two letters from the track team. I even had the goodwill of Mr. Fosbeck, the guidance counselor. He wanted me to be the Senior Class President.

"Owen, you're the perfect candidate. You look good, and you've never been in trouble."

He smiled and added, almost as an afterthought, "And besides, you've never had any ideas."

10

You see why I wanted out, why I wanted a new version of my life? I wanted to be something besides a cipher for other people's mediocre dreams. I wanted to have an idea I could put to use. The trouble was, I hadn't taken any courses in accounting or investment banking or computer engineering. I didn't know how to do real jobs for pay. All I could do was memorize a script and walk across a stage as if I lived there. What I didn't know how to do was go to the Personnel Department and ask for a job.

Vern Clark, who was the closest thing to a rebel at Elmira High School, talked me into trying out for the school play. I was Ben in *Death of a Salesman*. You know the character. He's the one who claims, "When I walked into the jungle, I was seventeen. When I walked out I was twenty one. And, by God, I was rich." That was my first play, and I've never forgotten those lines.

Vern—goddamn his foolish, rebellious soul—caused me no end of problems. He was Happy in the play and trouble everywhere else. His last piece of business, before getting kicked out of school for good, was forming The We-Don't-Have-To-Take-This-Anymore Party complete with hyphens in the correct places.

"Always strengthens your cause if your punctuation is correct," Vern said then.

Vern researched the school's Constitution, which (as I recall) said that students had the right to govern themselves. Vern took this to mean that we could decide how to spend the student government fee. Vern had become a Communist and thought we should invite the head of the Communist Party so we could hear the other side.

Well, you can imagine the fuss this caused in 1960, but Vern held to his argument and talked me into running for Senior Class President on the platform of returning the students' money to the students.

"Owen, you've disappointed me," Mr. Fosbeck told me. "While I knew you were tall, I never thought you had so much ambition."

"The Constitution supports us," Vern told everyone. "It says we can do this in the Constitution."

Mr. Fosbeck finally ended it all.

"I don't care," he told our Assembly one Wednesday morning, "what the Constitution says. People who write constitutions always say things like that. They don't mean anything. It's just words."

And that was that. Vern was gone from school by Thursday. By Monday, we had a new Happy, and I kept on leaving the jungle rich, or at least I did on the Elmira High School stage.

The newspaper ad about South America meant that, perhaps, I really *could* leave the jungle rich and that I could become rich without learning calculus. What's more, I could imagine a speaking part on a treasure hunt. It was the kind of a role I'd dreamed about. I could be tall for treasure. Vern would've been proud of me.

On the evening of July 22, I closed my thumb-worn copy of *Variety*, got in my Volvo, and drove to the Paradise Motel.

It was just close enough to the airport so that its ads could say "near the airport" and just far enough away to be called budget. It had been built in the early 1950s when its neighborhood was at the edge of the city and when the modest frontage road it now faced was a major highway. Like so much else from that period, the motel had been left in its peculiar little backwater. It now looked like the sort of place you'd come to drink or fornicate on a rainy afternoon.

I parked the Volvo next to a Trans Am with a golden eagle painted on its hood. My car was over ten years old and a model out of date. It looked like the kind of a car a diplomat from an impoverished country would drive and sounded a little puffy when it ran, but it didn't look bad from a distance.

Next to the Trans Am, however, it looked like a spinster librarian beside a bathing beauty. I wanted that Trans Am.

A ring of chairs was set up in the middle of the parking lot. Stale crackers and gritty cheese and styrofoam cups of warm soda were arranged on the dresser of a room that opened onto the parking lot. I'd guess that thirty men were wandering back and forth between the room and the arena of chairs.

These were not successful people. They never would've been taken for a group of corporate managers or a meeting of salesmen who'd met their quotas. No, they looked as if they'd just finished their shift and had stopped by the local tap for a boilermaker. Or perhaps they'd stopped by for a drink even though they hadn't worked any shifts for a while. Some of us that night were the men of no fixed address, the ones who came from their rooming houses and smelled of Old Spice and bourbon. Some of us were the men who spent their afternoons drinking pints of brandy with friends who'd been dead for years.

We all looked either a little too old or a little too heavy or a little too out of it for adventure. Some of us looked as though we'd have trouble walking over a bridge that spanned the Amazon; an expedition seemed out of the question.

"Good cheese, eh?" a man at my side offered.

"Right," I said. I thought my reply was sarcastic, but the man nodded his head and closed his eyes, as if in the ecstasies of Final Cheddar.

It was getting harder for me to be ironic. I wanted the Trans Am, and I wanted my opportunities all in capital letters. I wanted the serious nouns of that ad to apply in my life. Indeed, I even wanted the cheese. I was surprised to discover that I'd eaten three or four pieces and was disappointed to find that there wasn't any more when I went back for another helping.

Two of the men didn't belong to the group of prospective adventurers. One was heavy set and had a shaven head that looked like the thick point of an artillery shell. The other man was much smaller. He couldn't have been over five feet tall. He had long, spun white hair and moved as if his feet were padded. There was something slightly feminine and menacing about his presence, especially next to the Teutonic masculinity of the other man.

When the soda ran out, we all stood around the chairs but didn't sit down and didn't speak to each other. We looked down as if we'd just discovered how interesting the tops of our shoes were.

The small man walked quickly back and forth between the room and the parking lot. He brought out two large metal cases and then carried a portable screen to the front of the chairs and set it up. With a screen there, the area looked more focused, and we began to sit down. He unpacked a slide projector.

In a few minutes, the small man had finished setting up his show and slapped his hands together loudly, signaling the start of our meeting. The men who were still milling around shuffled to their seats like reluctant students on the first day of school.

"I'm Jason Rotbart," the small man said. He brought a kerosene lamp from one of his suitcases, set it on the camp table at the front of the chairs, and lit it. The other man closed the door of the room where the food had been. While we had waited, the sun had gone down. The western rim of the sky had an arc of orange bars.

Illuminated from below by the lantern light, Rotbart's face was full of shadows. As he moved, you could see the working of a muscular body. His hands seemed too large for his small frame. He flicked the projector on. The motorized lens ground back and forth as he brought the first slide into focus, and the image of a South American map appeared to the right and behind him.

"Men, I am not here tonight by choice. If I had my own way, I would go with my associate and some reliable natives and wrest my fortunes from the tentacles of that jungle the way great men always have."

As he spoke I was silently capitalizing his nouns. I was ready to believe that he had walked right out of a Rudyard Kipling story into the parking lot of the Paradise Motel and was about to lift me up and out of St. Louis into more money and more nouns than I've ever dreamed about. I mean, I wanted to go to South America right then and there.

"But, alas," he went on, "I shall not be able to enjoy the fruits of my years spent sojourning in the tropical climes. Gentlemen, I fear that I have hacked my way through some of the most despicable vegetation on the face of the earth for nothing. I have endured unnamable and untreatable diseases in vain. I've gone weeks without . . . ."

Something ended my recollections. Something was wrong.

I tripped on one of the railroad tracks and almost fell down.

Something in the present of the railroad tracks in Illinois was wrong.

There was a brightness somewhere calling me out of my reverie.

I looked to the left. A bird—was it a hawk?—swooped down toward its prey in a distant cornfield. Nearby, cows swished their tails as they slowly ambled about their pasture. A moment later, the bird rose in an ascending arc.

For the first time, I could see a road. A four-lane highway passed just beyond the grain elevator. I had a landmark. I could figure out a way to get home. The sun was to my left, and I realized that I was headed north with the road. That was it. The light was a sign. It was a symbol. I was about to be free, about to rejoin the ordinary life. Along that road was a hamburger, a Coke, and a place to sleep. I was going to be all right.

But no. The light wasn't metaphorical. It was there. It was ahead of me in the middle of the railroad tracks.

The merest flicker of light that caught a tiny fraction of the sun.

I kept on walking. It didn't make sense.

A light in broad daylight.

And then, making even less sense, another point of light appeared, beside the first one. I slowed down to see better and almost tripped again on a railroad tie.

I looked ahead. I stopped and stared. For a moment, I thought the lights were part of a train. But no, I realized, trains have only a single light. Besides, I couldn't hear any noise.

As I walked on, trying to recall what the front of a train looked like, the lights became part of a shape.

Oh, good God, the bearded trainman was waiting for me.

He held up a gold coin, which glittered in the sunlight. The other light came from the gold in the middle of his grin.

# Three

**I DON'T KNOW WHY**, but I kept walking toward him.

He must've been three hundred yards in front of me. He just stood there grinning and holding up the coin.

My mind was racing so fast it passed potential solutions the way an Indy car went by telephone poles.

He said something.

"What?" I yelled back. I walked a little faster to get in hearing range. I mean, that's how scared I was. I didn't have sense enough to run away. At that point, I probably could've made it.

"You lose this?" He held the coin toward me.

"What?" I asked again. My mind was slowing down, though it certainly didn't seem ready to be clever.

What could I do? I had to face him. He'd kill me if I tried to escape. He had tossed me off that train the way you might throw a Kleenex away.

It was suddenly too late to run. He could have friends hidden near me. He could have a gun.

I kept walking toward him.

"You heard me, bum."

"Yes," I muttered. "Yes," I repeated a little louder. I tried to sound sure of myself. I thought confidence might put him off.

Wasn't that what Rotbart's jungle survival course had taught us?

"Never run from an adversary," Rotbart told us in one of those rambling sessions he held after supper. We squatted on the ground.

Rotbart strode back and forth across the veranda in his jodhpurs and whacked a swagger stick against the palms of his hands to emphasize his points.

"Never run from an enemy," he repeated. "Running away gives the wogs a psychological advantage. They know you're frightened. Run toward them instead. Terrifies them. Turns the whole thing around. If they're armed, the chances of them hitting you are slim. Do you know how few people can hit anything with a gun, let alone a person who's moving toward them? Bob and weave. Threaten them."

That's what I did to the trainman, and it worked. I ran straight toward him at first, and then I cut back and forth across the tracks as I closed in on him. He put his hands out in front of him as if to stop me. He still smiled, but it was left over from another moment. His heart wasn't in it.

But what came next? I was trying to remember the script when I really didn't even know the name of the play. I hoped that he would just leave me alone.

Then I got lucky.

He ran into the brush along the track, and that made me remember what to do.

"If he runs away," Rotbart had told us, "you've got him. He's afraid. He may still try to get you, but he's scared. Keep after him. Move toward him and make a lot of noise. He won't be expecting that. He'll try to circle around you. It's a pattern as predictable as the seasons. Keep on after him."

I followed the trainman, even though every cell of my body seemed to urge me back the other way. But I kept going. I ran into the brush on the same side of the track and went crashing toward him. Small branches slapped my face.

I could hear the trainman in the brush. Rotbart had been right: he was trying to circle around behind me.

I decided then to bury the gold. Not all of it. I should keep, I told myself, enough to satisfy a robber.

I tried to memorize my location. It was as useless as trying to recall a particular wave on the ocean. All the bushes looked exactly like one another. Luckily, I had a rough idea of where north and south were, but my only real landmarks were the grain elevator in the distance, the Old Timer's Pigfeed sign, and the train tracks beside me.

I pulled the belt from my pants. It had a brass buckle ("Lacquered to hold its shine," the salesman in the outfitting store had told me). I ran out of the bushes to the edge of the hill beneath the railroad tracks. I was perhaps fifteen feet from the edge of the bushes then. I stretched the belt out on the ground so that its bright buckle was aimed toward the brush. I went back into the brush and dug a shallow hole with my hands. The belt pointed straight to that hole. With my Swiss Army

17

knife, I cut a branch and stuck it in the hole, leaf end down. That was another Rotbart idea: "An upside-down branch is like a neon sign to the person looking for it, but no one else will give it a second look."

I took two coins out of the case, put each in the toe of a shoe, and buried the rest of the gold—pouch and all—beside the twig. Then I stepped back a few feet from my cache. To someone standing right there, the markings of the belt and the twig were obvious, but as I stared up and down the expanse of gravel that went into both distances as far as the eye could see, I doubted that anyone else could ever find them unless he knew what to look for. In fact, I wondered if *I* could ever find them again. I looked at the grain elevator. I tried to commit its angles and signs and colors to memory. Here was nearly $30,000 buried in sight of an Old Timer's Pigfeed sign. I ran back into the bush, hoping no one had seen my little burial.

Once I was about ten feet in and pretty well hidden, I stopped to listen for the trainman. I heard the crack and pop of twigs, and then things got quiet. He was trying to hear me.

I had an idea.

"There's more gold where that came from," I shouted. "But I can't get it by myself."

I walked toward him, making as much noise as I could. He was still nervous about me. I heard him move away.

"I tried to tell you that in the boxcar," I said. "There's more than enough for both of us. I'm glad you came back."

I kept walking toward him. Sticks broke under my feet like small explosions.

"Really. I mean it. I can't get it out by myself." I stopped to listen for a reply.

What came next was light, and a searing through my right side. Then noise like the middle of a thunderbolt. The world on its side. The grain elevator like a gravestone. Then nothing.

# Four

"**YOU'RE A GODDAMNED FOOL**, Elwin McCoo. Always were. Always will be."

It was a woman's voice. A little throaty. In spite of what she was saying, the woman sounded calm, as if she were reciting facts obvious to anyone.

I heard a muffled reply and the sound of a chair scraping across the floor.

What I remember of waking up in that room was the musty smell it had. It was the smell of old cotton and mildew. It wasn't a bad smell. The sheets were clean, but the frame of the house had a little wood rot. I'll never forget that smell. What I recall of almost dying is not any profound insight on the human condition. Not at all. What I remember is the smell of old sheets and must.

For the briefest moment I wondered if I actually *had* died. I wondered if this was the life beyond.

Perhaps it was hell. What I saw around me would be just the sort of hell appropriate to the second half of the twentieth century in the United States. Heaven certainly wouldn't have been decorated with old *Saturday Evening Post* covers thumbtacked to the peeling wallpaper. The room had the feel of the normal gone bad, of Norman Rockwell children growing up to be Bonnie and Clyde.

I figured I'd been unconscious for some time. My right side from my waist to my shoulder felt like paper. I tried to lift my right arm, but I felt as if I were tearing the paper. When I finally got my arm back down, I was out of breath. Simply moving was a major exercise for me.

The papery feeling on my chest and side was caused in part by bandages. I guessed that I'd been shot—a conjecture my mind, somehow floating free from the sack of pain I called a body, considered the way someone from an aristocratic family might hear about the problems of a housekeeper. I even wondered where my notebook was. I wanted to get everything down.

Of course I couldn't have written my impressions if I had tried to. I simply didn't have enough strength in my arm. Besides, I don't know what I would have written about other than the look of the light through the tattered shades at the end of the room. There were too many questions I simply couldn't answer. I didn't know who my captors were or what they wanted.

I was, as the man in Louisiana said, lost and getting loster. This adventure business just wasn't all it was cracked up to be. Boy.

I heard muttered voices in the hall outside my room. I heard the door open. I closed my eyes and feigned sleep. Then I tried to peek through my eyelashes like a child. I saw a shape moving around the room. The shape disappeared behind me, and I closed my eyes completely, expecting some bad news I didn't want the details of.

Instead, someone began smoothing my bandage. I opened my eyes.

I blinked a couple of times, and things came into focus. The trainman hung against the doorway like a psychotic posing for his portrait. A woman I hadn't seen before came around the bed and stood at my feet. She wiggled my big toe.

"Well," she said and dropped it, "I guess you're going to live."

Her tone suggested that the matter had no great importance to her. She picked up my wrist with her right hand and felt my forehead with her left.

"You're both goddamned lucky," she said. "Him to be alive and you to be out of jail."

She smiled as she looked back and forth between me and the trainman. I half expected her to have us kiss and make up.

"Now, Elwin, get out of here while I change his dressing. Just because you shot him doesn't mean you get to see him in his altogether."

"But that's what you want, Mary Lynn. That's what you do with cousin Pole. I've seen you."

"Out of here, Elwin, before I whack your pee-pee."

"Mary Lynn, you know he might get away."

"Out."

"Now you know he might, Mary Lynn. You just know he could." The conviction seemed to go out of his voice like air escaping from a slow leak in a tire. He looked hurt. He looked like a slightly retarded version of James Dean in *Rebel Without a Cause*. He had that slicked-back hair that looked sexy on Dean but appeared merely greasy on him.

"Mary Lynn and Elwin." I spoke their names aloud, partly just to commit them to memory. "Mary Lynn and Elwin—it sounds like a dance combo."

"Does not," the woman said. "Doesn't sound like anything but us."

"Just us," Elwin agreed. "Just what our daddies made of us."

"Daddies?" I asked. This was getting complicated.

"Never mind," Mary Lynn said. "We're not the important ones around here. You are. The sooner we get to you, the better. It's your story we want to hear. Ours is flatter than downstate Illinois, and that's flatter than anyone wants to think about. Isn't that so, Elwin?"

Elwin looked up the way a dog who's caught a scent of something looks up, though in Elwin's case, I'm not sure he had the scent of anything.

Elwin didn't answer her question. We ended up staring at one another, while the sun turned golden, leaving a shimmering light on everything like a blessing. Then Mary Lynn walked toward Elwin and made this shooing gesture, as if he were a chicken. McCoo held up his hands and smiled at her.

"Be careful," he said to me. "She may not be armed, but she's more dangerous than I am. She told me, you know, that women can take men like they wasn't even there."

He said that as he walked away.

"Now what the hell does that mean?" I asked. "You mean she's going to rape me? Is that it? A male rape scene?"

He smiled, but he didn't answer my question as the door closed behind him.

"What's your name?" she asked after he left.

"Hill."

"A little higher than the rest of us. Is that it?"

"That's right. How'd you guess?"

"I can see it in the way you hold your nose above us all. You don't like us, do you? I can see that. I can figure things out for my own self. I've been around. Hey, maybe it's a small farm, but I've been all the way around it. You bet. And you—how do you feel?"

"Sore."

"You had a bullet in your diaphragm. I took it out three days ago.

21

You've been delirious ever since. I've given you some antibiotics. The stitches I'll take out in a day or two. By then you'll be three-quarters healthy. I'm not the Mayo Clinic, but you're doing fine. In a week or so you can take us to the rest of the gold."

I waited before I said anything. I wanted to concentrate. I didn't want to make any mistakes. I tried to look off in the distance for answers, but what I got was the last of the sunlight wavering in its beautiful way across the wall.

"Then we're near the place where I was shot?"

I tried to make this question sound like a statement. I wanted to be casual. And I wanted out of there alive so I could find that brass belt buckle.

"We're close enough. Daddy liked to hear the trains as he went about his work. Daddy was like the true and trembling brakeman in the song. He just loved the old Illinois Central highballing it past here."

"Your Daddy was a railroad man, then?" I silently wondered what the other daddy did. Maybe each of them had a different father.

"Well, you might say that. Daddy was a robber. He robbed the trains. He made his most money on the steam locomotives. They'd stop over just a few miles from here, in Beatrice, Illinois. You won't find that on any maps. It was named after the railroad president's wife. The railroad had a lake and a whole system to put water into those steam locomotives. It was at the edge of town. The trains would stop there, and the city people would get out to look things over like they owned the place. That's when Daddy would show up.

"Folks couldn't believe it. This was the twentieth century, and they'd be looking at a train robber. Oh, Daddy would dress the part. He had these old boots and these cartridge belts he wore. He used to study the way the outlaws looked in the movies. It was 1929 when he started. He always said he came like the stock market crash. In fact, his friends called him Crash McCoo.

"His last train he robbed in 1953. He was pretty selective. I mean, he didn't hit every train that came by. He got maybe two a year. Some years he didn't do any. He tried to get intelligence. He tried to find out when payrolls were on board. World War II was real good for that. He used to call it the Big Bill War. The trains carried nothing smaller than twenties for the payrolls of the contractors.

"But civilization finally caught up with us. The whole family was doing it by then. He'd send me out to stand on the tracks maybe a hundred yards in front of the locomotive. I mean, who'd run over a little girl?

"Mama would get a gun on the engineer, and Papa and Elwin would go after the mail car. That's where they usually kept the money.

"Pa robbed trains for over twenty years. Most of them he took in that train yard over by Beatrice. Until the end they never sent anybody to protect the trains. I guess they figured Daddy would quit. Maybe they didn't want the publicity. I don't know, but they never went after Daddy until the last time. It just goes to prove, as Daddy used to tell us, that there's a lot more in robbing than anyone would guess. No one ever expects a crook. And when one shows up, folks just think he'll go away.

"But the last robbing was sad. Some Federal man shot Pa in the neck, and he lay there dying and trying to ask me something. I couldn't make it out. He just couldn't talk through all the blood and mucous. I stood there by him. Mama hid in the hills. I knew she was watching when Pa went, but she never came back again. I don't blame her; I guess she'd had enough. I mean, would you want to spend your youth in the company of a train robber?"

When Mary Lynn paused there, I wasn't sure if I was to answer that question, but when I looked up at her, she was staring off in the distance, as if the last swatch of golden sunlight on the wall was going off to join her daddy.

"There was just this little moment I had. It was as if I was a movie camera above it all. There was Daddy on the ground with me beside him, blood and pieces of his body just everywhere. For a moment or two he crawled around in a little circle, trying to pick up these pieces. I mean, he'd pick one up, see that it was dirty, spit on it to clean it off, and try to put it back in his neck.

"And Mama—why I had just this glimpse of Mama halfway standing up behind this rock. She must have looked at the way all those years she and Pa had together were bleeding into the dirt. Pa was picking the pieces up, and Ma was staring, and Elwin was looking at his feet, and I was watching over the whole thing. And then, well, you can figure it from there. Pa just stopped like he couldn't put all those pieces together. He just quit. And Ma froze there behind the rock. She froze there as the Federal men came out from behind the train. The steam engine was still smoking, and people were staring out of the window. All of this was going on, and the wind blew up just a puff of dust as if to say what we were all really headed for, though especially Pa. It was a moment.

"I never heard from Ma again. I was thirteen the day my daddy died, thirteen the day my momma ran off. You'd think she'd send a postcard. You know, love from Anaheim—that kind of thing. But I didn't hear a word. Her sister raised me and Elwin. They were hillbillies. I mean that. Everybody thinks Illinois is flat black dirt with corn on top like the meringue on a banana cream pie, and they think that all our roads lead to Springfield or Chicago, but there are parts tucked so far away that Chicago and Springfield don't mean anything, and the roads don't lead anywhere. Talking about Chicago to people there would be like explaining Paris to the Indians Columbus met.

"Calla Lily was my mama's sister's name. It was some kind of awful fate that got her tagged with that. Her papa named her Calla, and she married a man named Lily. He said it was fate, but she said it was a bad accident.

"Ben Lily—that was his name—died, thank God. He was feeding chickens and just fell over. When we got there, the chickens had started to peck at him. At first it almost seemed like the chickens did him in. That was a scary scene—all those chickens climbing around a real human being.

"Then Calla marries Mr. Pee. That's all we ever heard. I never did learn what his first name was. We all called him Mr. He had four boys, and they were the meanest sons-of-bitches I ever knew. They would as soon beat on you as look at you.

"It was awful. I just lived in my head on what few dreams I had. I thought about my Daddy and Mama a lot. I imagined myself going into the robbery business. Elwin tried to, though I don't think he ever did any serious robbing. I mean, he hung around the trains all the time. When one slowed up enough, he'd ride on it awhile and then come back. Sometimes, he'd find things. He's brought us back sacks of potatoes, money, people's luggage, and now you. He's had quite a little career dreaming whatever it is he dreams. I don't understand him exactly, and I don't think I want to understand him exactly.

"I myself tried to be a good girl. I guess what I really wanted to do was fix my Daddy up. Since it was too late for him, I practiced on other people's lives. I went to nurses' training after I left high school. My biology teacher said I was smart. Hell, if I was really smart, I would've gone right back to robbing. Lot more money in that than in patting sick people on the hand. Teachers always think life is some long IQ test.

"Are you a teacher, Owen?"

The direct sunlight was gone, and the purple of twilight seemed to be rising around us like dark water.

"How do you know that? I didn't tell you my first name." I should've been surprised, but life was losing its ability to surprise me.

"It's not every day you meet a grown man who has his name on the label of his shirt. Do you think life is a camp? I mean, do you figure you'll lose your shirt somewhere and then be able to get it back if you can identify it?"

She was smiling as she said this.

"It was the man in the store. He said it would . . . . Look, it's a long story."

"We have nothing but time here. You can entertain us while you get ready to tell us about the gold."

"Why should I tell you anything? He tried to kill me." I gestured toward the door frame.

"Him," she said. She said the word as if the subject were annoying beyond explanation. "Him. Elwin is stupid. Me, I'm smarter, and I don't do things halfway. If I don't get half the gold, you're going to die. I saved you and I get to kill you."

I couldn't see her face as she said this. She was bent over me, pulling off the old bandages and putting on new ones.

When she finished, she turned to face me. I first noticed that blank, professional look of the doctor or the nurse. Her smile was out there like a fence.

Her eyes, though, what hard little eyes she had. Hard and black and small. They didn't seem to blink. Her face was a little like a mannequin's, attractive at first, then dead in a provocative and frightening way.

"But you might kill me anyway," I said. I thought briefly of giving her the two coins I'd saved, but I realized that I didn't even know where they were. I didn't have my shoes on. "I mean, I could take you to the gold, and you could finish me there."

She blinked then. Only her eyelids moved, and they came down slowly like those of some giant and calm bird of prey. The rest of her face remained oddly impassive.

"That's true," she said. "You're a bright fellow. But you must be a schoolteacher. You're bright about the wrong things. Yes, we could kill you. But then we might not. We might let you have half the gold. Not a bad deal, is it? It's hard to be rich when you're dead. If you don't take us there, you'll die. You'll be very dead and very rich. If you like, I'll send notes to your friends telling them how rich you were before you died."

I looked at her as steadily as I could. I realized that she had changed my dressing without an ache. She was good.

I kept trying to find a way over the wall of her confidence, but I didn't have the strength.

"I have to think about this," I said and heard the slur in my voice. I thought I saw her throwing a needle away.

Then I was gliding. I tried to stop myself; I was tired of sliding out of each episode. I wanted to stay and fight, but I felt as though I were tumbling in slow motion off the top of a high wall, and there was nothing I could do about it.

# Five

OF COURSE THE SUN WAS SHINING when I woke up. The room had the innocent charm an eight-year-old boy's room has. I half expected to see a baseball glove on the dresser and to find a collection of stuffed bears at the end of the bed. Nothing could be wrong in that buttery yellow light.

I could smell bacon frying and coffee perking. *The Saturday Evening Post* covers looked utterly quaint. I felt as if I were waking up in an out-of-the-way but charming resort, though the charm disappeared when I looked down and saw that someone had ripped old sheets apart and lashed them around me and the bed, cinching them with authoritative-looking square knots. It was a crude idea, threatening at the lowest level. The light took on a darker edge. It was only the look of innocence, as if evil were in drag.

I had to plan. If I took them to the gold along the railroad tracks, they might kill me right there. $30,000 might seem like more than I was worth. I was coming to notice how variable wealth was. The gold—which had seemed like a fortune two days ago—had become a nuisance to me. I would've traded it for my freedom in a second. However, they would believe it was a king's ransom.

I had to buy more time. With days instead of hours, something might happen. I couldn't just take them back to the tracks.

As I lay there thinking, the odor of hot asphalt wafted into the room. A road was being resurfaced nearby. I wished I were on it.

"How do you like your eggs?"

It was Mary Lynn's voice from another room.

"Scrambled."

"You'll get them over easy like everybody else," McCoo shouted from his part of the house. "This isn't a restaurant."

I couldn't imagine why anyone would get hostile about eggs, but then Mary Lynn appeared in the doorway, and I realized that McCoo was doing the cooking.

She paused in the doorway before she came in the room. At first I thought she was checking me and the room out, checking to make sure that I was still bound. But then I realized that she was doing this for effect. She wanted me to stare at her.

She was stunning in her way. She had the sort of shiny black hair that looks like patent leather. It was swept around her face in a bouffant hairdo that hadn't been popular for twenty years. Her skin was extremely pale, almost clown white, and had been heavily powdered. She looked frozen.

I tried to sound cheerful when I spoke. I figured a little banter might work.

"You offered me what you didn't have," I said.

"What do you mean?" she asked.

"You're not cooking the eggs," I said.

She stood leaning her back against the wall and arching her chest out. She was wearing a soft sweater. The sweater and her posture accentuated her breasts, which looked hard and pointed.

"So far we're even then, Owen. I'm not cooking the eggs, and you're not talking about the gold."

"Now wait. You offered me a choice of eggs. I haven't said anything about the gold. You lied. If you lie about eggs, who knows what you'll do about money."

I was a little nervous as I said this, but Rotbart told us to do our bargaining before the deals were done.

"You're right. Maybe you should tell me about the gold, and I'll make sure you get scrambled eggs."

"Great trade. Look, I've got to eat. I'm so hungry I can hardly see straight."

Her face softened a bit. As she turned away from me, I could see her chest sag, as if the toys were being put away. When she turned back around, the pistol she held was enormous. Her hands seemed particularly delicate against the blue and brown of the gun. They also seemed very practiced. The daughter of a train robber indeed.

"Well, that'll teach me to order scrambled eggs," I said. "Hey, I was just kidding. I really love eggs over easy."

I gave her my best smile.

"I'm going to help you get up. If you try anything, I'll shoot you in the nuts."

She said this in a clear, flat voice, as if she said things like this all the time. Then she stuffed the pistol into the elastic waist of her Capri pants. That seemed awkward, funny almost—the gun caused a droop in the waist of her pants and exposed the tops of her white underpants. I watched her as she untied the strips of sheeting from the bed.

I stood up carefully. This was the first time I'd gotten out of bed since I'd been shot. I was so dizzy that a Maserati parked two feet away on the new asphalt, a Maserati with its motor running and someone holding the door open for my escape would've done me no good whatsoever. I hurt. Oh, how I hurt. After the second or third wave of pain went through me, my thoughts vanished.

"You really think I'm going to escape?" I asked, putting ten seconds between each word to catch my breath. It was amazing how hard it was to function through pain. Even the simple task of walking required enormous strength.

I got to the end of the bed and held on to the bedpost.

"Elwin, get your ass in here," Mary Lynn yelled.

A moment later the trainman came. They put me between them and walked me slowly out of the bedroom, down a hall, and onto a broad porch where breakfast had been set out.

Once I got seated and got my breath back, I felt a lot better. I think my joints had seized up from inactivity. Just getting started may have caused the pain. I was like a car that hadn't been driven for a while.

When the hard pains didn't come back, I realized that I was getting better. And the porch was delightful. It was edged with Victorian gingerbread work and furnished with heavy old wicker furniture.

As I studied the porch, I had trouble imagining the two of them with a place like this. I just couldn't see Mary Lynn dusting the wicker or McCoo painting the delicate wood trim. But who said people had to be consistent? After all, Hitler did watercolors, and Alexander the Great studied under Aristotle. A world that accepted these large contradictions surely could include the modestly evil lives of Mary Lynn and McCoo in this innocent setting.

The three of us ate in silence, and they let me stay on the porch while they took away the dishes and cleaned up in the kitchen. Ever so often Mary Lynn came outside to check on me, the gun still conspicuously tucked in the front of her pants. Later on she came out without the gun and sat in a chair at the other end of the porch. McCoo went off to mow the lawn.

My pains were dwindling into a dull ache. I tried to think, though the ache tended to blur my thoughts. Images from weeks ago would dissolve into the recent present, and then everything would fall under the glitter of this pain or that. In fact, that's how I felt my wound, as an array of yellow lights falling against a dark background.

There on the porch, I slept and woke up several times, keeping track of time by noting McCoo's diminishing circles around the lawn.

Then it was dark, and I was awake in my bed. I thought I heard clatter in the distance. I sat up in the bed and realized that the sound was the laugh track from a television program.

Mary Lynn was there.

She was sitting in the corner of the room staring at me. She held the gun in her lap the way you might nestle a small house pet. The torn strips of sheet were gone; I was no longer tied to the bed.

"What time is it?"

"You got an appointment?"

"Hey, I'm hurt. I've been shot. Don't I get some slack, for God's sake?"

"You'll get your life and half the money when you show me where the gold is. It's very simple. Pretty soon you'll be well, and we can go. I'm not giving you my time and groceries for charity alone, Owen. You may be cute, but you've been very expensive."

I fell back on my pillow with the most pitiful moan I could summon up. I could feel her stare poking around for my weak places. At least I had graduated from kind-of cute to fully cute.

"OK, OK, you win. You let me go, and I'll tell you where the gold is. I don't want it. It's cursed. I never should've started out on this god-awful journey. I want to go home. You can have it all. I'll draw you a map."

I closed my eyes like a child waiting for the bogey man to go away. But my particular bogey lady didn't move. I couldn't see her face through my closed eyes, but I doubt if she even blinked.

"Owen, Owen." She said this the way a nurse might speak the name of an especially slow and tedious patient. "Owen, you know it can't work that way."

"What do you mean?" My lie was so hollow I thought I heard an echo in my words.

"Owen, I am not simple. Elwin may be, but I'm not. You know you've got to come along. How else can I be sure you're telling us the truth? Now this is how we're going to do it. You get a good night's sleep, and tomorrow you're going to tell us how to find the gold. You're going to write it all down, and then you're going with us. Why, Owen, we might just have us a good old time."

This time she said my name softly, almost affectionately.

"You're going to make me a rich woman, Owen."

She was standing beside my bed, taking off her clothes.

"Very rich."

Her tongue darted in and out of my ear while she slid my pants off. When she mounted me, her nipples brushed my face. She held the pistol against my cheek as she moved up and down on me.

In the distance I could hear the hollow laugh track of Elwin's TV show. A moment later I came in spite of myself. The little sounds I made arrived from someplace I never wanted to go again.

# Six

**WHEN I WOKE UP** the next morning, I was able to sit up in bed. As awful as I'd been feeling, I took my strength as a small miracle. I also realized that I wasn't tied to the bed with strips of torn sheets. I carefully swung my feet out of the bed and discovered that I could do a pretty good imitation of a walk if I stopped to catch my breath and hung on the furniture. After what seemed like hours, I made it to the bathroom. I spent a long time studying my face in the medicine cabinet mirror. As I went over its cuts and bumps and bruises, I thought that I'd become someone interesting. If nothing else, sailing out of the boxcar had gotten rid of Mr. Cute.

The longer I stood there, the more I noticed that my whole body seemed out of whack, as if hitting the ground had put me in a new way of approaching things.

I washed up, or tried to. Unfortunately, the pain of my wound prevented me from doing very much scrubbing on either my right side or the territory beneath my belt. I wanted to get rid of Mary Lynn's smell, but I had to settle for splashing Old Spice cologne on my hands and crotch and thighs.

I had just enough strength to finish up in the bathroom, slip on my shoes over my bare feet, and walk out to the kitchen, where Elwin was making another breakfast.

"Well look at here," he said, "the Lord High Asshole has joined us. My, my."

By ten, I was sitting alone on the porch with a pad of paper and a pen. At one side of the paper, I had drawn a Maltese Cross and, at the other side, a sketch of a three-masted sailing ship, which I named *The Golden Fleece* in tiny letters across its side.

I was feeling better. Just the acts of moving around and eating made me feel healthier. I'd also discovered that the two gold coins I'd saved were still in my shoes. That seemed a good omen of some kind.

I drew the shape of a jagged island around the Maltese Cross, and then I put a dotted line between the ship and the island. I filled the empty spaces with little squiggles meant to be waves. I sketched birds

32

flying above the ship and, at the side of the map, a dragon-like sea monster with the curls of its body going in and out of the water. At the bottom I inscribed, *Owen Hill III, His Map, In The Year of Our Lord 1979.* Whimsy, however, would not get me off the porch or rid me of Mary Lynn's smell.

I shifted in my chair and felt the dry semen cracking. The woman did have an imagination. She had taken me so easily. I didn't know things like that could happen. I could still feel the scrape of her pubic hair against my thighs as she got started. I could smell the scents beginning with cologne and going to old tuna.

But I also had to remember that these were people who looked on me as some kind of pack animal who would carry them to wealth. If I took them to the gold, I suspected they would leave me the way Mary Lynn had last night, uncovered and chilly, skin cracking with what I couldn't clean.

The longer I thought about that, the madder I got. I mean, how could I have let her do that to me? There's just no accounting for the sexual curiosity of males, but anger wouldn't get me out of there; I had to give them something. So, that evening, praying that an idea for escape would appear like the cavalry, I began my story while we sat in the kitchen of the farmhouse.

It was easier to tell than I had imagined. It was mostly true, and it was improbable enough that embellishments were simple. I quoted what Rotbart had told us, "Gold at the end in difficulty begins." The line sounded as though it had been translated—and badly translated at that—from German.

Anyway, I told them about the newspaper ad. I told them about Rotbart at the Paradise Motel. I tried to make it all sound important, but the events seemed rather ordinary as I explained them in that kitchen.

It had been decorated in one of those eras when the idea was to imitate a scientific laboratory. It had a lot of chrome details and translucent glass and linoleum and fluorescent lights and Formica counters. But the place had been neglected. The chrome was getting rusty; the Formica and the linoleum were cracking, and the lights flickered. Under that sickly and stuttering bluish light, the three of us looked pasty, an intimate family of fornication and foul play.

"That ad came into my life the way love at first sight must appear," I told them. "It was into-the jungle-at-eighteen-and-out-at-twenty-one-rich-beyond-your-wildest-dreams stuff. It was that big for me, you know."

"Who gives a shit about you? Get to the fucking gold," McCoo said. "I hate this kind of crap. It's what he tried on me out there along the railroad tracks."

It got quiet then, our silence punctuated by the crackling of a dying fluorescent bulb.

"Hush," Mary Lynn said. "Hush, Elwin. Why don't you go beat off? That always makes you feel better. Gets the poisons out of your system."

McCoo started to leave, but changed his mind and came back. He leaned against a door frame. That seemed to be a favorite pose of his.

"When I read that ad," I went on, trying to ignore McCoo and the kitchen. "When I read that ad, I felt it embodied, in capital letters, what I'd been looking for all these years.

"I was tired of my life. Oh, I had a sensible car and a decent place to live. I had prospects, I guess. I would keep on playing my minor parts and earning my $700 a month. But that ad, with its solicitation of men willing to court danger, played in my heart like Olivier. The evening at the Paradise Motel gave me an idea of how I might at least stand up in the tiny parlor of my life.

"The small, muscular man—his name was Jason Rotbart—showed the thirty of us bleached-out slides of him and his men buying supplies in a harbor town near the Amazon, slides of them going up the river with native guides and bearers, walking through the jungle past immense flowers, and holding up pieces of rock as they stood before what appeared to be a mine entrance. These slides looked like pictures from an adventure book, and the idea that I could walk into such an adventure intrigued me.

"The production at the Paradise Motel was amateurish, a bad version of scenes from *The Treasure of the Sierra Madre*. But still it got to me. It got to me because I could believe that I was standing just beyond the camera's range, that I was one of the out-of-focus men at the back of the group in front of the mine entrance.

"Rotbart showed us several maps—maps of the world, maps of South America. He had road maps and terrain maps. At one point he showed us a fairly detailed map of the Upper Amazon region where the mine was.

"'It's here,' he told us. 'Precisely here.'

"The shadow of his hand fell briefly over what must've been a two- or three-hundred-mile section of jungle.

"The tall man passed around ore samples of copper and zinc. Though I wouldn't have known the difference between rocks containing lead and those with gold inside, I didn't misunderstand the man at the back of the group who stood up and claimed that these were the purest samples he'd seen in ten years of studying minerals. He sounded like a mining engineer.

"It briefly crossed my mind that he might be a shill or that he was simply one of the other crazies, but I was so hungry to believe in the expedition that I didn't care if he was lying.

"I guess I suspected that Rotbart's presentation was all a con. It certainly was as slick as the hair oil on the head of a door-to-door encyclopedia salesman. But if it was a con, I wanted to find out how it worked. I wanted to know how he proposed to take the thirty of us—who looked like the overweight and out-of-shape winners of the Local Losers Contest—off on a treasure-hunting expedition in some of the worst terrain on God's earth. I mean, not one of us looked as though he could survive a long airplane ride, let alone a trip into the jungles of the Amazon.

"On the other hand, I thought, maybe Rotbart's story wasn't a con. Maybe he *was* going to take us all into the jungle to wrest our fortunes from the bloody earth. Maybe I had stumbled onto one of the great opportunities in history. I mean, great opportunities do happen after all. Andrew Carnegies and Henry Fords have to start someplace. Maybe years from now I'd be telling my grandchildren about the foundation of their wealth at the Paradise Motel."

I paused in my story and glanced at Mary Lynn and Elwin. They were both looking off into space.

"May I have something to drink? Do you have any beer?" I asked.

Mary Lynn dropped her fork on her plate as if I had interrupted her reverie. She jumped toward the refrigerator and was back to her seat in what seemed like one, cat-like step. She put a can of beer in front of me.

"So you went then?" She asked, fumbling with the snap-top. "You went to the Amazon? You brought the money back and changed it into Krugerrands?"

"Do you have a glass?"

She scowled and rinsed one in the sink and handed it to me. Then she stood there with her arms folded across her chest, as if to suggest that she wouldn't tolerate any more nonsense. But curiosity seemed to pull her toward me. A moment later she sat down.

What was it Rotbart had said?

"Don't kid yourselves," he had told us. "These wogs know what gold is.

"It's greed," he said with authority. "It's the love of money that'll make the natives work hard for you. Money's marvelous stuff. It rules the earth by capturing imaginations. And once you have a man's imagination, you have the man. Trinkets are too literal. You've got to explain what money will do."

"Really, Owen. Tell me." Mary Lynn's eyes were bright as she spoke. "Really tell me now. Did you go?"

"We'll get to that in a minute," I said. "You've got to let me tell the story my own way. Be patient."

She shook away my advice. "You must've gone," she said. "How else would you have gotten the gold?"

I took a sip of beer and went on.

"In the end it was a simple proposition. Rotbart wanted ten men. 'Able hands and true,' he called them. 'Men of will and passion.' His list of personal requirements was like a catalog of antique virtues. He told us his expedition up the Amazon would take about two years. He would train his candidates at his estate in southern Louisiana for about three months. We were to spend another month in a harbor town along the ocean in Brazil getting used to the climate and shaking down our equipment. Then we would head upriver in his boat *The Golden Fleece* to search for more wealth than we could dream about.

"It was the river that finally got me to go on the expedition. Rotbart had this slide of it taken from one of the banks. In the center was a fifteen or sixteen-foot boat with an outboard motor. The kind of thing you'd take along on a fishing trip. The scene looked ordinary at first. Two men in a boat on some brown and murky water. You could just make out the other shore in the distance. There was a small wake behind the boat.

"But as you looked more closely you could see that the boat was turning toward the camera. Somehow that was wrong. Something was wrong with the entire photograph. The man in the front of the boat, the man almost blurred by a shutter too slow for his movement, was not smiling. He stared with blank terror at the shore where the photographer stood. The other man, halfway standing up in the back of the boat, had both hands on the hood of the motor as if trying to wrestle it into control. He was attempting to steer the boat away from shore by turning the motor and was having no luck. The blurs in the picture were caused by the speed of their travel. The boat was out of control.

"It was hard to see any of that at first, hard the way noticing the start of an earthquake is hard. You try to stop the lamp from shaking, and then you're shaking, and then the whole world is shaking. The picture was like that.

"'You must look closely,' Rotbart said. 'It's like those puzzles where you have to find the hidden pictures. Except here you have to find the hidden terror. The river will get them. It will smash them against the shore as if it were simply tired of them. All their ambitions or their love of, say, the color blue or women with high breasts—all the lovely details of their lives will shatter against the shore, rise, and fall into mud, and disappear as if they had never lived and loved the color blue and the look of high-breasted women.

"'This kind of thing happens every few weeks on the river,' Rotbart went on. 'You get a tropical storm a little harder than the usual afternoon deluge. The water just comes down in sheets. If you stand in a rain like this, it hurts. It feels like God is throwing baseballs at you. It just crushes the vegetation. Huge trees bow down as if they just witnessed a tragedy. Afterwards, there's a hundred-yard-long bulge of water in the river coming down stream with the gravity of half a continent behind it. This is water with serious intentions.

37

"'These formations make a noise, and natives can recognize the sound ahead of time. They even have a name for these river tidal waves, though I've never learned it. But the tourists—why, the tourists never hear a thing but the beginning of their own deaths. The two you see in this slide are tourists, or they were.'"

I stopped again. Mary Lynn was staring at me as if I'd come to Illinois from the planet Mars.

"Can I have another beer?" I asked. I had gulped the first one down.

This time she brought two and kept one for herself. The lights in that kitchen cast their flickering pallor over the three of us.

"So you went then?" she asked.

"What do you think? It was as if the river were already pulling me along."

"That must be something," she said and hugged herself. "Really something."

"You're right about that," I said. "In the parking lot of the Paradise Motel most of us sat with our mouths open. I don't know why staring at the beginning of two deaths would impress anyone. You'd think we'd want to avoid that kind of thing. I guess that's how the Army gets us into wars. We watch everyone dying, and we think we'll make it. I guess that's it—we thought we would get away with it. We were better than the tourists.

"Then we got the pitch.

"'The difference,' Rotbart told us, 'between a good man and a well-intentioned fool is this: a good man knows the risks and has vowed to triumph over them. A fool hopes things will go his way. He believes in luck or God or Fate. A good man, knows better; he believes, just like the Boy Scouts, in being prepared.

"'I don't want any fools on this trip. You've seen two already. That they died is their business. That they cost me a boat and a good motor is every concern of mine. They were one reason my last expedition ended in failure. I don't bring spare equipment and extra men along. This time, with you men in my company, I mean to succeed. Is that clear?'

"I know I nodded as I sat there. Rotbart could have asked us to come forward for communion, and I would've gone.

"'Therefore,' Rotbart went on, 'I'm giving seminars. A three-month course at my Louisiana property to teach you how to survive and prosper on the way to that treasure. Three months to train you in how to survive some of the worst terrain on the face of the earth. I will then teach you how to get life's gold. When you're through, you'll know each and every one of the golden rules.

"'I'm not doing this for free of course. No, and you don't want me to. What's given away is hardly worth the getting. For the training and for the trip I'm charging the modest tuition of ten Krugerrands apiece. At today's spot prices that'll cost each of you about $3,000. These funds will cover my expenses in training you and the costs of transporting you from my estate to South America. You will of course have to buy your own airline ticket to Louisiana. You will also have to bring your own personal supplies. I recommend that you travel together. You should get to know one another. If you like, I will make a group reservation. For those of you who wish to sign up, I have a sheet of very complete instructions. Your first assignment . . . Oh, excuse me, the first assignment for those of you bold enough to undertake this mission will be following these instructions.

"'My colleagues and I will remain here until August 1. You have ten days to bring us your funds. I will take a mere three of the coins as a deposit, but I will expect to have the other seven on your arrival in Louisiana. Once you're at my estate there, you will choose one of your members to hold the money until you decide that mine is a legitimate operation.

"'But this is to become my money if you decide to go. I am bringing my skill and my knowledge to our enterprise. You are bringing merely your curiosity and a vague desire for wealth. I need something to assure me that you're serious. If you don't have $3,000, you need to work on a way to get it. Anyone who hasn't the imagination to find $3,000 in this great town of St. Louis won't be of much help in the jungles along the Amazon.'

"Then he held up a stiff sheet of buff-colored paper. It was filled with an antique script and looked like a document from another century.

"'This is what you get, my friends,' he said. 'Though this is merely a promise made of paper, it could become great wealth by the end of your journey. For $3,000 you'll become a member of the New Quest for the Golden Fleece. See, that's the title of our partnership agreement. And that's what we are, my good men, partners in this grand endeavor. In fact you're better than partners. When we divide up our spoils, you'll get sixty per cent of what we find. After expenses of course. There are some fine points you should study, and perhaps you'll want to have counsel examine the document. But all in all I think you'll find matters perfectly satisfactory here.'

"The heavy-set man passed out the papers. His movements broke the rhythms of Rotbart's talk, and I noticed that most of the men in the audience were reading with their lips as their fingers led their minds through the text.

"'Why should we trust you with our money?' one man asked. 'You could just run off with it. Anyone could make up these slides. What if this is all a big fraud?'

"He had a point.

"'I suppose you can't trust me,' Rotbart said. 'But then I really don't trust any of you. Look at yourselves. Who'd ask the lot of you to do anything? Why, if you spent as much on your brains as you did on your stomachs, you'd be something. But I can't get the gold without assistance, and you're never going to escape your dismal lives without help from someone exceptional like me. What if I take the money? What then? Do you really think a mere $3,000 will make any kind of difference in your lives? Be serious.

"'But if I'm right about the treasure, and you get your shares, why you'll be rich beyond your wildest dreams. Let's say we get there. Let's say I don't cheat you. Let's say we find emeralds like these.'

"He opened a wooden box that had been sitting on the table in front of him. We all leaned forward together. We were like men with springs inside. Then we got up and, one by one, filed by the box as if it contained the ashes of our dearest friend. No one said a word."

I paused and heard the crackle of the fluorescent lights in that Illinois farmhouse.

"What was it?" Mary Lynn asked. "What was in that box?" She leaned across the table and held my arm.

"Pieces of green crystal. I'd never seen so many. They were colored the deepest green you can imagine. They were like greed made tangible. You could've disappeared into those stones."

"Shit," McCoo interrupted and pointed at me. "I don't believe any of his bullshit. He just took everybody's money. He hasn't got the guts for emeralds."

"No. I don't believe that," Mary Lynn said. "No one would go to that kind of trouble just to pick some pockets."

She turned away from McCoo as if he were some kind of embarrassment.

"Then you went," Mary Lynn said to me. "You went to the jungle."

She was nodding as she spoke. "I just know you did. Oh, Owen, you're rich, aren't you?" She held my arm and looked into the distance, toward an Amazon of her own.

"Describe the stones to me again," she said. "Did you touch them? Did you run your fingers through them? Were they slick? I've heard that precious stones like that are slick."

"No," I said. "I didn't have a chance to before Rotbart closed the box. The man who claimed to know so much about minerals seemed convinced. He walked back to his chair like someone who'd had a religious conversion. The rest of us followed.

"'These are the most incredible raw emeralds I've ever seen,' the man said. He actually licked his lips.

"'OK, OK,' he continued. 'Let's say we give you the money, the $3,000 in Krugerrands. Let's say we sign the contract. Then what happens? I'm slow. I want to hear you say all the details over again.'

"'It's really very simple,' Rotbart said, 'if you call going after Fate Herself simple. After I have the rest of your deposits and after we complete your training in Louisiana, then we'll travel to a location I'd rather not name just now. There, my river boat is docked and awaiting us like a rich friend.'

"Again he urged us to have our lawyers read the contracts.

"'Discuss my proposition with them,' he told us. 'I rather doubt that they will approve. This is not an endeavor for a man who believes in desks and chairs and books.'

"We were to return to the motel with our Krugerrands. True to his

41

word, he didn't explain how we were to get them. As he'd told us earlier, I guess he figured that anyone who couldn't get Krugerrands would be useless on the trip.

"If there were enough of us and if each of our applications was acceptable, then he would call us. We were to depart in about ten days.

"'If you have affairs,' Rotbart told us, 'get them in order. If you have serious affairs, stay home. This is an expedition for men who have no prospects. I'm an outcast myself. I don't have much use for society, and I'd like men cut from the same cloth.'

"That's it Mary Lynn," I said. "That's how it started."

"Jesus Christ," she said. "How much did you get?"

"A lot," I answered in the softest voice I had. "More than I ever dreamed of."

# Seven

**THE MEETING** had been held on a Sunday night. We had a week and a half to come back to Room 212 of the Paradise Motel with the gold. That hardly seemed like enough time.

As if to leave us alone with our thoughts, Rotbart and the other man left right after their presentation in a dove-grey English car with the largest tires I'd ever seen. The soft rubber of those tires made kissing noises on the asphalt pavement of the parking lot as they drove away, and a good number of us hung around that parking lot watching the car leave. The sound of those tires was like the goodbyes of all the imaginary girls we had. We wanted them back and turned toward each other as if looking for answers. We were, I'd guess, the converted. This must happen after religious revival meetings.

We didn't know each other very well and didn't know what to say about Rotbart.

"What did you think?" began one exchange.

"I don't know. The whole thing's probably a fake, but . . . ."

"The *but* is what hangs me up. If he's telling the truth, we could all be rich. But maybe . . .

"But maybe nothing. If we don't go, all we got is the same nothing we've always had. But if we go and if he's right, then . . . ."

"Then still maybe we go and he screws us somehow. Runs off with our money."

"Well, then, we just have a different nothing. I for one would just as soon trade one nothing for another. I'm tired of St. Louis. I'm tired of the weeds along the roads and the way the bricks look in the buildings. I'll risk $3,000 for a look at something else. Hell, if I'm left in Brazil, I'll start over there. They have beer. The pussies are just as tight and wet as the ones here. Or have I been misinformed?"

That was the logic that won. We were all losers looking for another roll. That's what got me up and showered and shaved by eight the next morning.

After stacking the breakfast dishes next to the sink, I got out the Yellow Pages and checked the entries under Gold Dealers.

43

Arthur Fenwick, Esq., had the smallest ad and a name English enough for my sensibilities. I imagined a small office with cherry paneling, hunting prints, and brass scales. I got out my savings account book from its corner of the dresser and drove downtown.

I had $3,300 in savings and $600 in my checking account. Those little digits seemed rather sad as I stood in line waiting for a teller. I'd been saving money since I first had a factory job between my freshman and sophomore years of college.

All of my summer jobs were difficult and tedious and dirty and low paying. Now, after years of them and years of studying and years of acting, I had a grand total of $3,300. I had marked each of my modest deposits toward that total. My savings deposit book was filled with penciled notations of this $200 and that $50. It all seemed rather pathetic.

The man in the crowd at the Paradise Motel was right. I'd rather have a new kind of nothing than the nothing I had.

"Oh, sir, I'm extremely sorry, but I can't perform a same-day liquidation of an entire account balance. I'm terribly, terribly sorry, but I know you'll understand the rule. We'll have to mail you a check in a few days."

A *same-day liquidation* sounded almost like something sexual when this rather breathless young woman said it. But I insisted.

"It is, you know, my money, and I'd like it now," I said.

She went through her explanation again, but I held fast. I wanted my dough. I could feel the line behind me grow longer and more restless.

A moment later I was sitting in the office of the Assistant Manager.

"Well, you must understand we have our rules."

"Of course, ma'am, I would just like a check for all my money. It's not such a large sum these days. Besides, I promise to be careful with it, OK?"

"Sir, we just can't have everyone showing up for their money all at once. We've had this rule for just years and years."

I went though three assistant vice presidents before I got my money, and I thought I would have to go through three more when I asked for cash.

"Cash?" the last one I met said. "You mean cash like real dollar bills?"

"I certainly don't mean cash like fake dollar bills."

"Oh, I'm afraid we have a rule against giving out that much cash. You'll have to speak with the President. Besides, didn't you say you wanted a check?"

"Yes, that's where I started, but you know I'm a little worried that you folks don't have my money."

"Oh, sir, we've been in business since 1968. You don't need to worry about us. But we're a little worried about you wanting all that money at once."

I wondered if they would follow me around and comment on my spending habits.

The more I thought about her and about all the tedious people who tell you your library books are overdue or that your car title is incorrect—all those who keep the files of life straight while life itself drives quickly by them: the more I thought about them, the more I wanted to go to the Amazon.

Arthur Fenwick's gold dealership was located over a Chinese carry-out restaurant and a liquor store in the no-man's land of pawnshops and laundromats at the edge of the St. Louis ghetto.

Between the restaurant and the liquor store was a door with an old-fashioned pebbled translucent glass window in its top half. Arthur Fenwick, Esq. was lettered there in small and dim gold letters as if to whisper his presence. It never occurred to me that he might be poor and that he could afford nothing better than a ghetto address. What in all likelihood was poverty I took at first for understated elegance.

Inside the door was a hallway that smelled of urine and cigars. There were stairs that led to another door, though this second door had a translucent pane that covered practically the whole surface of the door, suggesting that things got better as you went up.

Next to the door was a twist-style doorbell. When I turned it, a buzzer clattered erratically. A moment later the door creaked open, pulled by an unseen power.

Inside, a counter barricaded off all but about four feet of a large room. It suggested that customers were either to conduct their business or leave. On the counter was a faded cardboard sign that read TUXES FOR RENT. A man and a woman with frozen smiles and fifties hairstyles looked at each other like cake decorations. *A Parfait Day in a Parfait Way—Parfait Cleaners. Your assurance of the best*, the print beneath the couple said.

There was nothing even close to cherry paneling on the walls. There weren't any hunting prints or brass scales. A sign hanging above the counter read STAMPS COINS COLLECTIBLES.

The room behind the counter was huge and mostly empty. It looked as though its largest enterprise was dust. Across one wall was a collection of tarnished trophies. The inscriptions I could read said *Mary Fay's Beauty Lives Forever in Our Hearts, 1959*. Against the other wall was a safe. Above the safe was a crudely worded sign on what appeared to be shirt cardboard. *The golden rules*, it read. *Them that's got the gold can make the rules. Isn't it time you got your?*

I wondered how powerful you could really be with bad grammar and poor spelling.

I heard a toilet flush and someone mutter. A moment later a bald man came from a room at the back.

"It's funny," he said, wiping his hands on his pants, "I sit here all day inhaling the smell of chop suey and worrying about somebody shooting up my liquor store and wondering if I'll have any customers. I get myself so stewed up my guts don't work right any more, and I have to spend half my life on the toilet. When customers do come, I miss a lot of them because I'm sitting back there taking another of the ten craps a day I do."

He stopped and looked at me. I started to ask about gold prices, but he was just pausing.

"Downstairs, oh boy, they think it's a shooting gallery. Irv's Liquor and Shooting Gallery, we should call it. Six shots for a buck. Right. Your choice—bullets or liquor."

He began chuckling.

"And the take-out place—why they're giving me heartburn just from the smell. Heavy grease over egg rolls. And over and over. I could just puke. Everyday the same food. I'd think they would lose their minds, but maybe their minds are as congealed as the gravy. And gold— do you think gold would go up? The government's giving money away like it was somebody else's dirty laundry, and still gold doesn't go up."

The man was picking up and setting down things on the counter as though he were looking for something. He lifted the tux ad twice and looked beneath it.

"Hasn't gold almost tripled?" I may have asked this with assurance, but I didn't really have any. I merely wanted to let him know I'd thought about gold. I didn't want him to take advantage of me.

He stopped picking up things and looked at me as if I were retarded.

"Tripled, schmipled. The way things are it ought to be a thousand bucks an ounce. I mean, good God, we threw away billions of dollars on that war in Asia. Just billions. And for what? To make the Japanese rich. Did you notice how you never saw much Japanese stuff before the War in Vietnam? You know, I think a lot when I'm back there on the toilet. I figure things out. I should take a typewriter with me. Shut myself in so I could shit and sermonize. *Sermons from the Shitter* by Irving Litewater. What do you think?"

"Then you're not Arthur Fenwick?"

"Arthur Fenwick. That's good. The old Esquire himself. Well, the old Esquire couldn't pay his rent. From the looks of the place I think he spent all his money on pints."

"But you sell gold?"

"You bet. I figure if the Esquire didn't pay me it would be OK to use his name. Besides, who'd shop at Irv's Gold Store? Get real. Sounds like the name of a place to buy steel-toed work shoes."

I didn't know how to break in on all of this, so I counted out $3,300 in bills and set them down on the counter. The man in the tux ad smiled out over the money and me and Irv as if he had better things on his mind.

Irv squinted at these the way a gardener might study a patch of dandelions in his otherwise perfect yard.

"They're no good," he said.

"But I just got them from . . . ."

"Not a silver certificate in the batch. Just paper, son. All you got is paper. Uncle's IOU, nothing more. Try writing a letter on the stuff or wiping your ass. No good."

He walked toward the safe.

"What you got there, $3,300?"

Though he may have thought the bills worthless, Irv knew how to count and count quickly.

"Yes."

He returned to the counter with a battered green metal box.

"Now here's the stuff you want, yessir."

The box was lined with old newspapers and held a variety of shiny gold coins. He reached beneath the counter and produced a threadbare piece of green velvet and, with great fanfare, counted out nine coins onto the fabric. He used his index finger to push them slowly across the fabric and line them up in front of me. They looked liked fat fifty-cent pieces.

"There are . . . ," I started.

"Krugerrands," he finished. "In God's good gold. Certainly worth more than your silly little pieces of paper."

"Wait. I thought . . . ."

"Oh," he said. "I forgot the dealer mark up. But you're a nice guy, and business is slow today. Let's just call it even. Let's forget the mark up. What do you say?"

He beamed when he asked me that, as if he were trying out for the part of Santa Claus in the school play.

"I don't understand," I told him. "I should've been given ten coins and change. Spot's around $300, right?"

Actually, I thought it closer to $290. Even with Irv's commission, I should've been given ten coins.

I looked at the counter. My bills were gone, and Irv smiled at me.

"Spot's up today," he said. "Besides, I get a little profit for putting up with guys like you."

"This spot must be a dog, because he's taken my money and left me short on gold."

"I like you," Irv told me. "I like a man with a sense of humor. I like a man who speaks his mind."

Maybe it was the hassle of getting the money. Maybe it was the realization that I was about to let go of almost all my money. Maybe it was Irv's smiling insouciance. Maybe it was remembering the awful summer jobs and the tired performances of Shakespeare when it took me weeks to save $50.

Whatever it was, it seemed to reach out from me and grab the front of Irv's shirt. His smile went from his face slowly, erased like a phosphorescent display. I could hear his stomach rumbling.

"Asshole, you either give me another Krugerrand or three hundred bucks," I demanded.

"But then . . . my profit . . . It's hard to make a living doing this."

His heart wasn't in this remark.

"Here," he said and handed me a coin. "Asshole is right. And right now mine is calling me. Shut the door on your way out."

He turned and trotted to the back of the room. Suddenly the meaning of *the trots* became clear.

I was shaking when I got to the street with my ten coins. As I started the Volvo, I saw a man stagger from the liquor store and lift a bag-covered bottle to his lips. A moment later he heaved the package at the plate glass front window of Irv's Liquors. Webs of cracks reached slowly across the glass. The face of a sales clerk appeared in the center of the cracks like a fat trapped fly and then disappeared.

As I drove away, I heard on the radio that gold had dropped in London. So far that day, Irv and I hadn't done very well.

# Eight

**A WEEK AND A HALF** after the first meeting, I took my three-coin deposit back to the Paradise Motel. The man with the shaven head opened the door when I knocked.

"Is Mr. Rotbart here?" I asked.

To tell the truth, I was a little frightened. I felt like a student coming in with his homework.

"No, not here," he said in a heavy German accent. I hadn't heard him speak before.

"He will be back?" I heard myself say, perhaps hoping that my Germanic syntax would be easier for the man to understand.

"Yah, soon. You have perhaps the money?" The man rubbed his fingers against his thumb.

I handed him the three coins, and he held each of them up in the sunlight. I half expected him to bite them.

"Yah, good. In you are," he said. "You will want this then, no?"

It was a photocopy of instructions for the plane flight between St. Louis and Beaumont, Texas, where Rotbart was to meet us and take us to Camp Fortitude, "a rare Eighteenth-Century Estate (I'm quoting the letter) that's been converted into a Training Facility to produce Men Suitable for Sojourns into Adversity." The rest of the letter detailed the clothing and gear we were to buy at a store called the Gentlemen's Chandlery. At the bottom on the letter was a rough skull and crossbones like a crude imprint from a pirate's intaglio ring.

I tried to look past the heavy-set man at the expensive looking leather suitcases on the bed.

"I thought," I said, "that Rotbart was to contact us, that we'd know we were going when he called us."

"True this is in the most cases. But in this one, for you, it is not. No." The man paused a moment, as if lost in the corridors of his thought. "What I am meaning is simply that Rotbart especially wanted the smart young man. 'The smart young man I hope for very much,' Rotbart had to me said. You go."

The man smiled at me, though you could tell there were other things

50

he'd rather do than smile.

This news buoyed me up enormously. I wanted to jump and click my heels together when I left the motel room.

There were six or seven others from the meeting who were at the Gentlemen's Chandlery when I got there. All of us had our letters. We didn't know what to say to each other and walked around the small store looking at the floor and the merchandise—at, in short, anything but each other. I noticed that every letter I saw (including my own) had the damp, brown marks of a tight and sweaty grip.

The proprietor of the shop wore a waxed moustache and one of those fly fisherman's vests with lots of pockets and epaulets. He, too, was sweating as he stood near his cash register at the front. I wasn't sure whether he was worked up about all the business or whether he was worried that we might steal the merchandise we'd gathered.

Rotbart had evidently contacted him ahead of time, for a table had been set up at the back of the store with parts of our outfit in various boxes. As if to strengthen our sense of mission, the original newspaper ad was taped up on the mirror in the dressing room.

"You know," the man with the moustache told me as I was checking out, "I almost wish I were going with you. Urban living is calcifying me."

After a great deal of fuss about my merchandise and about the cash register, he smiled when he announced my total of $232.16.

"Of course," he said, "it's getting easier to live here with totals like this.

"$232.16," he repeated like a mantra. "That's a nice number. If you wait just a moment, I'll print up the name labels for your shirts. It's a free service of ours. You know, our motto is *Camp Forever and Beyond.*

"Owen Hill III, that's a nice name," he said when he came back in a few minutes. "You know, you could be an actor or somebody important with a name like that. Oh, by the way, here's your Adventurer's Notebook.. We give them away with all purchases over a hundred dollars. You can keep a record for yourself. Good luck."

When I returned to my apartment around three in the afternoon, I dropped the bags from the outfitting store on the bed, got a beer from the refrigerator, and studied Rotbart's list. I had it all—from the

Dreadnought trousers down to the rot-proofed cotton socks.

As I finished my beer, I laid out the clothing on the bed, beginning with the steel-toed hiking shoes at the bottom and ending with the cotton-covered bushman's hat at the top. The various items of clothing lay together on the bedspread like a giant cut-out doll. I closed my eyes and imagined myself mastering the black water of the river, standing silent and jut jawed as the natives gathered around me with their faces painted in chromium yellow and red. I returned finally to civilization in a weather-beaten boat with the gold and precious minerals stacked around me like friends.

I thought very briefly about what I was leaving behind, but I hadn't accumulated much in my life, hardly even the costuming of an actor.

Within a few days, I sold my furniture and my car to a friend in the acting company. I gave away most of my clothes I wasn't that close to my parents, but I called them and told them that I was joining a new repertory company in Louisiana and that I was going to Latin America with it on an extended tour. My father gave me his old song and dance about going to business school, and my mother suggested—as she always did—that I should come home to think things over. I bid them farewell, and the next morning, with my Delta ticket in hand, I took a taxi to the airport and, I hoped, to the start of a brand-new life.

# Nine

"THAT'S HOW IT GOT STARTED," I said to Mary Lynn.

Returning to Mary Lynn and that ugly kitchen from the St. Louis of my story took a moment. Slowly, however, the sounds of Illinois overcame my memories of the airport.

Mary Lynn still sat huddled on the kitchen chair, and the fluorescent lights continued to flicker their blue and wavery shadows over us. The tick of the clock seemed loud in that silence. McCoo sat in a chair beside the door, his arms folded across his chest. He was gently snoring and seemed benign as the whimpers of sleep rose and fell. I noticed that it was almost midnight. Over three hours had passed since I'd begun my story.

"Very interesting," Mary Lynn said. "But let's take the Delta flight in the morning. We can't do much until you get well. You need your rest. Maybe you can travel in a few days."

She helped me up, and I did feel stronger, as if hearing the beginning of my story reminded me that my original ambitions were still true. I put my arm around her shoulder, and I tried to walk without using too many of my stomach muscles. It wasn't as hard as I imagined it would be.

And sure enough, she had me take up the thread of the story the next morning as we sat on the veranda after breakfast.

I began with the airplane flight to Texas and what happened in Louisiana after that.

# Ten

**THE DELTA FLIGHT** sank lazily down like some partly buoyant object resisting its descent. The heat from below was palpable, and the city underneath us seemed to shimmer toward the sky, as if it were very slowly rising and coming apart like something on fire.

Even though it was only nine in the morning, stepping out of the plane was like entering an attic room in deep summer. I had trouble breathing. Walking across the sticky asphalt of the runway, I was covered with a thin layer of sweat that turned chilly a few minutes after I entered the air-conditioned terminal. While I had the clothes for an adventure, I wondered if I had the body.

Rotbart kept his word. Arms crossed, he was standing by one of the baggage-claim areas as if he owned the place. The man with the shaven head was there too, along with two angular men wearing sweat-stained cowboy hats made of straw. I was glad to see the new men, glad to know that Rotbart had employees. They gave the enterprise credibility.

I counted exactly ten of us from the meeting at the Paradise Motel. All ten of us were easy to spot: we each had on a version of expedition clothes, and we were all patting our pockets or checking our bags to make sure we had our stash of gold coins. A pickpocket would've found us easy marks.

I was nervous. The world suddenly seemed bigger and more menacing than it had. It's hard to have your serious wishes come true.

"You are perhaps Hill, Hill with three sticks after your name?"

The question so startled me I didn't at first realize who had asked it.

"That's right," I said. I had to think a moment, and then I finished, "Yes, Hill the Third."

It was Rotbart. He'd only seen my name on the application form. I nodded yes and was, for the briefest moment, tempted to salute.

"You know, Mr. Hill, I'm delighted to have a man of your stature here on this trip."

"Yes," I agreed. I mean, what would you have said to that? While I liked the attention of our leader, I wondered where all of this was going.

"Mr. Hill, I spotted you right away as one of us."

He patted my shoulder and went on.

"Yes, I saw right off that you're one of those men who's born to live beyond the norm. You know, when we are done, and you have returned from the River a wealthy man, and you are sitting in, shall we imagine, a small cafe on the docks at Porto de Moz, sipping a Campari over ice, your coat will have the survivor's bright patina. You will, I suspect, attract many women with that coat."

I hoped that the sweat from my brief walk had left stains below my armpits. I hoped that my clothes were wrinkled. I wished for the stubbly beard of the adventurer, the look of the man who'd crouched in the fo'c's'le as the pirates came over the side. I wished for the narrow eyes of the man who'd seen hard things and lived.

Then Rotbart placed both hands on my shoulders. Although he was shorter than I, although I looked down into his sharp blue eyes, I could feel his power. I wanted to kneel down. I felt as if he were about to knight me.

"Mr. Hill, I've reserved a small conference room. I want you to gather our colleagues and their gear and meet me there. Room 308. Verstehen Sie?"

"Right," I said, having only the vaguest idea of what I was agreeing to.

"Good. I like a man who shares my opinions. I'm not afraid to admit it; I like a man who's like me."

That said, Rotbart squeezed my shoulders, shook me, and strode off with the bald man and the two cowboys.

When I turned around, I saw that our conversation had collected our brave little band in a rough semi-circle around me. Rotbart had effectively made me a leader.

"What'd he say? What'd he say?" It was the man who claimed to know so much about minerals. He no longer seemed so confident. "What we gonna do? What we gonna do? My name is Howard, and that's all I'm sure of. I'm worried. What we gonna do?"

Although we had all received the same instructions from Rotbart, we looked like a collective example of how well-planned things can go wrong. Howard was dressed in what appeared to be Army fatigues issued in the World War II era. They were simultaneously new and out of date.

One man was wearing an old football uniform with the number 28 on the back and *Central High* in black letters across the chest. Without the shoulder pads it was built for, the jersey drooped at the man's shoulders and made him seem small. We all looked, I think, as if we'd rummaged through the Goodwill Store of our fantasies. Our clothes embodied some element of what we wanted to be, but they ended up making us look silly, like examples of how reality ruins dreams. As I stood there and realized how we all must appear to outsiders, even my safari jacket seemed less like Porto de Moz and more like an L.L. Bean who might be in over his head. What's more, the clothes made us look out of shape and pasty—and even, finally, silly. Two or three of us didn't look like we could survive a long walk, let alone three months of training.

"What we going to do?" Howard asked again.

"I don't know," I said "I just don't know."

He had begun to tug at my arm, as if this might pull out the truth. His gesture drew the others into an even tighter circle.

"I mean," Howard went on, "do you think it's a good idea, coming all the way down here like this? I never been in no Louisiana before."

A red-faced man in a dirty Massey Ferguson hat spoke up.

"What the fuck you mean, 'Is it a good idea coming all the way down here?' Good God, man, we're already here, and the short guy's got some of our money. You should've thought about these things before. Besides, I can't see how Louisiana might be different than anyplace else."

There wasn't a way to answer Howard's question or say what he really wanted me to say, which was that everything was fine. On the other hand, I thought, I might as well make him feel better.

"Don't worry," I said, "everything's going to work out. For now, we've got to meet with Rotbart in a conference room. Let's hear him out I'm nervous too, you know, but let's hear what the man says. He still hasn't got all our gold, right?"

The red-faced man saluted me, and Howard gave me a tentative thumbs-up gesture. I couldn't believe it: a chain of command was beginning to form. I had never been in charge of anything before, and there I was—a lieutenant behind me, and a platoon trailing along behind him. I guess I led because they followed. I took them in the direction they wanted to go.

After we collected our luggage, we walked to one of those banal, cinder-block rooms that resemble high-school classrooms, rooms that suggest that we'll never quite get away from Miss Peterson and Vice Principal Neuhouse.

We stacked our baggage in one corner of the room and then stood quietly for a while, until one of the men said, "OK," and we all sat down in the chairs that had been arranged in lecture-hall style.

Howard and I sat at the side of a table in front of the others. Without saying anything to each other, we had left room for Rotbart and his associates. We waited in the room twenty minutes before anyone spoke.

Finally the red-faced man stood up.

"Owie, is it then?" he asked, or said really. He leaned forward a little, the way someone would tossing out dice.

"Right," I said just to be agreeable, though I've yet to find a way of making a nickname out of *Owen*.

"What's it to be then?" the man asked.

*Damned if I know,* I wanted to say.

But the man went on, "Then we're all going? That's decided, then?" He looked around the room for reactions.

When the man began to speak, Howard walked over to him and stood close as if to hear better. I think Howard meant this gesture to be threatening, but it merely seemed odd.

These people were all so strange. Next to them, a trip up the Amazon seemed normal.

"We have decisions to make and matters to decide. That's why we're here and why we're here," Howard said.

All ten of us looked back and forth at each other.

"Yes," Howard said in a voice become suddenly quite loud. "Yes again, I say. My name is Howard, which I may have already said; and I want you to call me Howard just like it says. I don't want Howie or Ho Ho, and I really don't want no 88. You can just forget that right now. And him. Him you don't call Owie or nothing else like that. It's

57

Owen Hill the Third as I heard them say. The next business here is gold. Golden gold, to make the point."

He pulled a small sack out of his trousers pocket and set it on the table.

"There's seven coins here. That's what's left from the three thousand of God's dollars I done over into gold. That was just about all the money I ever saw in my whole entire life. Here's the rest of my money. I'm in. I'm scared, but I'm in. It's go to that South America or keep on working as the night janitor in the Post Office. You tell me which is better. A government pension or rich beyond your wildest dreams? I'll take the dreams and go from there. I'm tired of pine-tar soap. I want more glitters than you get in the soap bubbles when you mop the floor. Yessir, I'm in all right."

He pushed the sack of gold toward the middle of the table, stuck his thumbs in the waist of his pants and walked toward the audience and sat down. He had the look of a man who'd accomplished something.

As he sat down, he said, "I had books on minerals from the other times I figured I'd get rich. I had so many books, I had books on books. I studied pictures of precious stones and minerals like they were the prettiest girls in the world. I studied them for years. For years, I've never seen anything like what Rotbart brought to that motel. If there's more of those stones, I'm going."

"I like that," I said and meant it. "I like that a lot. I'm a tired actor, and I'm throwing my goods in with Howard's."

I wondered what 88 was and dropped my own bag next to his. As I did so, I crossed my fingers and hoped he knew what he was talking about when it came to stones.

Then the rest of our group slowly came forward, beginning with the red-faced man. I suddenly noticed that beneath that Massey-Ferguson cap, he had the largest ears I've ever seen. He looked like a rat that was trying to become a human being.

"Lucky Beal. Count me in, too. Life ain't been the same since they shortened deer season."

Next came Tony LaCosta. He dropped his gold on the table and walked in silence to the back of the room. Then he came back and whispered to me that I should make a list of everyone's name and contribution. I got out my Adventurer's Notebook and began the list with Howard.

Then there was Murphy.

"Last name and first," he said, "Murphy was name enough for anyone."

Artie Hokum and Tyrone Butler came up. Merle Peppernow, who looked surprised to be there, dropped his gold on the pile. Haskel Fortune, who seemed rather gray and timid for such a large name, was next.

"You know, I've carried around this name of mine like a curse for years. This is the only chance I'll ever have of living up to it," he said as he put his gold with ours.

Saying "It's either this or working for a living," Stanley Smith was the last member of our group.

After I tallied up the gold to exactly seventy coins, I put a check beside each name. I never did write down Howard's last name and, in fact, never learned it. It didn't seem important at the time.

"Good," Howard said after I'd taken the coins out of their separate bags. We had ten neat stacks of seven coins each. Lucky Beal had a newspaper, and we discovered that gold had gone up. Even though the coins made a rather small pile for over $20,000, their increase in value seemed a fine omen for our departure.

Tyrone Butler said it for us all. "This is the first money I ever made by not working no regular way."

"You know," Tony LaCosta said, "it's something, what money together can do. I can see already what riches are. Each of those piles is now a little over $2,100. What good is $2,100? That's about the down payment on a mobile home, the first thing that gets blown away in a tornado. But $21,000—why now that's a sin worth confessing to. Good golly Miss Molly, I'll say. What a difference a zero makes. Of course we could just have us a lottery here. We could draw straws among ourselves for all the money. That way one of us could go home pretty rich. That way no one dies or gets hurt."

"No way, man," Lucky Beal said. "No way. I'm here for the big dough. We plan it right, we'll get so much money that we'll need help writing home about it. I mean, we'll have to have a Director of Zeros to keep the differences between your million and mine straight.

"Now here's the way I see it," Lucky went on. "We give the gold to Hamlet here. Somebody said he's a good actor, so we give him the gold. Anyway, when Rotbart shows up, we'll ask him to go over the deal again. I mean, we got to hear exactly what our cut is, comprende? When he's done on the fine points, Hamlet can ask for questions. If we're happy with the deal, we don't ask any. Then Hamlet gives Rotbart the gold. If there are questions, we walk. We walk hard and fast. OK, masked men?"

If nothing else, I'd become a star. While this airport room wasn't quite the stage I'd imagined, I was Hamlet at last.

"We've just got to be sure this trip is a big deal," Haskel Fortune said. "I've led a life of little deals way too long."

"What do the rest of you think?" I asked. I tried to squint my eyes like that sun-weathered explorer on the docks at Porto de Moz, but my eyes started to water and I quit.

They nodded half heartedly, and I took those gestures for yes. I guess I was learning that leaders, finally, have to shape the lives of the led.

"OK, then, I'll take care of the gold. Are we agreed on that?"

More nods.

Gold on the table, expectancy in the air, we waited for Rotbart to join us. I figured that he'd walk in just after we had put the gold into the bag Artie Hokum had made up especially for this trip.

"It's an expedition bag," Artie said and smiled as he set it on the table. He had been wearing it strapped to his chest beneath his shirt. "I worked it so it would be something special to bring my gold along. You see, I've never had so much money together in one place before, so I made the bag myself. What do you think?"

Scuffed and soiled, it looked like a leather ammunition pouch with straps attached. It was a leather-covered metal box with a leather flap, which had a brass snap to hold it closed. The pouch had leather straps to anchor it around someone's neck and chest. With leather-working tools, Artie had engraved the phrase *Rich Beyond My Wildest Dreams* on the flap. The words were a motto beneath a sun whose beams came down in streaks.

"Very nice," Howard said and held it up for everyone else to see. "Just the sort of thing to carry our goods. Just the sort of thing an adventurer would bring along."

That the bag looked like something from a shop class seemed just the right emblem for us. As it happened, all of our coins fit nicely inside the box.

But Rotbart didn't arrive and comment on the bag. His timing had been so impeccable I figured he would walk in the room just as we set Artie's bag full of gold on the table. But he didn't arrive then, and soon we all began pacing around the room. By any reasonable standards we shouldn't have been nervous. I mean, we had the gold and some agreement among ourselves. But our problem then—and our problem all the way to the jungles of our story—was this: we were all losers. We simply didn't know how to win. We expected another in the long list of failures the stories of our lives had become.

So we paced around that small room as it filled up with the sour smell of our fear. I don't know how many times I counted the courses of cinder blocks or how often I numbered the slats in the Venetian blinds. I knew the number of linoleum squares across the room and how many chairs there were. I knew that the folding wall at one end of the room was made by a company in Janesville, Wisconsin. I even tried to imagine what it was like to work in the factory where the door had been made.

At one point, Merle Peppernow looked at me and said, "Harriet told me I shouldn't come. She said I'm too fat to make money. She told me the trip's a fool's errand. But what does Harriet know? Can you answer me that? I mean really."

I confessed that I couldn't answer him, though I don't think he heard me.

"My whole life's been a fool's errand. Harriet was a fool's errand."

By the time Rotbart did arrive, we'd all passed into that funk you get from spending too much time waiting in close quarters with people you hardly know.

Rotbart finally walked into the room like good news coming by telegraph. We couldn't have been more delighted to have seen him. The bald-headed man joined him a moment later.

"I'm so very sorry," he said, "to have kept you waiting. But I've been busy with arrangements about our transportation to my estate in Louisiana."

He sat down at the middle of the front table, an act that caused all of us to return to our seats.

I suddenly realized that Rotbart's delay had been deliberate. We were so delighted that he hadn't forgotten us that our doubts had turned into relief. Most of us were smiling. Even Howard seemed to relax a bit and, for the first time that morning, sat down in a chair.

"Owen, your men are here and accounted for?"

"Yessir."

"I assume you have the gold?"

I nodded.

"Then I would like to have it counted here, on this table, please."

I glanced at Howard, who stood up, the smile leaving his face slowly, the way the picture used to disappear from old-fashioned TV screens when they were turned off.

Rotbart seemed to sense our worries when no one said anything.

"You must understand," Rotbart said, "I need my assurances. That's what the gold's for, don't you see? I don't want the money. Why, your amounts are nothing in comparison to what's out there. No, the gold only convinces me that you're serious. Do you really think I would go to all this trouble for what you have? And even if your gold were important, I could take it from you so easily."

Without taking his eyes off us, Rotbart gestured to the bald man, who now had a pistol in his hand. It was the longest small gun I'd ever seen.

"Helmut," Rotbart said to him, "you must give our friends a demonstration."

The bald man swung the gun around, pausing briefly as he pointed at each of us in turn. He then brought it back to me. He smiled and pulled the trigger. The hammer landing on the empty chamber produced the loudest click I'd ever heard.

"This," Rotbart said and smiled, "is a very effective weapon, especially in the hands of a connoisseur like Helmut. You should hear him talk about it. But, of course, you will hear him in Louisiana. Helmut speaks of this pistol the way some men talk about their women. And like the best women, the pistol is a foreign make."

Where, I asked myself, did this monologue come from? Where did he get such lines? Was there really, I wondered, a life that produced such thoughts?

"It is," he went on, "a pistol like a machine gun. It has a silencer and fires more than enough bullets to kill each of you several times over. It is a very effective weapon. To those passing by outside the sounds of the gun would resemble the dull impacts of hammering on a construction project."

It's funny how much smaller you feel when you realize that someone could kill you.

"You know, such a killing would stump the police. Ten dead in an airport meeting room. It would be a little like one of those gangster slayings in the thirties. They shot people down on the streets, and what were the clues? A speeding car, a man with a moustache who wore a dark grey hat. Nothing really. It would be like that—a front-page headline with a name like The Airport Murders. Oh, I like that. Let's see, it would go like this—Police said today that they have several clues about The Airport Murders."

Rotbart smiled.

"But enough. Please, let's gather up the gold and go. I don't want your money; I want you."

I glanced at the group.

"Are there any questions?" I asked.

"Yes, I've got one." Stanley Smith stood up as he began speaking.

"Actually, I've got more than one, but one's the only one I want to ask just here. Mr. Rotbart, sir, if we give you our money, will you quit pointing guns at us? That scares folks like me who don't like to think about dying any more than necessary."

"Right you are, Mr., ah, Mr. . . . ."

"Smith," Howard said. "He's Stanley Smith as I heard him say."

"Of course, Mr. Smith," Rotbart said and smiled. "Are there any more questions?"

As usual, the rest of us were studying the tops of our shoes.

I figured that our silence meant we'd settled on going, and once again I made ten piles of seven coins each. Ten little soldiers of fortune.

"Fine," Rotbart said, "you're all accounted for. The books on the entry fees are closed. Here is the rest of your money. Helmut, please add the thirty coins to the rest. Then, I want all these coins in a bag, please. A heavy one. Owen, I want you to carry it."

I slid Artie's pouch toward Rotbart, who stacked all hundred coins inside. Then I took my shirt off, strapped the pack to my chest and put my shirt back on. You really couldn't see the pack under the fabric unless you knew it was there.

"Perfect, men. Just the thing. Looks like what Long John Silver would carry," Rotbart said. "Men, are you ready?"

I nodded yes and then, slowly, everyone else did too.

"I know you're worried. I can feel it. You're afraid I'm going to take your money. You're afraid that you're going off on an eccentric's mad adventure.

"But you're not going to lose your money. Oh no, your money will come back to you a hundred times over. I promise you that. You'll return with rubies the size of baseballs, with emeralds like bars of Palmolive soap.

"Now we must, as they say, abroad. To Camp Fortitude, my estate in Louisiana. Do you like the name?"

I don't know if anyone besides me was following this. Howard was staring into the middle distance, and Merle Peppernow was watching a fly dive at the Venetian blinds.

"It's wonderful," I said. In fact, I thought it *was* a marvelous name. "But let's abroad, then. Movement is less wearisome than rhetoric. We've been sitting in this room for two hours."

"Ahh," Rotbart said, "I like a man who's anxious, Owen. That sort of fellow gets going. He changes the world, if only because he can't stand the gnawing void of inactivity.

"You will get on a bus I have converted to our uses. You must allow me to keep the location of Camp Fortitude secret. I've covered the windows of the bus so you won't know our route. The vehicle has rest room facilities and some food. The trip will take about three hours. We'll arrive about one in the afternoon. My good man Junior Junior will be your chauffeur. His brother Junior Senior will load you and

64

your things. Like all excellent men, they are quiet and reliable."

Once we began moving it was amazing how rapidly we ended up standing outside the main entrance to the terminal, our bags stacked neatly by one of the men in cowboy hats. We stood there like aging basic trainees.

A few minutes later, an old passenger bus with its windows painted black pulled up to the curb. The illuminated space above the front windshield—the space that usually said Main Street or Route 30 or Poughkeepsie on ordinary buses—was empty, as if the bus didn't know its destination. Inside the bus, a crude partition with a door had been fitted behind the driver's seat. Beyond this door, the darkness of the bus's passenger area seemed palpable. Just as I was about to walk beyond that rough door, I glanced back at the people hurrying into the terminal and the usual destinations of civilization.

The leather pouch felt hot against my chest as I turned around and stepped into the dark bus.

# Eleven

**IT WAS THREE HOURS ALL RIGHT**. By my watch, it was three hours to the very minute.

It was spooky. Afterwards, I wondered if Junior Junior had merely driven around near the airport and then headed to a location nearby. It seemed hard to believe that a long journey could be timed so well.

With the windows of the bus blacked out and a partition covering the front, we stared straight ahead into darkness. The cool and dusky interior of the bus resembled a black-lighted night club, and we all sat transfixed, like people waiting for the show to begin, for the chanteuse to sing, though the song was less likely to be "April in Paris" than "All Along the Watchtower."

The little plastic lights over each seat framed us in the darkness. Our faces seemed, after awhile, to stand out like masks. The scene felt vaguely oriental, like a noh play. Our lives were masks in the darkness, I thought. Happy, sad, or unimpressed—we each went through life with just our expressions of our little share of human history.

"What the fuck is this?" Lucky Beal asked. "I gave up three thousand bucks, a wife, and a three-bedroom ranch for a trip in this spookmobile."

He sat across the aisle from me. I could see small beads of sweat around his hairline.

"I don't have all that many spins left on the wheel."

Lucky must've been in his early fifties. Safely still in my twenties, I didn't feel quite so much anxiety. I had, as they say, miles to go. I tried to visualize being wealthy, and I tried to see myself dead. Neither vision came to me. I heard only the chatter of the bathroom door against its aluminum frame as the bus sped down the highway and saw only the dark around us like a costume.

"You went to college," Lucky went on. "You're certified smart, so you know. Are we doing the right thing? Are we going to be all right?"

"Of course we are," I said. "Quit worrying." I said this with so much authority I wondered if people in charge got their confidence by pretending to be confident. Is that what Churchill did; did he get rid of his own despair by getting rid of everyone else's?

I napped in fits and dreamed of getting older.

In between the naps, I drank cans of warm soda and ate watery tuna salad sandwiches. When the bus stopped, the hiss of the air brakes sounded like the opening of another soda can. A moment later, I felt the shudder of the motor as it was turned off.

Junior Junior opened the door between the driver's compartment and the rest of the bus. The sudden touch of light was almost unbearable. Lucky Beal turned away and covered his face with his hands, as if the possibility of the future was just too much. I saw large gold spots that contracted into themselves and went black and then away like black holes.

"OK, lambs, out for the shearing," a voice called from outside.

# Twelve

**AFTER I HAD BLINKED AWAY** the darkness, I began to study the landscape, which seemed to have a peculiar combination of the worst from several geographies. While there were pine trees that suggested cool northern climes, their resinous smell mixed with the humid air and created a palpably sticky atmosphere. Breathing was like inhaling varnish. Even the sand—as fine as that on a Mediterranean beach—turned out wrong and menacing. To walk in it meant sinking down a couple of inches in the earth and then sliding backward with each step forward. Trying to get someplace, breathing in that awful air which began to chafe your throat when you strained (and you strained with almost every movement) was frustrating and, for someone in ill health, deadly. I was probably the youngest of the group, and my chest felt heavy when I took a breath. I wondered briefly if my colleagues, who were older and heavier and more out of shape than I, would make it. I had never felt such withering heat.

"So this is Louisiana," I heard someone in our group mutter.

The rough voice that called us out of the bus belonged to Junior Senior. I noticed that our driver, Junior Junior, now wore a pistol slung low in a holster on the side of his leg. With his sweat-stained straw cowboy hat, he looked like an extra from a western. And this was a movie I wasn't sure I wanted to see.

I was the last to join our little group, and it was obvious that someone had asked Junior Senior about his name.

". . . . never thought it was no big matter. I came first, and Little Junior came next—the one these Krauts call Junior Junior. I'm big, and he's small. He drives and doesn't talk. I'm mean, and I talk all the time. I don't like to drive. I'm so mean I get someone else to drive."

He didn't so much smile as draw his lips back across his teeth.

He paced back and forth and around and through the ten of us like a drill sergeant sizing up some new recruits.

He would stop occasionally and flick at an unbuttoned pocket or ask a question.

"Do you really think you're going to survive Louisiana?" he asked

Lucky Beal. "I mean, son, you're fat and you're pretty red now, and we haven't even started yet."

Lucky didn't answer, but he studied our surroundings very carefully.

All of us got lectures from Junior Senior on one point or another. He told Haskel Fortune to change his name.

"You just can't have a name like that. It's almost un-American."

He told Murphy that the Irish got in their own way. He told Merle Peppernow that he was a mistake. We waited for an elaboration, but Junior Senior went on to Artie Hokum and told Artie that he needed to apologize to his mother for becoming a son of a bitch.

"Excuse me, Mr. Senior. Excuse me," Merle said. "But what do you mean by your remark that I am a mistake? I would like that clarified, please."

"I don't clarify nothing except the butter. And that's for Mr. Rotbart and those that eat with him. The rest of what I mean, why you're so smart, you figure it out."

While Junior Senior gave us his thoughts on our lives, an old Jeep came toward us. A trail of dust hung in the air behind it and seemed to thread its way in and out of the pine trees. My eyes followed the dust trail back to the top of a distant hill and a large frame house with a veranda across its front. The trees around the house swayed slightly in a wind I couldn't feel.

Helmut was driving the Jeep.

Although the leather case filled with the coins was a heavy weight strapped against my chest, I felt like it protected me from things.

"This is not good," Helmut said when he got out of the Jeep. "You are too . . . too . . . what is the word?"

No one answered, though Howard was stroking his chin and seemed to be trying to think of one.

"Perfect in your language I am not. You are not helping me here out of this."

This was going somewhere, I supposed. You could feel the intensity of his speech. Even if he didn't quite have the words, his thoughts came like an engine warming up.

"It is not manlich to stand here so."

"Good gravy, man, we don't know what to do. We never been in no Louisiana before and never were in nothing like this before, nosir. No one's given us the rules. If you would tell us what to do, why we'd go for that treasure like gophers after their holes. And that's the God's truth. The God's truth and more. Why, that's as good as money in your pocket."

It was Howard. Not Ho-Ho or 88, but Howard pure and plain.

"I don't know what you're after," Howard went on. "but I'll do what you tell me to. Yessir, I will. I'm a good man true. You give me the door, and I'll walk on through."

Helmut snorted.

"These here man I like and take with us along."

He walked over to some brush and pulled a packing crate painted a military green out from under the leaves. With the precise gestures of someone who loved machinery, he assembled a machine gun on a tripod. With Howard's help, he set the machine gun and the tripod on top of the wooden box. Helmut fed one end of a cartridge belt into the gun and released its bolt with a sound that made all of us stiffen a bit.

The rest of us paced back and forth. I noticed that the backs of almost everyone's shirt were soaked through with sweat, and I could feel rivulets of moisture going down the centers of my chest and my back. When I moved, the leather pack of gold stuck to my chest and pulled away like something wet.

"So," Helmut said at last. Almost in unison we all stepped back. "So, so, so," he repeated.

He pointed the gun barrel at a clear space in the trees along the road, dropped (almost, in fact, fell) to a kneeling position behind the gun, and fired at an unseen target up the road of our arrival.

None of us moved, except to flinch when the firing began and when it stopped.

I wanted to go home then. I remembered my mother and my father in a pleasant light; I wished, suddenly, that we hadn't grown apart. I recalled scenes from my childhood. I remembered walking out among the flowers behind our house. I wanted to go back there. I wanted out of Louisiana.

Once Helmut was done firing, everything seemed to hang in the air

70

like the smoke from the expended shells and the smell of gunpowder. He'd shot away our arrival, and we were left with the hard weather of staying in Louisiana. The day was still hot, and the humidity covered us all.

"Why does he keep doing this?" Howard asked. "He keeps pointing guns around as if we are the enemy. Shit, we're here for him. Does he think we came all this way to take his guns away?"

"And now, now do you see?" Helmut stood up from the gun. His eyes seemed to stand out from his face. "Die Weiblichen, ja, die Weiblichen. You see, yes."

I didn't know German and I didn't know much else, but *die Weiblichen* kept repeating itself over and over in my head like an overture to an opera. I guess he'd shown us that we couldn't escape whatever fate Camp Fortitude held in store for us.

Then Junior Senior made us get our bags. He had us stand in two lines so that we marched two by two toward the house carrying our things. It was about 2:30 in the afternoon when we started, and the heat was oppressive. I felt as though tons of air were weighing down on our heads and on our backs. The air was so heavy, the hundred ounces of gold hardly seemed like anything at all.

I began to feel light-headed. It was, at first, a rather pleasant sensation. In my head I was this very small person at the top of my body's enormous mountain. The usual ground of the ordinary earth was miles away. But then I had trouble walking. My feet were in another realm and didn't get the proper signals. They kept getting mixed up with the sand, and I began sliding on my feet and rocking with the rest of my body and hearing Lucky Beal say "Are you OK, man?"

I wasn't. I wasn't OK at all, but I didn't say anything. I thought I could beat my feelings. I thought I could wish them away. I was young and fairly healthy. So I concentrated on moving and on keeping my feet on the ground. But the earth kept rising up to me and going back down, and soon I was getting disoriented. I didn't know where the ground was supposed to be. All the while, I kept getting hotter and sweatier. All the while, I kept listening to Howard and Lucky chatter on about how hot and difficult everything was. I wondered how the others were managing. Their ages and their weights must've felt like chains.

"It's hotter than it ought to be," Howard said. "It isn't right to be this hot."

"Now what kind of thing is that to say? I mean really," Lucky said. "How do you know how hot it ought to be? Have you ever been on a gold rush before?"

As they began arguing, again, about whether Rotbart was telling the truth, I tuned out the world. I gritted my teeth, and—rocking and swaying along—I tried to manage the light-headedness. I thought to myself, hey, I'm not really light-headed. It'll go away. But it didn't go away. Nor did the pounding from the heat and the tons of atmosphere go away. It was in my head at first. It pounded like Dr. Death himself trying to get inside my head. I tried to shake it off. I was walking along with a pouch of gold against my chest, shaking my head back and forth, as if someone was asking me questions. It pounded and pounded.

"It takes awhile, doesn't it?" Rotbart asked from where he stood waiting for us, arms akimbo, on the veranda of the house at the end of the road.

"What?" Howard asked. He spit the word out as if it were the last one he had.

I was so involved with simply moving I didn't realize that the march was over. I walked into Howard and knocked him down. He felt light when he toppled over, as if the heat had taken substance out of him. He lay on his back looking up at the rest of us.

"Getting up this hill," Rotbart continued, "is harder than it seems. The house appears so close from below where Helmut put on his artillery lesson. But it's almost three miles, you know. You've all been walking for an hour. It's amazing how the eye compresses distances here. Everything seems closer than it really is. Life is much harder than it appears. It's a wonderful metaphor for the place. We are here to train you in how to overcome difficulties, and difficulties are everywhere. Isn't that marvelous?"

"Right, right, and double right," Howard said, gasping for breath between each word as he sat up on the ground. "But when do we get our breath back, please? I need it to get going again."

Rotbart looked down beneficently at Howard, like a priest, but didn't answer his question. He went on with his monologue.

"Three miles in that dreadful sand. Three miles in that heat and in the bad air. It's like walking through a tannery carrying weights. You know, I'm surprised that you made it. None of you appear to be in very good shape."

Howard stared mildly up at Rotbart, and the rest of us stood around, trying to bear up under the heat. No one thought to move into the shade.

Rotbart squinted down at Howard, who sat there blinking.

"Are you all right?"

I was so hot standing there that I couldn't think anymore. I began feeling dizzy again.

Merle Peppernow sank down in one continuous slow motion like someone who'd been hit on the head. His skin began to turn, first, the color of watermelon meat and, then, white like the part near the rind.

The heat seemed to have robbed us of our fellow feeling. We didn't do anything, except stare at him the way we'd stare at any mess.

"The climate here is difficult," Rotbart said. "One doesn't believe the heat at first. I suppose it's the wind that tricks us. It's always blowing; there's always a breeze. But the temperature and the humidity are ugly twins. They're both ninety or ninety five. But one survives, if one is careful, isn't that right, Mut?"

Helmut had come from someplace to join Rotbart on the veranda. He stood a little behind and to the side of his boss, as if in deference. Helmut crossed his arms and nodded slightly.

"We shall become, I hope, good friends. You must call him Mut, too, men. But sound it carefully with an *oo* sound on the vowel. Otherwise, he becomes a simple mut, a rough and homeless and mangy dog, though to tell you the truth he's sometimes that as well."

Rotbart seemed vastly pleased by his estate and by Helmut and by his charges before him on the ground.

Merle Peppernow's shirt was open. He was on his side, and his white stomach lay like a puddle beside him.

"I hope you don't mistake my good humor for callousness, men. Our fallen comrades are suffering from heat exhaustion. They should revive after resting on mother earth for a bit. If they don't, well they'll rest inside mother earth for a longer while. In any case, there isn't much we can do. I purposely don't have a dispensary at Camp Fortitude. I figure that people with health problems should find another line of work. It's a risky business, this hunting for treasure. Those who cannot survive these minor trials would certainly fail the major test of our expedition."

I wanted to be angry or frightened. I thought I ought to have an emotion of some kind, but the heat had robbed me of all sense except the instinct for survival. I wanted to live, and that thought didn't leave much room for anger or fear. And when I did have room to think, I got greedy. The survivors would profit from casualties, I realized. If some of us died, the survivors would have more money. I rubbed my hand against the leather case.

"Cool water helps sometimes, though it can also cause pneumonia. No, we shouldn't risk chilling them or even disturbing them. Let's wait. Their distress should pass."

And wait we did—Rotbart pacing the veranda, Helmut walking off to the woods and returning, the eight remaining members of our brave little band stepping back and forth around our fallen colleagues. We finally moved Merle into the shade, but even the shade was hot and humid, so we didn't bother with Howard. No one thought to take the two of them in the house and put them to bed. And if one of us had that thought, he didn't share it with anyone else. Merle got to his knees and rocked back and forth like someone locked in prayer, while Howard lay on one side in a fetal position moaning very slightly. Their color changed from a bright pink to a luminescent white and back to pink.

An hour later, Merle died.

He quit rocking back and forth, sighed once, and then tipped over on his side.

"Ja, ja," Helmut said as he walked back from one of his nervous trips to the woods.

Was this really happening? A little voice in the valley of my brain asked. No other voice answered it.

"Oh, shit, shit." That was Howard. He stood up briskly, as if this death had revived him. "Now what we going to do? This is terrible, and I mean terrible. One of God's souls just gone when he was right here like people are. I mean, I never been around no death like this before. When people died, they went off someplace else to do it. They didn't do it in front of strangers. Oh, shit, shit."

"We will bury him, of course. We won't leave him here."

I guess Rotbart was trying to comfort us in his way.

"Of course, we'll bury him," he repeated. "This Anglo-Saxon custom has its inconveniences, but it has its uses and its precedence as well. Burial was, I think, invented on the battlefield. It was a way of keeping one's enemies from discovering one's position and one's losses. In the jungle it's so much simpler. One leaves the dead or throws them in the river. That way, God gets a carcass that's been to the best cleaning service in the world. All the muck and matter of daily life are gone.

"Of course we'll bury him," Rotbart repeated again, as if answering an unstated objection. I glanced at Howard, who seemed horrified.

"We're not uncivilized men. After all, what's the good of great wealth if one isn't civilized enough to know what the joys of money are? Mut will bring you shovels."

Burying Merle was, in all kinds of ways, an awful chore. Stanley and I carried him. Stanley had his feet, and I hooked my arms under those of the corpse. He was overweight and very heavy. The going went slowly. I hitched the pack of gold tighter against my chest, and we went on. The longer we walked in that heat, the more I was convinced that he hadn't deserved to live. Stanley and I slid back in the sand with each step as if the ground didn't want us to go on. The limpness of the body made it heavier than a living one, and soon Merle's butt was dragging in the sand.

Every twenty or feet or so, we had to stop and regrasp the body. We were soaked with sweat. Our clothes were so wet, it looked as if we'd been standing in the rain. Several times I began to be nauseous. All of our jiggling around was mixing up the body's chemicals with its undigested food, and I walked in a halo of putrescence. I wanted to be sad or even horrified about Merle, but he smelled too bad for that. Lucky Beal walked beside us with a shovel. He kept glancing sideways at Merle and us, and managed to look more ratlike than ever.

"Lucky," Stanley asked, "can you help us out? This dead soldier seems to be gaining weight as he decays, and I'm not feeling so good my own self."

It was true. Merle's weight seemed to be sliding toward his middle and then sagging down.

Lucky grabbed Merle by the belt and held him off the ground.

"I don't know about you fellows," Lucky said, "but I'm getting a little worried. My mama used to tell me that bad starts bode bad finishes, and this one bodes about as bad as I have seen."

By the time our slow procession had reached the edge of the pine forest, it was almost five o'clock. We had been in Louisiana less than a few hours. I rubbed the bag of gold for luck.

The light in those awful woods was filtered through the dense pine branches and was like the light beneath the surface of a lake. The air was full of resin. Breathing was difficult.

"We go fifty meters, ja. It's easy, the digging. The trouble you have is little. Entirely little."

All of us except Helmut were sweating and breathing heavily. Because of the resin, sweat stuck to our skin. The air was filled with cobwebs and gnats.

Merle's body hit the floor of the shallow grave with two little thumps, as if a life were summed up by bass notes that faded the moment they were sounded. The earth seemed easy and accommodating; it was used to death.

"I don't like this," Howard said. "I don't like this at all."

Rotbart came for us with his usual large nouns and fast verbs, but the remaining nine of our brave little band were quiet as we walked back toward the main compound. Rich *beyond your wildest dreams* didn't add up to a death and the horrors of burying one of us.

Out of the woods, the air was cleaner and easier to breathe.

Rotbart escorted us to a long shed behind and above the main house we'd seen earlier. The building had once been a sawmill and had a line of bare light bulbs hanging at intervals along the ceiling. There were forty or so beds fashioned out of rough-cut timbers with thin mattresses rolled up at one end of each bed. The place looked like a prison or a military barracks.

"There are linens and blankets in those cabinets at the back of the room," Rotbart said. "There are showers and sinks outside the door at the end. For toilets you have the woods. I advise you to wear boots and check beneath you. Our snakes are rather vicious if you drop excrement on them. It drives then into a biting frenzy."

Helmut found this amusing and slapped his thigh. I had never seen anybody really do this before.

"After you clean up and store your gear away, we'll serve dinner on picnic tables behind the main house. The evening is yours, and I hope you'll use it to meditate on the challenges ahead. If you intend to win, you'll have to be strong. Tomorrow we will begin at six am, Are there questions?"

Of course there were none. Questions could only come from those who knew part of the lesson, and we didn't know any of it. This was terra incognita. This, in fact, was terra double incognita.

I unstrapped the gold and lay the leather pouch beneath my pillow. I wanted to say something important against the dark as I lay down, but I didn't know what to say. I simply let the dark come on with what it knew.

# Thirteen

"WHAT WAS IT ALFRED HITCHCOCK LIKED?"

He was talking to us as he paced back and forth across the veranda of the white house. Rotbart studied the sky, which was blue and beautiful and, because of the heat that increased with each minute of the morning, seemed to weigh on us like beauty gone bad.

"What he liked was a clear day with nothing on the horizon."

He squinted just beyond us as he answered his own question.

We stood before him in an approximation of a military formation. Helmut was beside him like an extra in a movie about Nazis. He looked us over with such menace that I wondered if he practiced before a mirror. For the briefest moment I had this vision of Hitler studying himself in the mirror as he fastened up his uniform. I don't suppose he saw the figure in the glass as evil. He probably fussed over his moustache and tried to keep his hair from falling across his forehead.

Rotbart had first explained that we had to decide how we wanted to present our—what was his word?—deposit.

We were digesting our breakfast of greasy eggs, bacon, and waffles. It had been served to us on metal trays handed out by a black woman who stood behind the bottom half of a Dutch door at the back of the white house.

"There is your gold to consider. I'm sure you're thinking of it now that your compadre has departed this life to, we hope, a better one. You're each a little richer than you were, isn't that so?"

The pouch of gold felt sticky against my chest. I wondered how much longer I would have to carry it.

"How many of you believe in heaven and in hell?" Rotbart asked.

I don't think any hands went up. I looked at Howard and at Lucky Beal. Their hands were clasped behind their backs like men handcuffed to themselves.

"But of course. I forgot. You're thinking about your gold," he snorted. "Your gold is hardly worth thinking of. It's rather like the glass of water you down at bedtime compared to all the water in the world. Your gold is nothing, though it's mine, of course. You know that, don't

78

you?"

He spun around as he said this, spun around on his heels and giggled. His laugh was brittle, like the call of a little bird. The laughter ended too quickly in the soft Louisiana air.

"But don't go quivery on me, lads. Oh no, stay a bit. I won't take your money from you until I've trained you into good men, loyal and true. Truer than our brother in the wood. I like that. 'Truer than our brother in the wood' sounds like a title to something, now doesn't it?"

As Rotbart walked back and forth across the porch, I noticed that he wore jodhpurs.

"Ah yes, getting and keeping wealth, significant wealth, requires great discipline. That's why you might call John D. Rockefeller the Leonardo da Vinci of capitalism."

Listening to this was hard. The day was getting hot, and our breakfasts seemed to be hardening in our systems like spilled syrup. Rotbart talked like this for almost an hour. He was like someone who had stayed too long in graduate school. Standing there in the heat, trying to follow the Byzantine circuits of his thought to some kind of point about gold in South America, I wondered if we all hadn't made a terrible mistake. Perhaps *that* was the fleece—he brought us to Louisiana and talked us to death. I mean, maybe we were losers, and maybe we had everything to gain if the trip panned out, but, Jeez Louise, how much longer would we have to listen to explanations of almost everything? I wanted to get going.

I must've tuned Rotbart out for ten or twenty minutes. When I came back on his wave length, he seemed to be answering my questions.

"You have, to be sure, no reason to trust me. I told you about this God-forsaken place, seduced you with my and Mut's oddities, and then allowed a colleague of yours to die. You must, in fact, wonder if I'm, to use the current slang, for real. Why, yes I am. I am for realities, though the pathway to this grand noun is sometimes fraught with unrealities. . .

"Fucking A, can't we dispense with this shit and get on with the gold?"

"Succinctly put, Mr., ah, Mr . . ."

"Lucky Beal."

"Quite. Yes, quite, Mr. Ball. But the point of the matter sometimes is the shit, you see. Don't you see that, Mr. Ball? But no, I guess you don't. These are rituals we are performing now. Don't you see that? These are rituals as delicate as those performed by Navaho Indians."

"Beal. The name's Beal. And Jesus Christ, man, get to the fucking point. We're out here frying in the middle of nowhere, three thousand bucks shy of where we started out, and you're talking like someone in an old book."

"Mr. Ball, have you ever heard of heat exhaustion?" Rotbart went on as if he hadn't heard him.

"Well, I guess I have. Now I guess I have."

"Now, that's good Mr. Ball, because what we're doing here is getting you lads used to this terrible heat. That's half the training, you know, just coping with the heat. You start out standing, maybe do some brief projects. Your friend that we lost yesterday went, you know, from heat exhaustion. Now we could have you, Mr. Ball, take over the speaker's duties. I mean, someone's got to help us get through these next few days until you all are acclimated, but I'm rather tired of the word *fuck* and would, frankly, rather hear myself rhapsodize about this and that. In fact I wonder if that over-used word *rap* came from rhapsodize."

"Beal. The name's Beal. It may not make much difference to you, but it's something that was ever so important to my now dead Mother, God rest her soul. Now that you've got my money, that name is about all I have."

The plan for storing the gold was easier than the discussion that preceded it.

The nine of us dug a hole into which we planted a twenty-foot pole. It stuck up about twelve or fifteen feet out of the ground after we planted it in the hole we dug. Into its top we drove a large nail. Riding piggy back on Howard's shoulders, I hooked one of the straps from the leather case over the nail.

There, in the center of the compound, to be guarded by one of our group in eight-hour shifts, was our gold.

Putting it there was Lucky Beal's idea. He proposed it the way an exasperated child puts together the puzzle his younger brother has been fretting over.

"It's fucking easy. I mean, anybody tries to get our goods will be spotted in a second. We rub the fucker out just that quick."

Lucky slid his thumb across his fingers like someone who was an expert in rubbing people out.

"Mr. Beal," Rotbart said, "your ingenuity is, well, simply remarkable. Simply remarkable. With your permission, I'd like to make you the foreman of our little crew. Yes I would. Will you take on the challenge, Mr. Beal?"

"Me, sir? No, you've got the wrong laddie, and that's a fact. No, sir, let the college boy take charge. That's why they had to learn Shakespeare and things like that so the common people can't understand what they're talking about. Those are the people that are good at being in charge. That's how you can tell there's some bad shit coming down, when people start saying Shakespeare. The college boy will do your job, yessir. I can't think things far enough through."

That turned out to be a nice observation. He could see what was right in front of him, while I—well, I could take the longer view of things. Whatever Lucky did, he did with little or no thought.

"Yes," Rotbart agreed. "I'm rather fond of Owen myself. He got all of you this far. He's a subtle leader. I like that. He has that slight pause in his thinking that lets others discover the truth for him. He lays down the premises of the syllogism, and others find the conclusion."

After more talk and some time spent cleaning up our bunkhouse, it got to be lunch time. Junior Junior brought out sawhorses and boards to the parade area by the pole. The black cook then pushed out a wobbly grocery cart filled with pans and trays. Both of them set up a lunch of limp hot dogs, sour coleslaw, and melted ice cream. Even the Cokes tasted bad. After lunch I was sworn in as a kind of platoon sergeant to Rotbart's company commander.

"Will you promise," Rotbart asked "to obey me under all conditions?"

I glanced up at the sack of gold hanging like a weighted flag from its pole, and then I looked at the remaining seekers of the golden fleece. They appeared harder, as if some of the training had already taken hold, but they also looked more frightened.

"Yes," I said. "I guess I will."

"Guess, Owen? We don't have any guessing here. You will or you won't. The future isn't tentative, you know. It comes whether we want it to or not. The way we triumph over it is to decide that we are ahead of time. Ambiguity has no role in my affairs."

"Obey him, for Christ's sake," Lucky shouted. "I don't want another lecture. I want to get going. Just say yes."

It's very difficult to argue with a short red-faced man. It's like trying to reason with a vicious dog.

"OK," I said. "Yes. I'll obey you." I realized that I was shouting to be heard over Lucky Beal's commands, which he kept repeating over and over. "Yes. Yes. Yes. I'll obey you."

"Good," Rotbart said quietly. "Good. Now the rest of you—do you swear the same? To obey me and Owen under all conditions?"

There was a mutter of *yes*'s tagged with *I guess* and *I suppose.*

We chose Lucky Beal to be the first guardian of our treasure. Junior Senior brought out a rifle from someplace and tossed it to Lucky, who caught it like a man practiced in things military. He did a few twists and turns with the rifle and tapped it on the ground a couple of times as if he'd been a member of a drum and bugle corp. I guess these gestures made us all feel better. At least no one would steal our gold when it was guarded by a man with so much skill with a gun. Or that's what Rotbart said.

"Ah, my men, it does my heart good to see a gun turn through the air like that. All this twirling—it's like lace, you know, all this fuss around some empty space."

"Right," Lucky said. "You took the fucking words right out of my mouth. Is this thing loaded?"

He held the gun to his shoulder and pointed it at each of us.

"I'm really getting tired, and I mean, tired-the-way-you-are-when-you-can't-go-on-any-more tired. That kind of tired, I am, of people pointing guns at me," Howard said. "Every time there's a free moment around here somebody's sticking a gun at my nose, and my nose doesn't like it, I can tell you that."

Rotbart went over to Howard and eyed him the way a drill sergeant might look at a recruit. He walked around him a time or two, whapping his swagger stick against his jodhpurs.

"You want things to work out, don't you, my good man?" Rotbart asked Howard. "You're worried that things aren't going to go the way you thought. Is that right?"

"Let's just say I'm getting more and more scareder as we go along," Howard said. "I haven't seen no emeralds and no gold. All I seen is one good soul gone like puffs of cigarette smoke in the draft of a fan."

"Ah, but life in this vale of Louisiana is the stuff of disappointment and sadnesses," Rotbart said. "And you, my man and all my men— why you are here to triumph over adversity and death. The world, if not your oyster, is certainly a clam or two, at least a bit of fresh cod."

What came next was an expedition.

"What nobody quite understands," Rotbart began, "about those grand-looking ancestors of ours, the men in their mustaches and stiff shirts, the women with their Bibles and their tight hairdos, is that they just took off when things went bad. What was it Tennyson said?"

He actually waited for an answer. My God, asking our little group in Louisiana about Tennyson would be like asking Elvis Presley if his song phrasing had been influenced by Dante.

"'To strive, to seek, to find, and not to yield' is what Tennyson said a man's duty is."

Lucky Beal interrupted him.

"It's Shakespeare. Jesus Christ, it's the old Shakespeare trick all over. I'm damn fucking tired of this. It started when I was on a football team in high school. The coach would say that poetry Shakespeare shit to us. That meant I was going to get my teeth kicked out. It meant we were going up against some Godzilla team that would tear us into little tiny pieces. It's a rule with me—when you hear that poetry stuff, things are going to be pretty bad."

"Well put, my friend," Rotbart said and smiled. "I don't think matters just yet are so serious. No, not at all. What I propose are simple training exercises. Little expeditions into the country at first. Nothing hard. A little walking, a little sleeping out. You'll get used to the heat, and then we'll take on more difficult tasks. On this first trip, Mr. Beal will stay here to guard your gold with the splendid turnings of his gun. Mut and the two Juniors will come along by truck with our equipment, and Mathiley our lovely cook will bring us dinner. All we have to do is walk a few miles."

It was, as expeditions go, a mild one surely. I don't think we could have gone more than four or five miles, and we stopped several times to rest from the heat. We set a jaunty pace at first.

Tony LaCosta said he'd been a Drill Sergeant in the Army and sang out a cadence or two.

> I don't know but I've been told
> It's Jason's Boys that gets the gold
> Go to your left, your right, your left.
> Go to your left, your right, your left.
> What I've seen is awful clear
> The quest for gold it starts right here
> Go to your left, your right, your left

Then Tony would chant *Sound off three four,* and we'd come in with *Left* pause *Left* pause *Left, Right, Left.*

After an hour of this through the woods, after an hour of marching along a sandy path in and out of the shafts of sunlight that came down from the treetops fifty feet overhead, we all started to get tired. Our march turned into a stumbling walk punctuated by curses instead of cadences. Soon we were sounding off with *Shit* and *Fuck* and *When the hell we going to get there?* and *I wonder if I can have my money back?* instead of rhymes about the gold.

Rotbart ambled along with us, whapping his swagger stick in time to the cadences and then just whapping it to his own beats as we lost our group stride. He didn't seem very hot or very tired or very upset by the way our march came apart. After awhile he began whistling classical tunes with complex melodies.

"It isn't much farther, my good men. Have stout hearts. You'll get there," he told us after awhile.

And we did. We came out of the woods into a large clearing. In a cooler place, this site would have been a pleasant meadow. But here it was a light brown patch of burnt-out grass and brush. Near the middle, under a solitary tree, the black cook and the two Juniors waited for us. Equipment was stacked beside a station wagon.

"This will be our first main camp," Rotbart said when we'd all staggered into the circle that formed around the circumference of the tree branches. The cook and the two Juniors and the equipment took up so much space around the tree, there wasn't room for us to stand in the shade. Still, we tried, though the shade didn't seem all that much cooler than the open areas.

"I'm excited," Rotbart said. "Our first camp. Why, this is a moment— a moment like the time you start to open a girl's blouse and she helps you, a moment like the time you punch a guy and he goes down. It's that kind of occasion to me, men. Junior Junior, bring us some beer. You men have earned a treat. You survived your first small march. I can't tell you how excited that makes me."

It must've been about three in the afternoon when we sat down. I looked at my watch, but I had forgotten to wind it. While its dark military face and radium-yellow numbers seemed rough and ready and competent, the watch wasn't much good unwound. I told myself I had better learn to take care of details like this if I intended to wrest my fortune from the bowels of the jungle. As I drank my beer, I kept saying words like *wrest* and *fortune* and *jungle* over and over as if they could turn me into something. I tried to say them in capital letters to myself until, in my beery reverie, I saw myself as a figure in a woodcut. In my sweat-stained safari jacket I stood there, my arms crossed, a victorious expression on my face, surrounded by uncountable wealth. Beneath me was the moral of my heroic life: *HE WRESTED HIS FORTUNE FROM THE JUNGLE.*

Unfortunately the supply of beer gave out, and I kept coming back to reality when I looked at the watch. I was afraid to ask anyone what time it was, so I gave the watch an approximate setting.

None of our little band was much good after those beers got hold of us. Conversations would begin in the middle of thoughts and end as abruptly as they had begun. Rotbart lay down in the back of the station wagon, and that seemed to be a signal that we could all rest for awhile.

At one point, concluding a silent collection of evidence, Stanley Smith looked off into space and said, "I wish all of this was over and that we were old friends laughing about things in a bar."

And then Howard began his story.

"You know," he said to no one in particular, "success is going to ruin me. All my life I've been studying success, and I haven't succeeded yet.

"The first success I aimed for was success in rocks. Rock success is what I was aiming for, all right. My daddy was a farmer, and he said to me, over and over, that rocks were always better than dirt. 'Dirt will grow things,' he'd say, 'but rocks, oh my God, rocks can multiply your money the way nature never could.'

"So I got these books on rocks from the library. I studied them high, and I studied them low. I studied them every which a way. I memorized the Mohs hardness scale. I learned how to use a streak test and a flame test. I learned all that I could know about minerals.

"But all that I could learn about rocks couldn't tell me anything about earning a living in 1949. The rocks were out west, and I was still in Illinois. I had to eat. After I gave up on studying the rocks, I signed up for the first TV repair school. How about that for success? The very first TV repair school in the whole country. They sent you some books, a few tools, and a box of parts. You put together this TV set. When it finally worked, you knew you could repair TVs. Folks even drove out from the school to answer your questions. One time, a fellow came all the way from Chicago to answer a question about a tuner.

"Great prospects I had, I can tell you that right off. Then I set up my own shop. I had just gotten married. Eileen Benten was her name. She had the most beautiful set of tits you ever saw. They poked straight out in front of her like they was showing her the way through life. But, oh my oh my, did I ever pay to get my hands on those tits. You know, they say nothing comes for nothing, and I don't know if that's an all-around true statement, but it sure is true when it comes to tits, I can tell you that.

"Eileen had a little money. A hundred, maybe two hundred dollars. That was a fortune then. I mean, my God, I thought you could buy and sell heaven and keep the change for two hundred dollars. I mean, I thought I had the bases covered and the team owned. Two hundred dollars and tits.

"'Two hundred dollars would buy you whole suites of furniture or a pretty good car. But I didn't want none of that, nosir. It was turquoise then, wasn't it? Or was that later? No, I think it was turquoise. That's what the two hundred dollars would've bought, a lot of furniture covered in turquoise fabric for the living room.'

"I wanted to get ahead. I wanted to invest. I wanted to own something. That's what I'd tell my wife after I got over looking at those tits. 'Eileen,' I'd say, 'I want some distance between me and what I am.'

"'Why, Ho Ho,' she'd tell me, 'you're a silly boy, why yes you are. You just come over here and sit by me, you silly boy. Now you just listen to mama. Why, Ho Ho, you get ahead, and you'll spend your whole life looking back at your friends. Why yes you will. Let's just stay where we are. It don't get no better than this, now do it now?'

"And she'd stick those D-cups out like she was about to give them away.

"'This TV thing, Ho Ho, is probably just a flash in the pants, and that's the truth. It'll sideline us, and that would be the worst of all.'

"Well, sir, I didn't listen to her. I never did. For a while, I just tried to flash in those pants if you get what I mean, but it was hard to come in under those D-cups. You know, that's another thing. Everybody thinks big tits are just great, but tits are trouble. Every magazine in America shows you big tits like they're Corvettes. Well, they're not, I can tell you that. They're a lot of trouble that's what they are.

"And let me tell you another secret. Women that have big tits are used to being stared at. Oh, of course, they tell you they don't like it. I mean, they say they don't like being stared at. But try not staring at their tits once. Never let your eyes travel below their neckline. You'll see. Pretty soon the ladies put a hand up to that neckline, and maybe they start rubbing their necks like they're tired, and you can just feel the shape of that tit moving up on you, like a soft ambush. Then they slowly move their hand back down, and if you follow with your eyes back to those tits, their expression will throw you away like an extra booger. If you don't follow that hand, if you keep looking above that neckline long enough, she'll fall in love with you. She'll think you're hard to get, and she'll want you more than anything.

"That's how I ended up with Eileen. She couldn't figure it out. I never looked at those tits. When we'd neck, I'd never try to touch one. She was the easiest fuck I ever had. Back in those days it was hard to get a fuck. But since I never went for her tits, her alarm system didn't go off. You know, women had this alarm system you triggered by touching a tit. They'd let you go that far, but if you moved below it was all over. No is all they'd ever say if you went south of that Mason-Dixon Line. Eileen's alarm system never went off, you see, and I don't think she ever quite figured things out until I was pulling on a Fourex rubber and she was wetter than Singapore in the monsoon season.

"We did that in the back seat of my '46 Ford. It was huge back there. You could've hung pictures it was so big. But it didn't seem to be big enough for those tits. Even then they got in the way. You had to work around them the way a road builder goes around the mountains. If she sat on top of you, why they bounced all over the place. It was nipple here and nipple there until things got distracting. If she was under you, they sort of sagged off to the side, and you had to be careful so you wouldn't pinch them.

"Like I said, those tits were trouble. And I never listened to her opinions. Hell, she talked all the time. I just got so I tuned her out. Tits this way and talk that way, I got lost.

"'Get into me,' she'd say on our sheets with the flowers on them. 'Get into me like you never been no place before.' And, oh, it was lovely, yes it was, with her thighs heaving up and down like all creation was to come from us. In and out and in between. That was it.

"But, oh good Christ, how she could talk. One time, I woke up in the middle of the night, and she was talking even then. It was Howie this and Howie, have you done that, and Howie every sort of thing. It was like her head was about to bust open she had so much in there. She just had to get rid of those words the way you and me have to go pee and get rid of all we've had to drink. Speaking of that."

We all sat in our circle beneath the lone tree in the meadow watching Howard walk off toward the woods at the edge of the field. All of us—Helmut, the two Juniors, the cook, and the remaining fleecers—stared off where he'd gone, as if we expected him to return with some message for all of us. I thought briefly of going to the woods to pee myself but realized that I had sweated away whatever excess moisture I had.

It must've been about five. While the sun was still overhead, it seemed to have relaxed its hold a bit. The air was slightly cooler.

"It was success that failed me. That's what I'm trying to explain now, you see," Howard said when he got back. "I ignored what Eileen said, all thousands and thousands of hours of her talk. I just forgot about it.

I went and got the money from the bank, and that was that. I rented a shop. It was out there between an A & P and the end of town. I was the first to go that far, and I was the first TV repair shop in Maynard, Illinois. The real estate man told me I couldn't miss. Had to be successful, the man from RCA who sold me the tubes said. The newspaperman who wrote up my advertising told me I had to make a lot of money. I remember standing with him in the doorway of my shop, right under the Howard's Television Repairs sign, as he swept his hand across the horizon.

"'How How,'" he said. He never got my nickname right. "'How How, there'll be televisions out there as far as the eye can see and even farther. And you, How How, I dream of what you'll be. You'll be the rescuer of all of them. They just can't last forever, and you'll make them well again, and people will thank you, and they'll tell their children who you are.'

"I was excited, I can tell you that. I figured I had the world by the ass, and my little section by the tit. Eileen's uncle gave me one those old Philco console radios to put in the window, and the RCA man gave me the Master's Voice dog. You know, that's the dog with his ear up listening to the big horn. Well, I had the dog but not the horn.

"I didn't know what I needed then. You know, you never know what you need in life until it's gone right by you. I figured I had it all. I never noticed that fifty of the dollars had gone to the real estate man and that fifty had gone to the RCA man and that fifty had gone to the newspaper man. I figured these were dollars that slicks you down to where the real dollars are. I sure never figured that these dollars were all there were. Nosirree, I didn't. I figured they were here to help me out. You see I had the dog but not the horn.

"That's been my trouble right along, I guess. The dog but not the horn. You have to have everything to succeed. It's like you got the *E* without the *mc²*. What would Einstein have done?

"You didn't think I'd know about Einstein. *Old Ho Ho now or How How, he doesn't know no Einstein.* But you see, I do. I know how the world works, even though it doesn't really work.

"Well that store didn't make a nickel for anyone except the man who sold the real estate, the man who sold the tubes, and the man who sold the advertising. If that store was a bladder, it couldn't pee. I was just too early. None of the TV sets in Maynard had broken yet.

"I suppose I'd eventually have figured out to sell TVs. You know, I could've had a line of TVs and radios and furniture, but Eileen was shrieking and shaking those tits at me, and I couldn't take it anymore. I'd spend hours in my shop taking the model TV I'd gotten in the course apart and putting it back together. I'd sit in my back room doing that and listening to old Glenn Miller records. I was good at following instructions. You put a little sketch and some step one two three in front of me, I become the Norman Rockwell of accomplishment.

"I finally sold my stock and my store in 1951. It went for $76. Can you imagine that? I mean, seventy-six fucking dollars for what was a future like no future ever was before. Shit. I thought I was getting off OK. I got some of Eileen's money back anyway.

"The guy that got the place ended up with appliance stores all over Illinois. I mean, he grew stores like some people grow corn.

"Then Eileen left. Big tits doesn't mean you can't do math. Even she figured out that $76 wasn't her original $200. I tried to make it back; I promised I would. I went to work at the pickle canning factory at the edge of town. Worked the second shift, 3:30 to midnight. Got a half hour off for dinner at 7:30.

"I tried to save money, but they didn't pay squat. I mean, if that money had been paper, there wouldn't have been enough to make a Kotex for a flea. Nosir. I wasn't making the money back, and Eileen knew that.

"So I came home one night just worn out. Hours of sniffing vinegar pretty well ruins your outlook, I can tell you that. So I came home, and the doors were open, and the lights were on. And they're gone. Eileen and Jennie our daughter were just plumb gone. No note, no nothing. I never did find out where they went.

"And then it got to be one thing after another. I lived in Chicago. I lived in Gary, Indiana. Lived in Akron. Then Toledo. I'm in New York twice. They're a blur, they are, all the years tumbling by. They're a blur with little moments that seem clear inside.

"One clear time, I remember, though I don't remember what city. It's one with Mexicans in it, that much I know. Mr. Rameriz brought this guy up to my room. I'm just drunk. I've been drunk for days and maybe weeks and maybe all the time since 1949.

"Anyway, this guy told me I won a contest. Told me they been looking all over for me. For winning this contest I get a free set of success books. They'll help me get ahead, the books will. The guy and Mr. Rameriz smile like they're my best friends. God, how I laughed at that, but what the hell, I say. Maybe this is my moment at last. This is a future where at last I step through the rose-colored glasses. I sign the papers.

"Maybe that's my problem. Maybe successful people don't ever sign any papers.

"Well you know what happened," Howard said and pointed around the circle at the rest of us. "You know. I get this bill for $500, except I'm so drunk I don't know it's a bill. I thought it meant I was going to get a check. I was waiting for it when the sheriff comes. I didn't get a check, and I didn't get the books. All I got was the choice between a city jail and a county one.

"This is it—over and over success keeps failing me. And now you bet I'm worried. I'm out $3,000, and I'm no closer to success than I ever was. My daughter would be thirty now.

"At first I wasn't worried about this little trip up the Amazon. Nosir. I was the one who identified the rocks and the emeralds, remember. I was the one who was excited. Why, it made my day and most of my month when the Shellhead told me 'Ja, especially we want the wise old one who knows the stones. Him we especially like.'"

My heart skipped a beat. Helmut had told me virtually the same thing.

"That's my story. No more to tell, except now I'm worried. I think I'm farther from succeeding than I ever was."

We didn't say anything when Howard finished. I'm not sure what we would've said if we'd wanted to talk.

"Faith, man" had been Rotbart's answer a day earlier, but rats were nibbling away at our storehouse of faith.

"I don't see no South American," Howard said. "Don't see no rubies, ain't got no gold. Ain't no pearls around here. I wonder if we shouldn't just take our money back and go home."

"It's South America," Tony LaCosta said quietly. "And pearls are out of the question here or there, you know. Pearls are found in oysters not in mines. There isn't an ocean here, and there won't be one where we're going in South America. Helmut told all of us, 'Ja, especially I want the whatever one.' I was the quiet one who would be strong. He had to tell us things like that. I mean, how many people would set off on something like this without a little ass kissing?

"Come on," Tony LaCosta continued, "you know people are always getting worried about the wrong things. If I were you I'd relax, Howard. Don't get scared and pee all over yourself. You might just succeed this time. At least that's what I hope. Because, by God, if you make it, then so will I and the rest of us."

He punched Howard in the arm and winked at him.

A half hour later Rotbart got out of the station wagon and came back to our little group.

The rest of the evening was given over to setting up our camp and fixing our first meal. Although Juniors Junior and Senior and the black cook had sorted out the parts and tools of our tasks, even the simplest project became difficult when we did it together. I don't care what the coaches say. Most of life doesn't consist of teamwork; it consists of a few gifted people doing the work. While it's easy to fry a hamburger, it's hard for a committee to do it.

A bit of everything went wrong. The sides of our tents sagged because someone had mistaken the tent poles for kindling wood. Howard and Tony, who both claimed to be experienced cooks, ruined our dinner by salting all of our food with sugar. The sugar for our tea and coffee was, of course, salt. Artie Hokum, who must be one of the most literal people on earth, emptied two spray containers of insect repellant into the Kool-Aid.

"How could anyone be that fucking stupid?" Murphy asked him.

"Well they call it bug juice, for God's sake," Artie answered.

Even our post-dinner campfire sputtered and fumed and then died out like a bad idea because its wood was too moist or too dense for burning. By sunset, most of us were asleep, our dreams troubled by insects and indigestion.

I woke up sometime in the night with the feeling that I was flying away. But no, I realized as I thought more about it, something was carrying me. I was wrapped by something. Above me were dark wings, below were the misty woods. I was carried higher and higher by, perhaps, a large, dark bird. And then I was falling—spinning toward the shreds of fog between the trees, toward what glittered and got larger. And then it was gold, gold, gold and then maybe death behind the glitters.

I never found out what came behind. I woke up and I could hardly breathe. An oily taste was in the air. I had this sense of being wrapped up. I kept waking out of dreams within dreams within dreams. I kept waking up into an atmosphere that got heavier and heavier and heavier. I tried to see the gold, but I couldn't.

Of course. The mysterious usually turns out to be the mundane in disguise. What had grabbed hold of me was hardly a large, dark bird. Of course not. The tent had fallen in the night, and its flap was around me. When I awoke, I was staring at one of the brass rings on the tent's border.

I pushed the tent away and stood up. The air was cool and clean smelling, as if the resin smell had been scrubbed out. Part of my dream was true: shreds of fog were breaking around the trees, like an old order of the night giving way to the legions of the day.

I looked back at the tent and saw the bumpy outlines of the sleeping voyagers. We were all funny. The nine survivors trying to survive a little longer.

I was Lucky Beal's relief and woke up Junior Junior to have him drive me back to the main camp.

# Fourteen

"**I'VE BEEN VERY PATIENT,**" Mary Lynn said as we ate lunch on the porch of her Illinois farmhouse.

I'd been telling my story since breakfast.

"Very patient. If you had made Elwin sit through all this, he would have killed you."

It was another one of those days of hard blue skies and fluffy clouds. The green of the corn stalks out in the distance was almost luminescent. We seemed to be—as Shakespeare might have put it—embowered there in green. Unfortunately, *there* was such an ugly place.

"Where's the gold, Owen?"

"In Louisiana," I answered. "It's hidden there."

"Did you get to South America?"

"I'm coming to that in the story. It's the most interesting part."

"How much money is in Louisiana?" she asked.

"I'm not sure. It depends on what spot gold prices are."

"Owen, please don't be coy anymore. You have a lovely voice, but I'm getting tired of it."

"Thanks for saying that. Most people think I sound pompous."

"To tell you the truth, you do. I was just being polite. The best part of you, if you want to know the truth, is your hair. You can have the rest. Did it ever occur to you that we're just as tired of you as you are of us? What do think the gold is worth?"

"$40,000 or $50,000. Something like that."

"That's enough," she said.

"For what?"

"To go. I'd go to Louisiana for $40,000. Rest up. We're leaving in a day or two. You can tell us the end of the story later."

# Fifteen

**AS IT TURNED OUT**, she gave me another week to recuperate.

"Can't hunt for gold unless you're healthy," she said.

Actually, I felt pretty good after that week of rest. What's more, Mary Lynn and McCoo both left me alone. For some reason, she never asked to hear the end of the story. I spent most of my time eating and wandering around the farmyard and reading old magazines. While my side had a kind of steady ache, the hard pains were gone, and I had that euphoric feeling of health you get after you've been sick. My appetite was good, and I was getting excited about the trip. I hoped I'd find a place to escape.

The day we left, they put me between them in the Ford pickup truck. It had a metal dashboard painted to look like padding. That dashboard worried me; I could picture my face in pieces on it. I rubbed it with my right hand as though petting it might make it safer. My left hand was manacled to Elwin's belt.

"You think there's a genie in there?" Mary Lynn asked me. "You think that's who's going to save you, bucko?"

"Just hoping we don't have an accident. I wouldn't like to hit that in a hurry."

"Hey, life's dangerous. If you think Ralph Nader and padded dashes can keep the bogey man away from you, well you better think things through again. Say, if we're going to have all this stroking, we might as well get some use out of it," she said in that flat voice of hers. She took my hand and slid it between her thighs. Her face was powdered and neutral, but her crotch was wet, and the muscles inside her vagina sucked on my finger as if it were a Popsicle.

If you like manacles, and if you believe that rubbing crotches though downstate Illinois is a great way to travel, it was not an unpleasant ride. The summer cornfields were a deep and peaceful green. The spruced-up towns we passed were filled with plain white houses and neat yards. It seemed hard to believe that anything could go wrong in all that neatness. The three of us could've been a farm family on a Sunday outing, though we were a family with strange ties to one

95

another. We were also a farm family that carried with it the heavy odor of sex and violence. I can smell that scent to this very day, just as I can feel the greasy slide of my finger in and out of her until it felt wrinkled and old.

I dozed on and off through the day. I woke up about noon, just as McCoo was leaving the freeway in St. Louis. Ahead of us was an enormous Standard sign. At first I thought I was dreaming. The sign took over my whole consciousness, as if everything behind it were certified normal. I longed to get back there; I was homesick for the ordinary.

It took me a moment to wake up. When I did, I realized that my homesickness was quite accurate. The Standard sign wasn't ten blocks from my old neighborhood. I once had been an actor behind that sign.

While McCoo had the boy fill the gas tank and Mary Lynn went off to the bathroom, I could almost imagine getting into my rusted-out Toyota and driving to the Theater Company's office in University City. I used to hate that drive. Pulling into the parking lot and searching for an empty spot among the unreserved stalls seemed to symbolize my insignificant life. Usually the only slots left when I arrived in the early afternoon were in an unshaded corner near the highway. In the deepest shade at the front corner of the lot, in a parking stall that was three or four feet wider than any of the others in the lot, sat the Artistic Director's forest-green Mercedes 380 SEL. Every time I saw it, I was reminded of the things I would never have.

Since the roles I played seldom had lines, my rehearsals and those of the three or four other minor actors like me in the Company were often held in the early afternoon while the rest of the cast relaxed after lunch. Usually a technician would walk us through our stage positions. The closest I ever came to a starring role was standing in for Hamlet while an Assistant Director showed us the structure of the scene when the players come to Hamlet's castle.

But even being an underpaid actor was an improvement on sitting in the front seat of that Ford pickup.

"Where the fuck . . . ?" But McCoo's question went unfinished as Mary Lynn sashayed—there is simply no other word for it—out of the ladies room in a low-cut white blouse and a matching hoop skirt. She looked like she was headed for a pornographic square dance or the filming of an R-rated *Oklahoma*. The teenage gas station attendant dropped his greasy rag as she went by. When he bent to pick it up, he looked like a courtier bowing.

"Let's go have us some good fun," she said. Her smile was as tight as ever when she got into the truck.

"Well, goddamnit, Mary Lynn," McCoo started to say. "Goddamnit anyway."

The more I heard of McCoo, the more I realized that he simply didn't have enough words.

"Listen," I said. "We can all debate this in a minute. I've got to go to the bathroom."

If the gas station attendant had thought Mary Lynn a sight, I wonder what he made of me and McCoo walking back-to-back across the parking lot and into the men's room.

"Just drive" was what Mary Lynn said when we got back to the car, and drive we did.

It was hot that day. I don't know if the temperature was higher in the city than it had been in the country, but the concrete seemed to focus the heat. You could feel it rise up through the floor of the truck. When we stopped at red lights, you could see patches of thistles and wild flowers growing in the cracks of the sidewalks.

"Mary Lynn," McCoo began after we had driven around for an hour, "we got gold to get to. I don't like this messing around."

I was lying back in my seat, half in a drowse from the heat when McCoo said all this. I remember, I wanted to write it down.

Mary Lynn smiled at Elwin for, I think, the first time since I'd met them.

"Why, Elwin," she said in this breathless little voice like Marilyn Monroe's, "maybe we can find you a good little girl. Goodness knows you need one. Elwin, you going to pull on that thing till you pull it off."

McCoo blushed and speeded the truck up, and Mary Lynn held my hand with both of hers and shrugged like a girl on her first date.

I don't know how long we drove around, but we passed Hamburger Heaven and the Sporting Club and Good Eats/Good Gas and The Last

97

Time I Saw Paris.

We must've driven around for an hour until Mary Lynn spotted a corner tavern with a broken neon sign that read CORDIAL DANCING.

"I like that one, oh yes I do. Why, *cordial* means nice, doesn't it? I love the nice."

I stifled the urge to say something sarcastic and agreed with her. I imagined us in there. I pictured the dim red light. I saw myself dancing some version of the Texas Two Step while the Wurlitzer played away. I began to think that I might escape. I was so happy I started stroking her thighs.

She slapped my hand.

"It isn't time to get fresh. At least not yet."

She smiled at me, looking more girlish than ever.

"Mary Lynn," McCoo broke in, "I know you like to dance and socialize, but it's only three in the afternoon. There ain't no real dancing till after dark. That's when people dance, after dark. You see what I mean."

His hand swept out in front of him, where bad air was heated to a milky smear.

"You know, I've lived in half-baked Illinois nothing all my life. Where I grew up, the dirt and then the corn were the main events. I want something more."

"But the gold," McCoo started.

"The gold," she snorted. I could feel the small beads of her spit on my hand. "The gold's what gold can do, and gold ain't done nothing yet. Without fun, it ain't worth its glitter."

"All that glitters isn't gold," I added, though my cliché didn't do much for our thoughts. We were in a land beyond clichés. I rubbed my toe against the coins hidden in my shoes.

"Well, we ain't had no glitters or no golds."

"That's not quite true," I said, an idea beginning to form. "Elwin's got that coin. That coin will buy us a thing or two."

I again thought of the coins in the toes of my shoes.

After a few wrong turns, we ended up near where I began all this on Delmar Avenue, across from the liquor store and the Chinese restaurant, which had become Cajun Creole in my absence.

McCoo and I, his arm hooked around me as if we were the closest of friends, mounted the steps to Arthur Fenwick's.

The old-fashioned twist door bell was gone, replaced by a button that tripped a distant electronic noise when I touched it. A moment later the door swung open, moved by some unseen power. The stairwell had been painted the dull green of old dollar bills. The stairs were carpeted in the deep green of new ones.

The cramped little waiting area and the tux poster were gone. Instead, a blonde receptionist sat at an antique library table. Birds, in flamboyant and aging colors, stared down at her out of old prints as if in shock at what the future had become. Behind her were panels of old glass that distorted the vista beyond of polished mahogany desks. An expensive-looking young man sat behind each desk.

"Gold must be up, and up a lot." I said to no one in particular.

McCoo gave me a hard look, as if he were practicing for the film *noir* account of our visit. He probably was scared. Even McCoo, in his sub-literate way, understood that men in button-down collar shirts and English silk ties could be more dangerous than *banditos* any day.

I felt better when I saw that. I don't know why, but observing a thing is somehow powerful. I could even tie Rotbart into this. "Get close enough," he said, "and you can read people like books."

"Yessir."

"Pardon me?"

"May I help you?" the blonde asked.

"We want to sell some gold," I said.

"Have a seat there." She fluttered her eyelashes as if we'd just become important. "I'll ring Mr. Johnson."

Mr. Johnson arrived a few minutes later. He was all gestures. He rubbed his hands together when he greeted us, bobbed up and down while we walked to his desk, raised and lowered his eyebrows while he spoke to us.

"Yes," Mr. Johnson nodded, "I can certainly help you, yes I can."

"What happened to Irv?" I asked.

"Irv?" Mr. Johnson replied with a pained expression. He looked as though I'd said a coarse word. "Perhaps you mean Mr. Fenwick. He's away on unexpected but important business."

"Right," I said, "we just wanted to know what this coin is . . . ."

"Mr. Fenwick is such a good citizen. Why, he's on panels."

Mr. Johnson spoke of Fenwick as if he'd just won the Nobel Prize.

"But yes," he came back to us as if he were attached by a rubber cord, "we can certainly help you place your minerals. That is, after all, our business here. That's what Mr. Fenwick would want us to do in his absence.

"And, ah, how much gold exactly do you have?" His eyebrows went up and down and seemed to catch just below his forehead. Then he sat back and smiled as though he expected the wealth of Croesus to follow.

McCoo reached in his pocket and tossed the coin on the desk.

"This is, ah . . . ." Mr. Johnson began. The sentence wouldn't quite come out.

"Of course there's more where that came from," I said brightly.

"You bet," McCoo added.

"Well," Mr. Johnson began, "with handling fees and dealer costs . . . ."

"How much is spot?" I asked.

"$320."

"So we get?" McCoo asked.

Mr. Johnson hunched over his calculator.

"$280 or so."

"You make forty bucks in five minutes," McCoo said, his eyes widening. "Why, it takes me days to make that kind of money."

Mr. Johnson tilted back in his chair.

"Well, of course there are expenses," he began. "And single coins are difficult to place."

I didn't care. Hell, I had more money than I'd ever dreamed about, or I'd have it if I could get to it and live.

"Make it $300," McCoo said. "We'll split the difference."

I wanted to crawl under my chair. I just didn't believe in dickering when you got around mahogany. Mr. Johnson wasn't the sort of person you grabbed by the front of his shirt.

But it was "Fine" I heard him say in a matter-of-fact voice. He didn't argue.

"No sense getting upset over twenty dollars," he said.

"Fucking capitalists," McCoo muttered as he put my handcuff back on when we got inside the truck. He buckled me to his waist. I briefly wondered if Irv had changed his name.

Mary Lynn still looked cool and crisp in her outfit. She seemed to float inside her skirt as she sat on that dirty truck seat.

# Sixteen

**THE AFTERNOON WAS FULL OF EXPECTANCY**. Of that much I'm sure, but I'm not sure of what we wanted. It was as if we each had a secret plan that we couldn't divulge, a plan that we ached to carry out.

McCoo made a noise once in awhile that sounded like someone gargling. Mary Lynn was quiet and cool and full of sex. And I kept longing for an escape.

We cruised the city like this for at least two hours. We passed white bungalows edged with neat little rows of yellow flowers. We went by grand apartment buildings constructed at the time of the World's Fair. They had been abused like old family fortunes that had fallen into the hands of a profligate third generation. We drove by men who hung around bus stops as if they were home and women who walked rapidly to some furious business.

I remember stopping at a light and looking up to see a man at a desk in a bay window. He was tilted back in a chair and had his feet upon a desk. He was smoking a cigarette and meditating on something across the room. For all I know, he could've been dreaming up a story like mine and disregarding it as too impossible. How I longed to trade places with him.

At six or so we stopped at a large restaurant. McCoo unlocked the handcuffs.

"Think you can trust me after all?" I asked, trying to be affable.

McCoo just looked at me. He appeared menacing, but I wondered if his dour look wasn't the result of stupidity. He simply didn't know how to reply.

The crowd in the place unnerved me. I hadn't been around people for weeks. The scar from my bullet wound began to ache.

As we stood waiting for a table, we were bustled by a matronly woman and shoved by teenagers. A man handed McCoo a baby to hold while he paid his check, and the child spit up on McCoo. A man with a Harley-Davidson emblem on his cap put an arm around Mary Lynn.

"How's about you and me having some good loving fun?" he asked.

By this time, his request didn't seem that unusual to me. I mean, a few months earlier I would've been one of those straight little souls who gets upset if someone drops a tray in McDonald's, but now—hey, it was all becoming rock and roll to me. And besides, one of these characters might just get me out of my little mess.

But Mary Lynn seemed surprised at first. One of her eyebrows arched like the back of a cat.

I felt—and I can hardly believe it myself—a little protective and even jealous. In some perverse way Mary Lynn was my girl. I thought I ought to look after her.

"The McCord party," the hostess shouted into a raspy loudspeaker system. The microphone went dead with a metallic click, and the system went back to playing "I'm in the Mood for Love."

The biker joined us as if he were a relative. He sat down next to Mary Lynn and put his arm around her. Mary Lynn was smiling as if her dreams had come true. I had been merely a prelude to this fugue of contentment.

"Yes, we're going to have us some good fun tonight," she said as she snapped open a menu.

"Mary Lynn, I've got to speak with you this very minute. I mean right now." McCoo sounded a little desperate.

Mary Lynn looked at something far way. The biker was paging through the menu with his free hand as if love and food were equally matters of appetite. He had, I noticed, a tattoo on his right cheek. I studied it more closely. A tiny heart was surrounded by the words *Go Fuck Yorself.* The misspelling was as menacing as the sentiment.

"Mary Lynn, we got to talk."

"Well a fine good evening to you folks and a great big welcome to Smith's Eats. Can I get you folks a drink?"

At some point I tuned out of all this. My mind went to the place it goes when I sit in a dentist's chair. I simply couldn't cope. My bourgeois sentiments couldn't handle anymore.

A few minutes later we were served what appeared to be a pitcher filled with strawberry milk shake, and Mary Lynn began pouring some into all of our glasses. After she finished with McCoo and me, she filled the biker's glass and snuggled closer to him. Then she began stroking his leg.

"Pee Pole, I just love strawberry daiquiris."

I don't know how she learned his name.

"Shit," he replied.

I suspected he said this in many contexts. It sounded more like a statement about the human condition than anything really critical of our situation. We looked at him with glasses raised, about to drink.

"Don't mean nothin," he went on. "Don't mean nothin at all."

The more I heard of Mr. Pee Pole, the more I suspected that he and McCoo were soul mates.

I think we had chicken for dinner. After the third daiquiri, things got a little slushy. I remember trying to get in on the flow of events and grabbing at the waitress. I almost flew out of the booth, and I don't think anyone noticed that I ended up face down on the floor counting the linoleum tile squares until McCoo dragged me back up. After I was sitting again, I studied McCoo in my drunken way. He was stupid and greasy and dangerous. I could hardly bear to look at him, though when I looked away and caught my own reflection in the darkened window of the restaurant, the visage looking back wasn't much of an improvement.

Sometime later, McCoo and I ended up back in the truck. He was out of breath from the exertion of getting us there. He cuffed me to the passenger door.

I heard the chugging and the roar of a large motorcycle starting up. McCoo fumbled at the controls of the truck as he tried to get the key in the ignition. Just when he got the motor started and lights on, I looked out in the glare of our headlights and saw Mary Lynn—her white, hooped skirt crushed over the rear fender of the motorcycle and her hair done up in one of those voile kerchiefs—wave as she and Pee Pole sped off into the dark, the white of Mary Lynn's dress getting smaller and smaller and then disappearing completely.

"Fuck, fuck, fuck," McCoo said like a litany. "I just hate it when she does this. Hate it, hate it. I don't know what to do."

"Well, after her, man," I said. For a moment I wanted to say "On King, on you huskies," but that was another and simpler story.

And after her we went.

They were out there for a while, Mary Lynn's white dress shimmering in the corona of the truck's headlights. The soft night air was so humid it was almost wet and seemed around us like a messy embrace.

We lost them at a traffic light. McCoo tried to run it and keep up, but a white Cadillac came squealing through the intersection from the right. The truck stalled, and McCoo couldn't get it started. By the time we were going again, the motorcycle was gone.

"Fuck, fuck, fuck."

"My thoughts exactly," I added, for I suddenly had this vision of McCoo and me driving on to Louisiana alone. I didn't like that at all. My plan of escape, half formed as it was, included Mary Lynn. Dealing with an inarticulate imbecile who threw people off trains was a little scary.

My mind, which had been sliding on its way through a daiquiri high, was getting clearer. Unfortunately, the more sober I became, the more frightened I got.

# Seventeen

**WE DROVE ON FOR ANOTHER HOUR** before we gave up. We both wanted to find her. At one point, I remember exchanging worried looks with McCoo.

We drove on and on. We passed stretches of residential areas, where people sat on their stoops watching television outside, the flickering of the screens turning their faces into moving masks of light and shadow. We passed a movie theatre that had been turned into a church. Its marquee read *Coupon Special: Jesus Saves More Than 20%.*

There was no shimmering woman in white. There wasn't even one of those huge American motorcycles. Sometimes the clattering noises of a small Japanese bike went by. They sounded like gastric distress, like too many belches coming out at once.

"Fuck, fuck, fuck," McCoo kept saying to himself, as if these curses would bring her back.

I soon heard myself saying the same words over and over in my head.

"Maybe we should stop," I offered, "you know, for a beer or something. Maybe it would help us get our bearings."

"What the fuck we going to do?"

He turned to me as he said that. I realized he hadn't been listening. His face, red from the taillights in front of us, looked tired and drawn. He was scared without her.

"A beer. Let's get a beer. Say, I know a friendly place we could ..."

"Don't want friendly; that's what got us in all this trouble. I want Mary Lynn."

"Right. I know a quiet place where we can figure things out. It's back the way we came. It's not far from the Standard Station. Just turn around up here."

That was a Rotbart trick. "Get them interested in the process," he told us from the veranda in Louisiana, "and the wogs'll forget all about the larger questions. Give them lessons in mining or in how to run the supply trucks, and they'll forget that they never agreed to work for you in the first place."

And it worked. McCoo turned the truck around, and we headed back.

The name of the tavern was Hyde's. It was a place where some of my artistic pals hung out, and I hoped against hope that someone I knew would see me there, that something would happen to get me free of McCoo.

It felt good to walk in the door and smell the beer and the cigarette smoke—the scents of ordinary evils. McCoo had cuffed us together in the parking lot outside, and his coat hung over the manacles.

When my eyes adjusted to the dark, I could see ten or twenty people seated either at the bar or at one of the tables scattered around the place.

On the juke box Bob Dylan sang:

> Don't put on any airs
> When you're down on Rue Morgue Avenue

McCoo must've felt my happiness at being there, for he pulled me tighter to him and walked me to a back corner table.

"I just hate this kind of music," he said. "One beer and then we go, OK? We can figure out plans while we drive."

"Kind of butch tonight, aren't we, boys?" A girl in a green halter top bent over the table and cleaned it with a rag. McCoo tried to look over the top of her halter, and that seemed to calm him down.

The barmaid then straightened herself up, as if to suggest that further looks would require a purchase of some kind.

"Beer," McCoo said. "Two beers. Little ones."

The woman laughed. "Little bitty ones for two hombres like you? Come on, I figured you for a pitcher apiece and juke box change."

I tried to lift up the arm with the handcuffs on in the hope that she would see them and call the police, but he jerked my arm down.

McCoo smiled at her. I think that's the first time I ever saw him smile.

"Two'll be just fine."

"Two pitchers he means," I put in with the biggest smile I had. I even nudged McCoo in the side where the handcuffs were. "You're right. We're big boys."

As she walked off McCoo said, "Now, why'd you go and do that, huh?"

"You haven't got any sense, have you?" I hissed back at him.

"What do you mean?"

"Mary Lynn's right. You're an idiot. Look at you. You argue with the waitress. You annoy her. You draw attention to us. Why don't you just show her the chain? Or maybe we should just tell her to call the police." I rattled the cuffs and tried to raise them, but McCoo was much stronger than I and forced my arm down, hard, on the table with his right hand.

"I'd still like to kill you. Yes I would. I don't think the gold would be as much fun as watching you go away. Do you see what I mean?"

"Why didn't you kill me back on the track?" I asked him. I just realized; he had to carry me to the farm.

"In my head, I heard her say I shouldn't do it. I hear her all the time. She tells me what to do."

"What's she saying now?" I asked.

He suddenly looked scared. His eyes moved around like those of a trapped animal.

"I can't hear her. I'm worried."

"Elwin, there's something else I've always wondered about. Do you work on the railroad? I mean, were you working as a brakeman or something the day you found me?"

"No. I just would get on the trains. Mary Lynn had me do it. She said I was a modern version of Daddy. I'd get on the trains at Rosedale or nearby, and I'd just ride to see what I could find. I found all kinds of things. Of course one day I found you."

He said that ruefully, as if I was the source of his trouble.

"And now I've lost Mary Lynn."

I took a chance.

"Don't worry, Elwin, I'll help you out of this. I'll take care of you." I patted his arm with my free hand.

The waitress in the green halter brought the pitchers and some glasses, and I poured each of us a beer with my free hand. He took a sip and stared off in the distance. He almost looked as though he was thinking.

"What if we can't find her?" he asked.

"It's simple. Go to Illinois and wait. She'll come back. This famous adventurer once told me that's how you kill game. You go to their lair and wait. Tracking them often just gets you lost. No, you go back to Illinois."

"To Illinois . . . ? And forget the gold?"

"Go after it later, after you find her."

"Shit," he said, "I don't care all that much about the gold. I don't care about money."

"You know, Elwin," I began and took the deepest breath I could, "I don't either. It's too much bother. I almost died for a few gold coins. It's not worth it, you know."

He looked at me carefully. I tried to look back as earnestly as I could.

"I don't know how to get back to your place," I went on. "Hey, why not both of us quit right here. Finish off our drinks and go our separate ways. Hey, you'll never hear from me again, and you'll get back to Mary Lynn."

He didn't say anything.

"Hey," I went on like the best salesman I could be, "if we can't find Mary Lynn, you'll have to go back anyway. What do you want me for?"

He smiled. "Why, the fun of it. You didn't forget, did you? I'd like to kill you."

His eyes had no depth when I looked in them.

"Oh, you're serious then?" I asked.

"You bet I am. You bet I am."

# Eighteen

**WE WERE MAYBE HALFWAY** through the first pitcher when the waitress came back.

"I hate to be nosy, but why do you guys sit together like that?"

"We're just good friends," McCoo said.

He amazed me; he really did. I mean here was this half-illiterate, half-murderous creature who should have been put away. He could hardly function without his sleazy sister, but he could still come up with lines like this. I was the one who was educated, and I hadn't been able to get myself free.

I glanced around the room again, but I couldn't see any of my clever friends. I wanted to try something, but I would've felt better if a friend had been there.

Of course there was the waitress. She was still standing by our table with an amused look on her face, and McCoo was still interested in her chest.

Since most of my friends were physical cowards and wouldn't have done me much good if they actually had been there, I decided to trust the waitress.

"That's right," I added to McCoo's declaration. "We like each other so well we stay chained together."

For the briefest moment I looked straight into McCoo's eyes. My glance came back to me like a ball off a back board.

I lifted my arm out from under the jacket casually, so she could see the cuffs.

I thought there was an intense silence at our table, a black hole of quiet that drew noise out of the tavern.

Or maybe it was the silence in my head, for in a moment the juke box got to the next song (I think it was Jackson Brown's "Running on Empty"), and the bar conversation returned to baseball scores and Polish jokes. I was so on edge I seemed to hear this talk with a special clarity.

McCoo jerked me toward him so hard he almost tipped me over in my chair.

The waitress kept standing before us. She had the remains of a smile

110

and was trying to figure out the dynamics of our complex little situation.

"Guys, I'll be right back, OK? I just want to get my friend."

My heart leapt. She was going to call the police. I was as good as free. I kept my face turned away from McCoo so he wouldn't see my smile.

She pointed her finger at me.

"OK?" she said.

She then pointed at McCoo.

"OK?"

"Yes," we said in unison like two schoolboys as she walked away.

After a pause, McCoo said, "Fucker, you do something like that again, and I'll make it so you never do that again. Got me?"

"Right," I said, suppressing any desire to explain how idiotic he was. At the same time, I started bearing down on my thoughts the way I did when I was a child. I concentrated as hard as I could so that the waitress would read my mind. *Please, oh please call the police, please, please.*

"You waited for me. I'm so glad. This is my friend Karen. I'm Maybellene."

I realized that I'd been wishing so hard I'd closed my eyes.

They were seated across from us before either McCoo or I could say anything, though I'm not sure what we would've said.

Maybellene was the waitress in the green halter top. Karen had on a T-shirt that read *There Is a Penalty for Early Withdrawal*.

"Well," I said.

"Right," McCoo added.

"You could order two thirsty girls a drink," Maybellene said.

"And you might as well start talking, the both of you, because we've been studying you from, as they say, afar," Karen said and nodded toward the end of the bar, where a small group of people were staring at us. They all looked as if they were in the middle of a laugh.

Another waitress brought us a third pitcher of beer and some more glasses. I absently wondered what had happened to the first two pitchers, but details like that didn't seem important anymore. McCoo was leaning back in his chair like a man who was about to enjoy things.

111

"As they say from afar," I repeated. "Is that what you said?"

"Karen and I are educated," Maybellene said. "Though you shouldn't hold it against us. Two guys chained together like you must be desperadoes, and we just love outlaws."

She put her feet up on the chair and hugged her legs when she said this.

"Don't hold it against us," Maybellene went on. "I'd like it just a whole lot better if we could hold you against us. What do you think?"

She took a sip of beer after she asked this and winked over the edge of the glass at McCoo. His chair came forward and hit the floor. It sounded like a shot.

My God, I thought, I might get out of this yet. I'd never seen McCoo so taken with anything. Oh, I hoped she was serious. I wanted her and Karen to fall for McCoo, to sweep him right off his insecure little feet and away from me.

Well, no, that's not quite right. I wanted just Karen to do this. To tell the truth, I was quite taken with Maybellene.

"But maybe we're too forward," Maybellene said to Karen. "I mean do you really think we should go through with this?"

Maybellene was nodding her head back toward the group at the bar. I suddenly realized that they had come over on a bet or a dare. Of course. How could McCoo and I take ourselves seriously? We were idiots. No one wanted us.

I was tired of being a joke, of being the jester to someone else's king. Howard, bless his heart, was right. It was time to stand up and see who was standing there.

So I did. To hell with the consequences. I stood up. Just that simply, yes, I stood up. I jerked McCoo into a half-erect stance. I must've looked like an animal trainer with a reluctant bear.

"Owen, I just don't think this is a good idea for any of our healths, do you? I mean someone could get hurt here." It was a moment, all right. McCoo had never spoken my name before.

Just then, Karen walked behind McCoo, put her arms around him, and gave him a hug.

"I really like you, I really do, cowboy," she said "What's your name anyway?"

112

"Be careful," I said. "He's got a gun."

She tousled his hair.

He could've killed us all. He could've forced us into the alley and killed us. But he didn't. He just stood there.

Maybe he was in love. Maybe the loss of Mary Lynn was slowly getting to him. Maybe he was like a machine whose batteries were slowly running down.

McCoo was looking around—at us, at the bar, and back. All the time Karen was caressing him as if he were—if not Mr. Right—then at least Mr. Right Now.

"A gun," she said. "My goodness, a real live gun. Now what are you doing with that?"

She pulled it from beneath his shirt and looked at it as if it were a specimen of an unusual insect. Then she pointed it at McCoo and wiggled it back and forth.

"Aren't you naughty now, just aren't you? A gun just like the big boys'. My, my, my."

"Jesus Christ," Maybellene said, "you really are outlaws."

"McCoo," I asked, "is the safety on? Someone could get hurt."

"You dumb shit" He practically hissed when he spoke "It ain't even loaded. Mary Lynn took my bullets away. She was afraid I'd hurt you."

Karen began studying the gun. She was about to look down the barrel when Maybellene grabbed it from her.

"God, girl, you're as dumb as he is." Maybellene popped something, a clip fell out and dropped on the floor. "Empty," she said after she knelt down and looked at it.

McCoo seemed a lot smaller then.

"Do you mean to tell me," I started, "that you've been pushing me around with an empty gun?"

McCoo smiled, and then his grin spread into a laugh.

"You dumb shit. Mary Lynn took my bullets away after I shot you. She figured I might just do it again."

Maybellene handed me the gun, and I stuffed it in my back pocket. I looked out from our little scene and saw a circle of frightened faces looking back at me from a haze of smoke. I finally had a starring role.

113

"Now let's just all sit down, folks," I said to our audience. "Everything is under control, and no one is going to get hurt."

They did. They all went back to their drinks and their quiet little lives as if nothing had happened. I tried for a moment to imagine myself in that group. Surely I would sneak away and call the police, surely I would feel the menace in the air. But no one moved, except one man who went to the bathroom and returned a few minutes later. I suppose no one really cares about tragedies. We drive by car accidents, glance a moment to see if there's been blood and death, and then drive on to our business and our destination. What we remember of our trip are the cold French fries we had in downtown Madison and the surly gas station attendant just outside of Butte. The man whose last sight on this earth was our Chevy going by—why, we didn't see him and didn't really care to see him.

I sat down beside McCoo. The women were sitting across from us and had the pursed lips of those who'd come to a serious conclusion.

"I don't suppose you have the key to these cuffs," I said to McCoo.

"No . . . ."

"No, of course you don't," I said to finish his sentence. "Mary Lynn's got it."

"How'd you know that?" McCoo seemed genuinely puzzled.

"Oh, just a good guess."

The women were taking all of this in.

"What Jesse James once said," I began, "is still the truth."

Maybellene bit her lip and thought a moment. "What's that?"

"'We are in serious need of a hacksaw' is what he used to tell his colleagues. 'Serious need.'"

Karen got up and walked into the back room. While we waited, Maybellene smiled tentatively.

"I'd like this a lot better if you'd tell me what's going on," she said.

"Oh, it's a long story." I was so tired that I learned of my weariness when I heard my voice. "We're treasure hunters. We're *Treasure Island* meets *On the Road*. We're on the trail of The Golden Fleece. We're low comedians after high stakes. We're after easy money in these hard times."

"Come on. Tell me really," Maybellene asked earnestly.

"Tell me really, tell me true. Is that what you really want?" I asked.

114

"I know you think these are great lines," Maybellene said. "And you're right: they're not bad, but I'm getting bored. I like to know how things stand. Ambiguities don't interest me any more. I want to get on with a life I can believe in. I mean, tonight I vowed to get myself squared away, and I run into the two of you. Instead of squares, I get rectangles. Hell, I don't even get shapes. It's more like a connect-the-dots drawing without any numbers." She looked off in the distance when she finished. I thought she was gorgeous.

"Will this work?" It was Karen. She handed me a hacksaw that seemed like it came from the Tiffany of tools. It had a varnished walnut handle and a blade so shiny it looked as if it were made of a precious metal.

"Where'd you get . . . ?" I began.

"Let's just say I'm resourceful."

Karen and Maybellene held the bracelet down while I went to work with the saw. When I began sawing on the handcuffs, pieces of its chrome peeled off like birch bark, revealing a darker metal beneath. That dark stuff was hard and made harder by our difficulty in holding the metal still while I tried to move the saw back and forth.

McCoo sat quietly as we worked. In fact he was so docile that he let Karen hold his arm against the table to keep tension on the chain. He seemed almost somnolent. It was as if Mary Lynn had turned him off. I halfway expected a violent gesture, but instead he sat there quietly.

Maybellene spelled me on the sawing. It must've taken us an hour, but finally the metal cut, and I stood up, abruptly stood up, as if suddenly free of something sticky. McCoo just sat there, at first looking around. Then he seemed to realize that I wasn't next to him.

"Well, it's over, isn't it, Owen? Isn't that right?"

After the bracelet fell from my wrist, I was free. It might come down to a fight, I supposed, but I had the gun, and I was less weary than McCoo. But he didn't seem interested in me any more. In fact, he stretched one arm on the table and put his head down. The arm still had the cuffs attached.

"I'm tired of you, Owen. I wanted to kill you, and I didn't get to do it. Mary Lynn wanted you like a pet. That's over now, isn't it? Why don't you and your girls go? Just leave me my truck, OK? I'm going back to Illinois. But you—you should go."

I did. Karen and Maybellene and I did. We got up, walked to the door, opened it, and stepped out into the night air, which had become cool and clammy. I peeked through a corner of the window, and McCoo was still sitting there, the chain of the handcuff dangling down like a loose exclamation point.

# Nineteen

"**YOU MIGHT SAY** I've been kissing frogs to find a prince," Maybellene said as she rolled off me and onto her back.

"What am I?"

"I don't know yet. You're not bad in bed. Not great, mind you, just better than average."

"Thanks, I guess."

"Neither frog nor prince," she told me and touched my nose with her finger. "What do they say about wine? Grande Bourgeoisie?"

"The big middle, right? Not too good and not too bad."

"Something like that."

"Do I get to rate you?" I asked.

"I'd rather you didn't."

"You know," I began, "I'm tired of this. I'm tired of appearing in someone else's play. Even worse are the reviews. Some asshole like you comes in here and figures he can explain me. Owen's this, and Owen's that. It's not right. No one but me knows what's been going on here." I tapped my head.

"But everyone's an expert," I went on. "Rotbart's got an opinion. McCoo's got one, and so has Mary Lynn. I thought you were going to be my true love, but I suppose you're going to figure me out when I thought you were going to love me."

She was silent when I finished. I looked over and saw her in the tangle of her hair.

"She," Maybellene said.

"I beg your pardon."

"She. You were talking about some asshole like me, and you called me 'he.' I'm a she, in case you hadn't noticed."

She sat up and shook her hair. She leaned back against her arms, her breasts out and her stomach in. Then she shook her hair again and stood up. She walked away and returned with a brassiere. As she put it on, her crotch was just at my eye level, and her pubic hair came down in a little curl like an upside-down question mark.

"My, my, my." I said. "That's the stuff."

"So I'm told," she replied as she pulled on her jeans. She didn't put on any panties, and I remembered the delight I felt when I first reached inside those jeans last night and discovered just soft, bare flesh and the kinky tangle of her crotch. My my my indeed. I felt as though I'd been given a prize, a well-deserved one after my time with McCoo.

She shook her hair again, tossed a blanket that had fallen on the floor back on the bed, and walked to the kitchen.

"You're too sensitive," she said from the other room. I could hear her opening and closing the refrigerator. "You're taking things the wrong way. Sometimes criticism means affection, you know. We only dare to criticize the ones we like."

I had come to the frame of the kitchen door as she said this. She was kneeling in front of the open refrigerator when she spoke.

"Besides, he's a cute little guy," she said and flicked at the end of my penis. I had forgotten that I didn't have any clothes on. That was something, at least. Before I went to Louisiana I would have done a lot of things, but I never, ever would've forgotten that I was walking around a woman's apartment without any clothes on.

I blushed. I could feel the blood coming to skin surfaces all over my body. Blushing was, I suddenly realized, like a defense. We could all make fun of the blushing while the real emotion went scurrying away, unnoticed, back into the depths of the body.

"I'll get dressed," I said because I didn't know what else to say. "In fact, what I'd like is a bath, a nice hot slow bath with as many pleasures as the adjectives I've used."

"You know what your trouble is, Wee Mr. Owen? You're too much of an actor. You keep putting on costumes for a play that hasn't started."

While I sat in the hot water of her bathtub, I tried to work through the dynamics of our relationship, but I couldn't. I simply didn't know enough about her.

Later, I used the word *relationship* with her, and she didn't quite hear me. "Elationship? Is that what you said? I like that I'm elated to be in this elationship with you."

The bath was delightful. The tub was one of those claw-footed affairs from early in the twentieth century. I had used some pink bubble bath that was on a shelf above the tub. For a moment I felt what transvestites must feel: the joy of slipping into feminine things.

She knocked on the door and was in the room before I could say anything.

"I'll bet you drink tea. Any truth to that rumor?" She put the cup on the floor beside the tub and gave me a kiss. Then she sat on the closed toilet seat with her feet in front of her and her arms around her knees.

I reached out from the protection of my bubbles for the cup, but I couldn't quite reach it. I suddenly felt modest and didn't want to get out of the tub, though I certainly wanted that tea.

"Could you?" I looked at her and then at the cup.

She jumped off the toilet seat and handed it to me.

"You look like Mae West, darling," she said.

"I suppose that makes you Cary Grant, then."

"I don't think Cary Grant has ever been as receptive as I have, my dear. Now, tell me what you'd like for breakfast. You can have anything you want as long as it's granola or fruit."

"Both. I'll have both." I really felt shy and wanted her out of there. I also felt awkward. I couldn't set the tea cup down without getting out of the soft warmth of the bubble bath.

"Breakfast will be ready in twenty minutes." She tousled my hair as she walked out.

I felt like a different person in that bathroom. It was as if the bath—or perhaps my whole stay with Maybellene—had somehow changed me. I didn't want to act anymore. For that matter, I didn't care about being rich either. Getting rich required work dirtier than I wanted to do. Instead, I wanted to seize something like our love making had been and make that my life. That's what I wanted, and wanted a lot.

"You must remember this," I began singing to myself as I put on her deodorant. It had a sharp chlorophyll smell and was called Queen Helene. "A kiss is just a kiss.'"

I liked that name. Queen Helene, I repeated to myself. It somehow echoed what I wanted to begin. I wanted what Queen Helene was monarch of. Queen Helene, the Cajun Queen, I'd call her.

As I opened the bathroom door and went in for breakfast, I'd never felt so light and clean and happy.

While I waited for breakfast, I studied the books on her shelves.

119

There were mostly books about other books. *The Princeton Encyclopedia of Poetry and Poetics, Understanding Poetry, Ruskin's Carpet, Nobody's Nabokov.* They looked like hard and serious titles that would go into the brain slowly and stay there like a great weight against the day-to-day world.

On the floor, however, stacked next to a large pillow that was propped against the wall, were very different titles: *Think and Grow Rich, How I Became a Selling Success, How To Get Rich in Spite of Yourself.*

I especially liked the last title. It was what we all wanted, to be able to walk through God's bright day, good people in love with their neighbors, doing all the right things, but still collecting wealth the way our lungs collected oxygen.

I loved that little apartment. It gave off such wonderful and eccentric vibes. The books said the place housed an English major and a car dealer, though maybe the car dealer had the most forceful personality. The self-help books had crushed spines and notes in their margins. The serious texts looked new and unread. And the sunlight that suffused it all said that everything would be all right.

"I want you to keep this breakfast in perspective," she said as she began setting dishes on the dining room table. "I'm just doing this to pay you back. This service won't be a regular thing. You did most of the work last night. I mean, I just laid there and took it, so now you get yours."

"All part of the Food for Love Program?" I asked.

It was her turn to blush.

"Well, you could say that. I have granola and navel oranges and homemade bread for toast and jelly my grandmother makes and hot tea and orange juice."

"That's more than you advertised," I said.

"Well, I liked the loving," she said and blushed as she looked down.

"Hey," I said, "maybe next time we can have blow jobs turn into bacon."

She just smiled.

I didn't know that breakfast could be sexy, but watching her eat into the orange had me all over her in a minute. Then we were back in that bed, and the blanket was back on the floor.

The light had never felt so graceful.

"Does that mean there'll be bacon next time?" I asked when she finished.

"You talk about the wrong things," she said.

# Twenty

**A VERY SMALL VOICE** told me that I should get out of there.

I really didn't know very much about her, and my common sense kept ordering me to ask her some hard questions. About the only facts I learned was that she was finishing up a Master's Degree in English and thinking of becoming a saleswoman because she was sick of school. Every time we got very far into her life, she deflected the questions and started talking about me. She found my life as an actor fascinating, she said.

But she didn't know I was an actor when she rescued me. Why had she taken so much risk? Loving outlaws just wasn't enough of an explanation. Maybellene had never answered the question.

But I was falling in love, a condition that doesn't allow much room for common sense.

Just as I would think up a hard question, it would soften into delight, and I only wanted to lay around in that bed for days and days.

Her apartment was on the third floor of a red-brick building in a student neighborhood. I remember that we stayed up there for days after the first meeting. I have this distinct memory of the two of us walking around in the nude with the windows open. It was like walking around high in the trees. Since the summer foliage was so dense, we could hardly see anyone else, and I had the feeling of being alone in a garden. It wasn't Eden, but it was awfully close.

I lost count of all the times we made love. After each delightful time, we sat back against the pillows reading while we got our strength up for another spell.

That's what Maybellene called them.

"It's my grandmother's word. She used to speak of a spell of weather or a spell of canasta or a spell of going downtown. Everything she did was a spell of this or that. So one time, when I was thirteen or fourteen, I looked the word up.

"'Grandmama,' I asked, 'what's all this spell stuff? A spell is a magic charm. It's what the fairies do.'

"'Of course it is, you darling girl. It's all a spell, you know. You think

122

life is real and earnest? Well, let me be the first to tell you it isn't. You plant by the light of the moon, and you pick in the heat of the sun. The best garden you'll ever have you'll gather near where the foxes run.'

"I've got one of her plants outside. A clematis. It's over twenty-five years old. Sometimes I think it's holding up my side of the building. I went out at dark to put it in. I was so worried about getting the dirt right I forgot to see whether it was the dark of the moon. But it's lived for a year. Big fat purple blossoms."

She looked out of the window into the trees and the light that came like a benediction.

"'This is a spell of love, my darling boy', is what my Grand-mama would say."

With that, she crawled on top of me again and took me off to some speechless place.

I think I lost five pounds in those first two days. I don't think we ever ate a full meal. I felt, I guess correctly, that love was making me lighter.

After several days had passed, I had this sense of floating out the front door as we made our first trip together for food. The front door frame of the apartment was covered with peeling varnish. That door and lobby seemed like a setting from another and harsher world, and I remember studying them carefully so that I would be sure to find my way back. As we stepped outside, I hung on to Maybellene's hand, because I was afraid to lose her and because I didn't want her to lose me. After so long indoors, even the light felt dangerous, and I got a little dizzy when we got to the sidewalk. The distances appeared longer than I remembered.

After a block or so, however, the world was affable enough. Everyone seemed to be about nineteen and smiled a lot.

There is something therapeutic about the produce department of a grocery store. It's comforting to know that good earth can bring forth so many riches of color that are also good to eat. I remember standing before a display of oranges like someone in a trance. They were so brightly colored the very air around them seemed orange.

We filled a grocery cart with oranges and cheese and bread and chicken and wine and granola. I plopped an issue of the St. Louis

*Post-Dispatch* on top of our groceries. I stood casually behind the cart as we worked our way to the head of the checkout line until I realized that I didn't have any money. When I reached in the back pocket of my Dreadnought Trousers for my wallet, I found nothing but dirt and pieces of sticks and my Adventurer's Notebook. I'd stuck a check from my old bank there as a page marker, but that account had been closed long ago. My wallet was probably lying in the brush alongside those railroad tracks in Illinois.

I was terror stricken. Even though I hadn't done so well in the wilderness, it was somehow worse to be standing in a checkout line with no money. Out there you didn't have to apologize for what was wrong or dirty. What was, well, was.

In that grocery line, though, my heart began to pound. I backed up the cart, apologizing as I forced two very stylish looking women with inch-long fingernails to move out of my way. Maybellene was just coming to join me. She was carrying a package of Tampax. At that moment I felt very close to her. Is this how it happens? You see a woman coming toward you with sanitary products and you realize how much you love her?

"Are you all right?" she asked as she flipped the box into the cart. "Have I embarrassed you by buying these? They're a necessity, you know, unless you want me to wad up old sheets. Or do you want me pregnant? That'd be great. A little rug rat in the midst of all this sex and handcuffs. Just great."

"I don't have any money." I said this in a whisper.

"Honey? You want honey?"

"Money," I said as loud as I dared. "I don't have any money."

She smiled. "That's my boy. Why, that's all my boys. They never have any money. But that's what I get for working in a bar and bringing all the boys back home. I guess rich boys don't come home with barmaids, now do they?"

"Maybellene, I'm sorry. I really am. You saved my life, but my wallet's gone. If you want, I'll leave right now. I'll put all this stuff back and just go away."

"That'll be great. You can put the cheese with the oranges and the Tampax with the wine. We'll tell everyone we're reorganizing the store."

"You don't care? It doesn't bother you?"

"I've got money. I don't think about it. I mean, I've never worried about money that much, and I guess I never figured a guy in handcuffs would have any."

"Do you mean it?"

"Sure. I don't want you to starve. And I surely don't want you having to explain why you're putting the Tampax and the wine together."

"I'll make it up to you, I will. I've got all kinds of money. I mean, not with me, I don't." I could feel myself blushing. I didn't want to lie to Maybellene, but I wasn't sure if I should tell her the truth about the coins beside the railroad tracks or even about those inside my right shoe.

"Trust me," I went on. Then I made up my mind. "I have it. Honest. It's buried. It's an honest-to-goodness buried treasure. Thirty big ones, out there in Illinois."

I was beginning to sweat as I said all this.

"Calm down," she said and looked at me closely. For a second I couldn't tell if she was worried about me or if she was trying to see into my secret. I could feel the coins in my shoe. They seemed warm, as if they had been heated by my little lie about lacking money.

I felt better when Maybellene paid for the groceries and we were outside in the dazzle of the sunlight. Though all the way back to the apartment, the coins kept chafing my foot.

# Twenty-One

**I FELT MORE ANCHORED** to the world when we got back to the apartment. There's nothing like worrying about money to get you reacquainted with reality.

Maybellene was humming "The Old Gray Mare She Ain't What She Used To Be" as she put away the groceries. I curled against the big pillow on the floor of the living room chair with *War and Peace* and my own thoughts. Maybellene was giving my story a direction I hadn't intended to take. I was, as Rotbart had put it in the ad, a man WILLING to COURT DANGER, but I hadn't signed up to do the usual kind of courting.

"I'm going to take a bath," Maybellene said. "Back rubs for the ladies are more than welcome."

"Oh, right," I said. I tried to sound distracted, which of course I was. I also realized that I was beginning to feel extremely self-conscious.

I liked Maybellene. I had no doubts about that. Maybe I loved her. But there was also the $30,000 along that railroad track in Illinois. Those coins were beginning to loom in my mind like the statues on Easter Island. By now, I figured I'd earned them. I'd almost died for them, and that was enough for my own private medals committee.

*For Consummate BRAVERY under HOSTILE Conditions,* I wrote on an imaginary citation in my head. I almost wished I had Rotbart there with me to help me compose it. *For his Extreme VALOR in . . . .*

"Fucking."

"What?" I asked back of this word that had appeared out of nowhere, and then I thought. Well, sure, *for his Extreme VALOR in FUCKING, too, this AWARD is . . . .*

". . . . rubbed."

Of course, Maybellene was saying something from the bathroom. I hated to have my private awards ceremony interrupted. I guess the question was—was I ready for love in what had started out to be an adventure story?

"What?" I yelled back.

"What I said, dorkbreath, is, 'Are you just good at fucking? Don't you know there's a lady in here that wants her back rubbed?"

As I walked into the bathroom, I supposed I *was* ready for love. After all, the adventure hadn't been quite what I imagined. And yet, I'd lost at so much, I wasn't sure I wanted to attempt success in love.

I thought about all this as I massaged Maybellene's back. Or, at least, I tried to.

"I've got to tell somebody the truth," I said. "I'm tired of lies. I'm even tired of little harmless lies. Lies got me into this mess, and perhaps the truth will get me out."

"You sound like a philosopher, my dear. Can it all be that serious? I mean, does anything really that serious happen these days? Oh, by the way, rub a little to the left. That's it."

"Judge for yourself," I said and started in.

I told her about Rotbart and the meeting at the Paradise Motel. I told her about going to Louisiana. I told her about our training. I picked up the thread of the story I had begun to tell Mary Lynn and McCoo before they decided that they'd heard enough of me. After all, I hadn't gotten to talk about Sylvie Mae and the Flamingo Island Motel. What's more, I wanted to pass on the names of Howard and Lucky and Tony and Murphy and Artie and Tyrone and Merle and Haskel and Stanley. Somebody had to know that story besides me and Mary Lynn.

As she dried herself off, I told her the rest of what happened.

"We trained hard in Louisiana, Maybellene," I began. "It was more physical work than I'd ever done in my whole life."

# Twenty-Two

**WE TRAINED VERY HARD** in Louisiana. Every morning, we hiked out, carrying increasingly heavy pieces of our gear, into different parts of Rotbart's estate. We'd get up an hour before dawn to avoid the heat. Even so, the temperature would be in the low 80s.

I had never seen skies like those at dawn in Louisiana. The sky would be purple and gold and orange and then resolve itself into a delicate, Robin's egg blue before taking on the haze of the early morning heat. By noon, the sky became gray from the haze, even though there wasn't a cloud in sight.

As the days went by, we got less worried about our gold. I guess we figured that Rotbart could've taken it if he wanted to. If this were really a con, he would've killed us all at the start.

We had begun with eight-hour shifts for each of our turns at guarding the gold. The guard stayed back at the compound to watch the gold. But making arrangements to move the men back and forth ultimately seemed too complex, so we finally decided to leave a guard for the day, and then we agreed that the guard could stay until the rest of the men came back from their outing.

Since I was troop leader, I didn't have to take a turn as guard, but I decided to take a shift anyway. After several weeks of training, I wanted to vary my routine. At first, I felt strange standing all alone beneath our stash while I watched everyone else go out of sight with the *Left, right, left* of Tony LaCosta echoing against the barracks and the main house. I was used to being part of a group.

Rotbart, who was in my usual place at the rear of the formation, lifted his arm and his closed fist to salute me and the trees as the marchers wound their way out of sight.

Then this huge silence settled over me and the camp. I tried to make time pass by marching. I set the gun on my shoulder and played drum rolls in my head as I walked around. I was in Napoleon's Army and that of George Patton. I imagined myself pinned down by enemy fire and shelled by howitzers. I tried a couple of times to roll into a crouching position, but I kept catching the gun in my shirt.

As I marched, I tried to invent cadences like Tony's, but my rhymes were off, and my meter wasn't very good. Pretty soon, the gun got heavy, and I sat down on the steps leading to the veranda around the main house. After awhile, I got back up and paced around the compound.

I stared at the gold hanging from its pole and then concluded that looking at the leather case was a waste of time. I should, I decided, be looking around for the forces that might arrive to take the gold away. Then I roamed the compound looking for possible attackers. There were so many places for an attack that I made myself nervous and then afraid. I began to see shapes lurking behind every bush, assassins in the trees. I got more and more scared and soon realized I couldn't see the gold. Someone could've taken it while I was walking around. I rushed back to the pole and found that, of course, the pack was still hanging from its nail.

This went on for hours. I kept going from confidence to fear to boredom and back to fear. I'd watch the sack, get concerned, and start to check on the whole compound. Then I'd get scared and run back to see if the gold was still there. On one of my nervous walks around the perimeter I imagined that someone had taken the gold and left the bag. So I dragged three chairs from the front lawn over to the pole and set them on top of one another. I climbed up this unsteady structure and made sure the gold was still in the bag.

I think I began to hallucinate as the day went on. I had to pay attention to everything. Every shift of wind's direction, every rattle of an acorn through the leaves, every flurry of the birds scared me. The very air seemed dangerous. It was as if the wind was full of knives.

This kind of thing can be very wearying. After awhile I started to see shapes skulking up on me just at the far edge of my peripheral vision. When I would turn around with the gun, they'd be gone.

By two pm, I was almost delirious with hunger and the heat. I felt ill. I felt like I had a temperature. When I got so dizzy with it all I could hardly walk, I looked for the nearest place of refuge, and suddenly there it was. The main house loomed before me like fate, and I walked up the steps and onto the porch.

That was such a radical act. While Rotbart had never said that we couldn't go up there, I guess I'd always assumed it was off limits.

I thought I should knock. Even though I felt quite sick, I thought I should knock rather than just go in. The door knocker was a long piece of brass shaped like an upside-down hammer. Except the head of the hammer had been replaced by a gargoyle figure, whose rump hit a brass striker. The sounds of that rump hitting the door seemed to reverberate all through the house.

Standing on Rotbart's porch, I smelled the sullen humidity. Louisiana was strange that way: it was as if the heat forced the plants to grow faster than they wanted to, giving the world this sour smell.

No one answered, and I finally pushed the door open and stepped inside. I mean, good God, I just went in. I went in there as if I owned the place. Sneaking in wouldn't have protected me from harm. No, skulking would've invited trouble. Rotbart had prepared me for that. "It's the hidden man we fear," Rotbart had told us, "not the one striding toward us in the sun. We are such hopeful creatures. We assume that the man coming toward us has good news or gifts. We seldom notice how pale he looks or that he carries a scythe beneath those robes."

Besides, I was following orders in my way. I was looking over things. No one had told me that I was to stay in that hot and stinking heat beneath our bag of gold. Good God, I had to eat. I had to get out of the heat for some little while. No one could begrudge me that.

Yet the place was such an emblem of Rotbart that I trembled a bit from fear (and hunger and exhaustion). The house was like a repository for all those capitalized thoughts Rotbart had told us, and I felt as if I were out of my league when I turned the brass doorknob.

It moved effortlessly. The air inside the house felt cool and filtered and antique. It took my eyes a moment to adjust to the dimly lit interior.

I saw mahogany and the deep colors of old oriental rugs. When I shut the door behind me, the air seemed rich and mellow, as if daylight were simply too rude for these halls.

While I knew very little about antiques, the place had the aura of another time, a time of gentlemen's clubs and leather wingback chairs. Sounding as if it came from a deep place in yesterday, a clock ticked off the current seconds with a tone that sounded like dignity made audible.

To the left of the front hall was a dining room with a setting for two laid out in crystal and silver and silence on a deeply shining table.

To the right of the hallway was the living room. Above the fireplace was an oil painting of a bird carrying off a small rodent in his talons.

As I walked around, the place slowed me down. It seemed to say that life on this scale was slower than it was out there in that harsh and sour world where everything was just a little too hot and humid. No, in here, with the chintz and the mahogany and the silver, things were just a trifle better. I halfway expected a butler to show up with a tray of caviar.

As I walked around, I adjusted my footsteps to the ticking of the clock. I toured the first floor from the dining room and the living room to the library and the kitchen. I felt as though I were wandering through the set of a movie. I didn't really know what I was doing. At first, I simply wanted out of the heat. Second, I wanted some food.

In the kitchen, I sat by a maple carving block—the kind of thing butchers have—finishing off some left-over curried chicken. I found a bottle of champagne in the refrigerator and had several glasses to wash the chicken down and the heat of the day out of my head. The meal was quite delicious. This was not a household of peanut butter and jelly. I felt like someone who'd come to the kitchen after the Grand Ball to have a snack. This wasn't a version of life I had lived. In my ordinary life, people couldn't afford to keep champagne around. This was life the way I wanted to live it.

I felt better after eating, though I'm not sure how clear my head was. I no longer suffered from heat exhaustion alone; now heated-up champagne bubbled through my system as well.

That champagne made me braver than I really was, and I decided to check out the house to see what I could learn about Rotbart and our quest. When I got up from the block of maple, the room seemed to swirl about me. I sat back in the chair and hoped that everything would calm down. I felt like the still center of the moving world. Kitchen cabinets, at first, and then the rest of the rooms and the ground outside with its barracks and its gold went round and round. I just sat there and watched things go by. At first, I thought I would gather some insight out of all this movement. I would learn, I thought to myself, the way the world works. I was in the house of a serious man, a man who knew how to find the world's treasure. I would learn things.

I'd never experienced a sensation like the one I felt that day. It was a curious result of the champagne and the heat and the training and the resinous air. I felt like I was floating around the house. I felt like I was about six inches off the floor. I was very happy. I was going to be rich. I no longer cared about the details of wresting (or, for that matter, simply getting) the gold out of the ground and onto a boat and down the river and out of the country and into the United States. The details of who did what simply weren't of interest to me. I didn't care who drove the boat or who did the digging.

I floated around and around the first floor and then I drifted (there's no other word for it; it was as if the air currents were moving me) up the stairs.

There was a tall and arched window at the end of the landing. The stairs then curved around and back and went farther up. I started to pass the Palladian window on my way to the mysteries of the second floor but stopped to admire the view. I had never noticed this part of the house from the outside. From inside, though, you had the feeling that you could survey everything, that the world came up this arched view, was shaped, and was sent on to better things. The view from this window was like having capital letters on the nouns. I stood there for a moment or two, having this bubbly reverie. For the briefest second, it almost seemed as if a ship's steering wheel could've been put on the landing. I mean, it seemed as if you could drive the landscape and the world from that view,

The window looked directly down on the bunkhouse. Off to the right, and almost out of sight, was the formation area and our pole with its bag of gold dangling down. The stacked-up chairs stood by the pole like a ruined monument. I could hear the birds twittering in the woods and watch the breeze stir up slight whirlwinds in the dusty patches of ground. It all seemed so peaceful.

I had my hands clasped together behind my back and rocked my feet back and forth. This must be, I thought, how Rotbart feels. I was like the lord of the manor, or I was until Helmut walked up to the pole with a long hook, knocked the gold down, and caught the case as it fell. I began to sober up as I watched him spread a handkerchief carefully on the ground. He emptied out the coins, and counted them. He counted so slowly that I counted with him. There were exactly one hundred coins.

When he finished, he put the coins back in the case, tossed it once in air, and caught it as if he were very happy with himself. He then stood there listening to someone I couldn't see.

At first all this seemed quite innocent. I suppose Helmut and Rotbart had as little reason to trust us as we had to trust them. Helmut was thus simply checking to make sure the gold was still in the bag. It was all right with me, what he was doing. Shit, I told myself, I'd done the same.

But something about the way he hefted the bag worried me. He held it as if it were already his, even though we weren't yet in sight of South America.

I backed away from the window, hoping he wouldn't see me. I started climbing the stairs to get an even better view from someplace higher up.

The stairs were elegant. As worried as I was, I noticed that. They were made out of a light hardwood, maple perhaps, covered down the center with an oriental rug that was, in turn, fastened by brass rods to the steps.

I couldn't get the sight of Helmut cutting down the gold out of my head. It was a con game, I decided. I wasn't sure how it worked, but it had to be a fraud of some kind. There was no foreign treasure, no South America that the remaining seven of us would ever see. No, there was just this expanse of dust and heat and resined air. There was just this fact that Helmut and Rotbart had our money.

As I walked up the stairs with these gloomy thoughts in my mind, I noticed that my steps were still synchronized with the solemn beats of the clock tick-tocking away its somber hours.

When I got to the top of the stairs, I was sad. I wanted to go to South America. I really did. I wanted to wrest my fortune from the bowels of the earth. I wanted stains on my safari jacket.

I looked around for another window to study the situation further. Perhaps I'd been mistaken. Perhaps Helmut was just checking our

133

money, making sure all the coins were still there. That's it, I concluded. He came and couldn't find me and got worried. He probably thought our camp had been overrun by thieves after our goods. I felt relieved when I thought it out that way. That made sense.

Ahead of me at the top of the stairs was an antique door with a latch made out of wrought iron. The whole business looked unmistakably old. I was sober now and getting scared. I lifted the latch, and the door swung open onto a low-ceilinged room whose walls sloped into the roof. The floor had the undulating patina of long years of steps and wax. In the light coming from the shuttered windows on a far wall, the room seemed to glow, as if seen through a bottle of lemon oil.

I walked to the windows and opened the shutters. I now had an unobstructed view of the parade ground, where Helmut and Rotbart stood talking while Helmut continued to idly toss the case in the air. Together, the two of them gave the distinct impression that they were more worried about their own concerns than our gold. The charitable explanation was simply that they were waiting for my return before replacing the gold.

I still couldn't see much of what was behind Rotbart and Helmut. Perhaps the rest of our band had come back and perhaps they were all discussing my absence. I realized that I'd been stumbling around the house drunk for probably an hour. I tried to back away from the window and stand in a corner of the room to get a better angle on the parade ground. As I started to move, I knocked over a stack of newspapers piled on a table beside the window.

I knew I ought to get out of that house, but I didn't want them to see me. I didn't know what to do, so I went back to the window. They continued to talk as if nothing was there but the gold and my stacked-up chairs standing there like a foolish sentinel. I bent over to pick up the newspapers and realized that I was sweating heavily. I put the newspapers back on the table and sat down at the desk in front of the window. The desk faced into the room and back toward the door, but I could whirl the desk chair around and look out the window if I wanted to.

What I needed was sleep, I realized. I was very tired suddenly, perhaps from all that alcohol bubbling through my system.

I sat at the desk the way I did at my desk in my apartment. I leaned back in the chair and held one arm out rigidly against the desk and drummed the fingers of that hand against the top of the desk, as if the marching cadences of those fingers would rouse me to action.

The desk had very little on its surface—a couple of pens, a pad of yellow legal paper, and a square magnifying glass. I held the magnifying glass up to my eyes and looked around at the blurred outline of the room. Everything seemed to be there. The chairs and the books and tables were there, except they were closer somehow, drawn into a circle of blurred congruence with me.

The desk was placed just behind a red and dark green oriental rug that said it was expensive by the density of its weave. The books on the shelf had gold-leafed titles. The two or three files on the leather-topped desk were held in place by silver paperweights. I was tempted to open the desk drawers, but I figured that Rotbart and Helmut might come in the house any minute looking for me. I got up and quickly ducked back to the corner behind the desk and peeked out the window. They were still pacing around the pole.

The room, I figured, was Rotbart's office and probably contained the real agenda of our quest. The contents of the room could tell me whether we'd signed up for a fool's errand or were off to be fools for gold. I moved back away from the window and began circulating about the place. But clues, if there were any, just weren't that obvious. Indeed, there was really very little that pertained to the present. In one closet I found some boxes of canceled checks stapled to various bills and thought they would, at least, give me his monetary history, but his monetary history—like yours and mine—was mostly a matter of gas stations (Kenny's Super Shell) and barber shops (Mr. Jose of Leland, Louisiana) and cleaners (The Phoenix Brings Them Back). The gas and the electric company were there, along with various charge cards, but nothing really gave his game away. I stood in front of the desk as if I were a truant boy standing before the principal. The answer was probably inside that desk, but I was afraid to open it. It gave off an aura of power. It was very old and said that it had been around far longer than I. I came back around again and realized, suddenly, that I was standing before the window and probably in plain sight of Rotbart

135

and Helmut. I stepped back quickly and, again, knocked over the newspapers. I squatted down and began picking them up. This time, I noticed that the St. Louis *Post-Dispatch* was there. There as well were the Cleveland *Plain Dealer* and the Denver *Post* and the Milwaukee *Journal*. It seemed an unusual mix, not the sort of thing someone trying to keep up on the world would have. Stranger yet, the dates were all far apart. The Cleveland paper and the one from Denver were several years old. The *Post-Dispatch* was from a few weeks ago, and the Milwaukee *Journal* was current. It was an odd collection.

Then it hit me. Of course.

The *Post-Dispatch* was the paper that brought us here; it held the ad for the Paradise Motel.

I thumbed through the Milwaukee *Journal,* and there it was: *EXPEDITION—Men of QUALITY sought.*

I rapidly glanced through the other papers. Each one had an ad. Each one had exactly the same wording. Only the dates and the names of the motels were different.

And that was it of course, the heart of our little darkness: the golden fleece was on our backs, and Rotbart was coming to clip us sheep. He would do so as surely as rain and stormy weather follow sunshine.

Shit. What was I going to do with such heavy knowledge?

I rocked back and forth in the chair reading each paper over and over.

*EXPEDITION—Men of QUALITY sought.*

At the end of this news story and that, it was the same story. It was *Men of QUALITY sought* after NIXON RESIGNS; it was *EXPEDITION* following PRIME GOES UP AGAIN. And two weeks from today there was to be a meeting in Milwaukee at the Bliss Motel. I figured it up. There were twenty newspapers spread out over the last five years. Twenty newspapers and twenty ads and ten good souls for each *EXPEDITION*. They probably weren't much, these *Men of QUALITY*. They were really the men of no fixed address, the men of uncertain employment. But they all must've brought their ten gold coins to Rotbart's little party. That was twenty or thirty thousand dollars a pop. Twenty or thirty thousand times twenty. Not bad in such hard times. Not bad at all. It was probably better pay than searching for real treasure.

136

I had it now—the whole enterprise, in all its dirty glory, was before me like the soft underbelly of an insect.

It was so obvious. Collect some lost souls in a city and charge them a few thousand each. No one would ever miss them if they didn't come back. Take Howard, for example. Who'd notice that old Ho Ho wasn't around the block? Or Lucky Beal—who'd ever see the closing-up of the Get Lucky Repair Shop? I kept reading over the newspapers in hopes of finding another explanation.

"Owen," the voice purred before I recognized it. "Owen, it's so good to find you here."

With that, Rotbart was sitting across from me.

"Right," I said, standing up and out of the chair in one movement. "Or sorry. I mean, I'm sorry to be here." I pushed the chair back under the desk and stepped away.

"Why, not at all, my friend. Not at all. Why, you're on guard. I understand that. You had to check things out. Of course. I couldn't ask for anything less, now could I? You're guarding my property. Our property, really, and you had such a large area. You came in from the heat of the sun. I understand. And there's such a marvelous view from here, don't you think? I think you could justify looking over things from here. Yes, I do. Let me get us some refreshment and cool air. We're not without our comforts here, you know."

He opened shutters in one of the walls, revealing an air conditioner. He then pressed a button to summon, I suppose, someone from the kitchen. The air conditioner went on with a thunk.

"Things will be much more cheerful in a moment, my young friend. You know, Owen, I'm just delighted to have you in our little group. I'm glad you're staying with us. I just can't imagine this expedition without you. We just couldn't get by without your thoughts. How are you feeling?"

"Fine," I said. I tried to be careful. I didn't know what sort of ground I was on.

The servant Rotbart had summoned with the button was Helmut. He arrived carrying a tray with two glasses and a pitcher of what appeared to be iced tea.

He seemed startled when be entered the room. He probably hadn't been expecting me. He set the tray down on the desk.

"Well," he started off, giving a guttural $v$ sound to the first letter. "Well, well, well." I half expected him to begin assembling a gun. "You are here for some purpose then, Herr Owen Hill? Is that true?"

"Why, yes," I answered back, my confidence appearing from nowhere like the cavalry. "I came into the house to escape the heat, and then I realized that I could see very well from up here. Staying up here made more sense to me than walking around in the heat."

No one said anything, but the pause was just a little too long. I guessed that Rotbart and Helmut were trying to figure out what I knew. I looked out the window and saw that the leather bag had been replaced on its nail. My stack of chairs were there as well, a foolish memorial to earnestness.

"You see," I went on, pointing out the window, "I have a perfect view of the gold from here. I counted the gold right along with you, Helmut."

He almost seemed to blush.

"You would like perhaps some refreshment here? We have the tea made just for you."

I wondered whether they had put the coins back in the pouch.

"Please, Owen," Rotbart said as he put his arm around me and led me to a chair in front of the desk. "Please."

He pulled the chair up before the desk and gestured for me to sit down.

"Owen, you've done your duties for today. The gold is quite safe. No one will disturb it."

As if on cue, Helmut walked over and closed the shutters on the window behind the desk. He turned on some small, shaded lamps at the sides of the room and set a glass of iced tea on a butler's table at my side. After making some small adjustments here and there, he left the room, quietly shutting the door behind him. After he left, I could hear the sounds of symphonic music and, a moment later, a dark, coloratura voice singing.

"Isn't this delightful, Owen? Isn't this just where you want to be?"

Rotbart bounced up and down on the chair behind the desk. I remembered how short he was.

"I guess," I replied. I tried to be cheerful.

"I sit here for hours, Owen, just hours in this amber light. After awhile, the push and shove of life in this tedious century ends. After awhile, a curtain seems to flutter over the twentieth century and take it far, far from here. I have so little interest in what most men find amusing. I guess that's what brought me here. I certainly don't care much about sports or selling the kind of foolish objects that make men wealthy or sitting around my suburban house on the weekends barbecuing sirloin steaks and tending the roses. I don't care for things like that. I always wanted to strike out into the Indian territories of our lives, go where few have gone before.

"But do you have any idea of how difficult that is? I mean, most of the land in this country is given over to silly little lots for houses and rows of crops. The country that's left is mapped and measured like a puzzle that's been put together many times. Hardly the kind of terrain that requires an explorer. So I had to invent my own territory"

As he spoke, he leaned back in his chair and folded his hands together as if in prayer. I noticed he had a ring with a purple stone on his little finger, a purple stone that glittered as he rocked back and forth in his chair.

"Owen, I spotted you right off as one of us."

"Us?" I asked.

"As one of the men who are uncomfortable within the boundaries of average society, one of the men who has to get outside the little rows of houses and of crops, one who must forge his destiny in the hard iron of great experience."

What marvelous, old words, I thought. What *dangerous*, marvelous, old words, I thought when I'd thought some more. This kind of talk was a version of tattoos; it flirted with trouble, invited trouble to the speaker, the way the arms of the tattooed man seemed to invite fist fights.

"Don't you love it here?" Rotbart asked, throwing his arms out in a circle. "Isn't it wonderful?"

I wasn't sure what he meant. The room, the estate, the search—his reach seemed to gather them all in.

"Owen, I sit here for hours and plan things. I sit inside this lovely

139

amber light and hear these notes of music, notes that are easily two-hundred years old. I sit around these antiques that are easily as old. This all came from an era when men had larger thoughts, greater visions. A man can expand himself in here, don't you think?"

I started to answer him, but I saw that his question was addressed more to himself than to me. He had the inward-looking expression I had seen on the faces of religious people.

"I believe, Owen, that there is a giant force inside this world, an intelligence so vast and deep and wise that we only have glimpses of from time to time. You know how it is, sometimes, when you're doing a complicated mathematical problem and everything falls in place or if you're writing and the story comes out in some unexpected way that looks as though it was planned for pages? When those things happen, you get to see a little of this intelligence. I'm not talking about the kind of God in churches. That's for suckers. Marx was right on that score; religion is the opiate of the masses.

"No, the Greeks got the closest with their Oracle at Delphi. They had these women priests who would stand where the vapors came from the earth. They believed this holy steam came straight from the gods in the underworld. Well, I think that's the right idea. You have to find the spot where you can best understand some tiny part of this vast intelligence. I think that's what great men have always done. That's why, at the highest levels, great men get together. Have you ever seen those wonderful pictures of Thomas Edison and Henry Ford and John Burroughs together? They knew. They understood that it's the spirit of the great intelligence that matters and not its mundane forms. What counts is not whether you invent a light bulb or an auto assembly method or a study of nature. These are but the merest instances of the vast. Don't you see?"

I didn't even think to answer this time. Part of my mind was nodding in agreement with his theory. I mean, it was a gratifying notion to think that little souls like me might strive to go the way that Edison had. I suppose you had to have enormous self-confidence to do great things. Serious money isn't given away.

I wanted to believe him. I wanted to believe that his other missions had ended in failures. After all, the photographs had suggested as much. Maybe we really were going to be versions of Henry Ford. But I wanted to have all those newspapers explained. What had become of the *Men of QUALITY* he sought?

"What about the ads?" I said. I was scared to break his train of thought, but I couldn't figure out any other way. My grandfather always told me to speak my mind. He said if people would've spoken their minds instead of fooling around, a lot more progress would've been made.

"The world would've gone right from Shakespeare to indoor plumbing and V-8s instead of fooling around with all the side trips," he told me once. I guess I didn't want any more side trips.

"The newspaper ads?" Rotbart looked genuinely puzzled. He was still thinking about Universal Intelligence and trying to sniff his allotment of vapors. "Newspaper ads?"

"There," I said and pointed to the credenza beside his desk. "The ones in there. I read them."

He had turned to stare at the stack of papers, and I couldn't see his expression. He stared at the pile for a moment as if he was trying to gather his thoughts.

"Of course, Owen. There have to be ads. I thought we understood one another. Perhaps not, perhaps you don't want to join me."

When he turned around, he looked at me in a hard and serious way.

"Do you, Owen?"

"I'm not sure what I'm joining. I mean, I already joined one group, and I guess it's not quite what I figured it would be. I mean, I thought we were going to South America to search for the tangibles of the I-want-to-get-rich-beyond-my-wildest-dreams story. I mean, I thought I was training to locate gem crystals the size of basketballs and so much gold it would break my back carrying it out of the mines. That's what I thought we all meant. Am I mistaken?"

Rotbart began to laugh, and Helmut joined in. I'd been so engrossed in Rotbart's story, I hadn't heard him come back in the room.

"It's a show for suckers, my friend. It's all theatre. It's theatre the way all capitalism is. What do you think our friends who find some ordinary item for a penny, wrap it in bubble pack and sell it for a

141

dollar are doing? How do you think the world works? The doctors with a two-thousand-dollar version of aspirin. Come, come, my boy. You can only be so innocent. This is your chance to be part of the world's great theatre. This is your chance to quit being a sucker in the audience and join the troupe. This is a marvelous opportunity for you. Opportunity is knocking very loudly on your door."

"What would I do?"

"I sometimes think Mut and I are a little too baroque for the folks out there. We need a plainer touch. Mut is a German aristocrat, and he can only take so much stupidity. I've also thought about expanding. This is a big place—over 1,000 acres. We could have two groups here at a time without much trouble."

"It's so simple," I said to no one in particular.

"Pardon me." Rotbart looked puzzled. I had interrupted his plans for expansion.

"I mean the whole thing it's so incredibly simple, isn't it? The con is so straightforward no one would guess it's a con. It's as obvious as the weather. That's why nobody suspects you."

Rotbart's smile got broader as I went on.

"It's a version of your glass house theory, isn't it?" I went on. "You told us once the glass houses are really the best protection against rocks. They stand so naked in the open that they threaten attackers. Attackers don't want to be seen. You and this con are so clear that you don't get attacked. Your critics are looking for something hidden, while you go from city to city picking up ten local losers. That's thirty or forty grand a city and . . . ."

"When we started out, we only got $10,000. It was harder then. But go on. Please."

He seemed full of pleasure to hear me talk about his work. I was like the artist's great critic, the one who could accurately describe each brush stroke with the love and effort that had gone into it.

"You must've figured on something like a 100 cities at ten grand apiece. Right? That's . . . ."

"A neat million dollars," Rotbart said, finishing my sentence. "Such a round and lovely number, don't you think?"

"Almost as much as you could take from the jungle, or should I say *wrest?"*

He winced a bit when I said that.

"You see," Rotbart said, "that's my problem. I'm too exotic for these clods. I'm like a peacock in a flock of ravens. When I fan out my gorgeous tail, I scare them off. I just can't help myself, and I think I'm getting in my own way. I'm costing myself voyagers in the quest. I need someone with the common touch."

"I never thought of myself as common," I said.

"Mut, would you mind getting us some more tea?"

He walked briskly out of the room. I could hear his hard steps echo down the hall. I wondered if Rotbart wanted to tell me a secret.

"Mut is delightful. I met him in the Congo. We were fighting rebels, or I should say we were being paid by the Belgians to fight the rebels. What we mostly did was sit around in bivouac tents drinking Heinekens. It was a marvelous time, actually, if you like a military setting, and God knows I do. We moved our camp every few days after radioing back to Headquarters that we sighted this chap or that. Once in a while we'd kill a burrhead or two. Nothing serious. Those Belgians loved their *pommes frites* and hated their revolutionaries. If you told them you'd found a commie or two, why they'd just shower you with money.

"Even then Mut thought we were getting soft. He hasn't changed. He's sorry he missed the Big War. He was too young. As a boy, he must've dreamed about being a Dreaded Hun the way other children dream of being President or Most Valuable Player.

"If you want to know the truth, I have a terrible time with him. I don't think he's quite figured out what we're doing here. I sometimes think he believes we really are training people for South America. He wants the training to be done by his little book of Prussian Warfare. Other times, he just wants to kill everyone and take the gold. He makes me a little nervous, if you want to know the truth. What saves me is Mut's inability to function without an officer around. Mut's like a permanent staff sergeant. He needs a Major or a Colonel to give him focus. I don't think Mut could survive without me. Of course, the question is whether you nine can survive with Mut. He's getting very impatient. As you can see, we're getting ready for Milwaukee. Portland,

Oregon comes after that."

He sounded like the head of franchising for a fast-food restaurant.

"Meaning?" I got a little clammy thinking about what I *thought* his meaning was.

"Well, you figure it out. There's thirty thousand hanging from that pole, and nine—no, excuse me—eight men in our way. What is it Helmut told you? 'The smart young man I hope for very much.'"

He smiled as he said this, smiled and seemed to relax into his chair. He looked at me the way a collector might, a collector who'd just discovered that an object was really an *objet*. He was beginning to count me in.

"So that's it then," I started. "I'm to help you get rid of Howard and Lucky and Tony and Murphy and Artie and Tyrone and Stanley and Haskel. We get rid of them, collect the money, and go on to the next town. Is that it?"

"Something like that." He had sunk lower in his chair and touched the fingers of each hand together again in that gesture that began *Here's the church, and here's the steeple.* "I started all this thinking of a million dollars."

"Excuse me."

"It is such a nice round number. Clean and simple. One million dollars. I said that number over and over in my head the way some men might say *Take that, you bastards* or *Take off your underwear.* It was my fantasy. A high clear number. Mostly zeroes. Hardly there at all when you look at it. It's like a little stick chasing all these fat nothings along. But the specifics got nasty. They always do, don't they? It all came down to George this and Edward that. It was all real people with fingerprints and histories, things the police could figure out, things Mrs. George and Mama Edward wouldn't like very much if they knew the truth. They lived in big old gray frame houses with cheap lace curtains and furniture so old and soiled its fabric stuck to you when you sat down on hot days. No, mamas like these never wanted to lose their darling boys, even though their darling boys were petty shoplifters and beery drunks with paunches, even though their little babies now were forty and were impotent on the few occasions when they talked some pudgy middle-aged woman into sleeping with them. Nonetheless,

144

these mamas didn't like it when their boys went off and didn't come back. But against their high, shrill voices was the calm and clear sound of one million dollars echoing over the green. It was as much as you could get from the jungle surely. Or should I say *wrest?*"

His smile was tight.

"Who'd notice the loss?" I asked. I felt I was carrying out his logic when I spoke. "I mean really. A hundred small souls. Men like ephemera. Men with families that really didn't count, the families that always take in losses like the best of friends. Miners and steel workers and television repairmen. Men with mamas and little else, and maybe not even mamas. Men almost out of chances, men willing to spend the last of their money for one huge roll of fortune's furious wheel down here in Louisiana. 'Whatever happened,' the neighbors might wonder, 'to Howard?' 'Who?' the answer comes back. 'Don't remember him.' Then talk of weather and how the evening's coming on. That's it, isn't it? Talk of how pretty the sunset is, and maybe how Howard, whoever he might be, is gone. A hundred souls like these, a hundred souls times a few thousand dollars each."

"A marvelous idea, don't you think?" He dropped the church gesture as if he'd thought of something better.

"Here." He held up the square magnifying glass. "This simple device is an enchanter of the highest order." He handed it to me. "Owen, hold this out at arm's length and look through it at me. Please, indulge me for a moment."

I did what he said.

"What do you see?"

"You. Out of focus and upside down, but definitely you."

"Now bring the glass slowly toward your eyes. What do you see? Describe it, please"

"You. You're still there. You're still upside down and getting larger and larger."

"Stop. Now hold the glass there." The magnifying glass was about a foot from my face.

"You see," he said, "how I become a tapestry of flesh. Or no, *tapestry's* not the right word. I'm more like one of those terrain maps where you can see all the rivers and the hills and flat parts. Now bring it closer.

145

What do you see?"

"It's dark, as if the scene came together all at once. It's kind of spooky, really. It almost seems as though there might be black holes everywhere, little spaces we could simply fall through, leaving nothing but blackness behind us. But wait, as I move the glass closer, through the dark place, why now you've gotten distant and small again, and you're right side up. Interesting. Spooky but interesting."

And I guess it really was, though when I put the magnifying glass down, I came back to the menace of that room. I still didn't know exactly where I stood. These recruiting gestures could be just another con. But I wanted out of there; that much was clear. And Rotbart had told us in a training session that we should always do the for-sure thing.

"It's the first thing you have to learn in poker and in life. You never bet until you see that you have a winning hand. And then you bet everything."

"Wait, Owen," Rotbart said as we sat together in his room. "I'm not done with our experiment yet. Please, pick up the glass again and bring it close to your eyes. What do you see?"

"There are two of you. A blurry twosome."

He laughed and clapped his hands the way a delighted child might.

"Tell me," I began, trying to force a confidential smile out, "how you got into this. This isn't a very common line of work."

"Ah, you *are* perceptive lad," Rotbart said and put his hands behind his head. He seemed to be in an expansive mood. "I'm greedy of course. That goes without saying. Most of us are, but most of us spend our time trying to camouflage our greed. The ones who try to act on it usually do so in such an unappetizing way that they don't get anywhere. These are the red-faced minions of commerce in small towns trying to work up some petty scam on the locals all the while wrapping themselves in the mantle of good citizenship. That kind of greed never gets anywhere. I'm speaking of major greed, the kind Rockefeller had, the kind Paul Getty had, the kind Lyndon Johnson had. This kind of greed is so astonishing we miss it, even though it's right in front of us.

"There aren't many grand gestures left for us, you know. We're running out of wonders. I mean, how much is left to discover? The real

Golden Fleece was probably found centuries ago. It was found and sheered and carded and made into God knows what pedestrian article of clothing. It's interesting to think how the great past turns into its ironic present. The grand fleece of legend becomes the word for a con. For the men whose ambition rages inside them the way Columbus' did—what's left for them? Those tall striders in the sun of centuries ago, what great ambitions they had. Here, listen to this."

He bounded (no other word would do) to one of the bookcases and brought back one of the leather-covered books.

"These are Captain Cook's papers. Here's his commission: *Resolution and Discovery to be sheathed and filled and fitted for voyage to remote parts.* Listen to this: *From the list of clothing required for the voyage: A pair of Fearnought Trowsers and a Jacket for each man and four or five good watch coats.*

"I wanted to live my life on those terms, to voyage into remote parts with a pair of Fearnought Trowsers. I wanted words like *Resolution* and *Discovery* cutting through the waves ahead of me, but we simply don't have any remote parts anymore. Someone has been everywhere before us.

"So I made up my own unknown lands. That's exactly what I did. I figured I'd just make up a new territory. I had enough money to buy this place, and I created a myth that went out from here, to Cincinnati and Louisville and Atlanta and Pittsburgh and Denver and San Diego and Seattle. It went all over the place and made me money on the way. The trouble is, the turnover of my inventory is slowing down. That's where you come in, my bright young friend. I need another partner. Mut and I are partners, you see. We've discussed this. If you join us, we'll split it three ways. There should be enough new business to cover us all. When I started out, I hoped to make a million altogether. Now, with any luck at all, we'll gross over a million a year."

"A million . . . ." I just stopped when I said the word. I simply had no idea at all of how to finish the sentence.

"Yes. It's such a lovely sum, don't you think?"

It was, certainly, a tempting idea as I began to let the resonances flow through. I suddenly could see myself with the rapt faces of the losers in Indianapolis around me.

As if reading my mind, Rotbart said, "Come, my friend. Let me show you something."

He led me into a room off to one side of his office. It was painted an institutional green and had fluorescent fixtures on the ceiling. It was furnished with a light green metal desk trimmed with aluminum. The desk stood at the head of a squadron of dark green folding chairs. Behind the desk on the wall were three green blackboards and above them were map cylinders with what appeared to be several maps in each. It looked like a military briefing room.

"I once worked for the CIA," Rotbart said by way of explanation. "We called these situation rooms. You know, something would go wrong in the Dominican Republic or Korea or Viet Nam Or Hungary— something would go wrong, and up would go the maps in rooms like this, and we'd all sit around chain-smoking cigarettes and drinking gallons of coffee and pretending that we could do something about parts of the world that had names we couldn't even pronounce. You know, they finally let me go from the CIA. Excuse me; they said we'd have to separate. I was, I suspect, a touch too flamboyant for the lads. They seemed to like the fellows who wore short-sleeved white shirts and clip-on ties, the ones who never said much and squinted at everything as if it were a fresh and overwhelming fart.

"Well, they went their ways, and I went mine. I guess the Dominican Republic worked in their favor, and I suppose Korea was a draw. Viet Nam, well, that's a loss. They're about even, I suppose, but I'm winning. I started winning the day I walked out of there. That's why I did the place up like this, I like the idea of the situation room. We come in here and think about situations. I have maps of this part of the world and that, and I have all sorts of plans. And more important, I have a lot of money and ways to get lots more. The question now, my young friend, are you in or out?"

Until he asked me outright, I would've said yes. I must admit, it was all very attractive. I even liked the situation room. It was very cool, in an institutional sort of way. Yes, I liked it all, especially the idea of having a third of a million dollars. What I didn't like, though, was the sense that Howard was there with me, a version of Jimmy Cricket to my Pinocchio. Howard was telling me that I couldn't leave my pals

148

behind. Pals didn't leave each other for a few dollars. Besides, I had no assurance that Rotbart was telling the truth. I mean, what had happened to all the other lads on all the other expeditions?

"It's a hard decision, isn't it?" Rotbart said, as if reading my mind. "You don't want to hurt your friends. It breaks the Golden Rule, doesn't it? You surely don't want them doing these hard things back to you, right?"

"My thoughts exactly."

"Well, I'd like to help you out, but friends are a lot of trouble when it comes to making serious money. They get in the way of the other Golden Rules, the rules about how to get the gold. They especially get in your way if they're losers. They have too many of the wrong opinions. Sometimes, you have to go for the main chance. You've got to leave them behind. Sometimes you have to strike out on your own. But you've got to be brave. You've got to walk where it's hard to go. Now let me ask you again. Are you in or out?"

"What proof have I got that I'll get my share of that million dollars?"

"Proof?" he said, not a little astonished. "Share? Come, come, Owen. Real life doesn't have any proof or share. Real life doesn't care about such things or about you, for that matter. Real life keeps plunging on, taking things as they come."

That's when I saw it. No, real life didn't care about those things, but the men out on that training march were friends of mine and that counted for something. What's more, there was something obscene about stealing the gold of a loser.

"I need something I can count on," I said, afraid to tell him what I really thought. I began to back out of the situation room into his office. "I've got to think about this."

"Think, man?" Rotbart looked incredulous. "What's there to think about. We'll make a fortune."

I almost stumbled up against Helmut, who had just arrived with more iced tea. He was holding out two glasses.

I gave him a tight smile as I backed right on past him.

"Thanks, Helmut, but I'm not really thirsty anymore. You can have my share."

By this time, Rotbart had come to the door between his study and

149

the situation room. He leaned against the frame and crossed his arms over his chest. It was exactly the same gesture I'd seen him make at the Paradise Motel. Both of them had these tentative smiles.

"I'm sorry," I said as I kept backing up toward the hall door. "I just guess I'm not your man. I don't want to set off in my Fearnought Trowsers to steal money from the hopeless. I don't think it's what Captain Cook would be doing if he were around today. I wish you luck, though. Hey, your secret is safe with me."

I realized I was doing a kind of shuffle as I went backward. I was shuffling and saluting goodbye in a rocking motion like a bad imitation of Stepin' Fetchit.

"Adios, goodbye, so long," I said when my butt hit the door, and I reached behind me to open it. "It's been good to know you. It really has, but I think me and the boys ought to go now. I mean, we'll take our gold and go. Milwaukee is yours, and Toledo will embrace you with open arms. Portland ought to be a piece of cake."

I looked back just once as I hit the landing in front of the Palladian window. Rotbart and Helmut were staring out of the door at me. They still seemed to be smiling.

I didn't feel a step beneath my feet as I went down the stairs. I just seemed to flow down the first section of stairs. On the second set, I think I hit one step.

"Oh my God," I said as I went down the stairs. "Oh my dear God."

The front door seemed to open itself, and I bounded out onto the veranda and down the veranda steps.

"Oh my God," I said. "Oh my God."

And then I was on the front lawn like a character in a silent movie comedy, going first this way with one arm pointing and that way with the other arm pointing. Is this how heroes go? I asked myself.

I finally got my bearings and ran toward the pole. I tried to listen for footsteps behind or the sound of voices, but I couldn't hear anything over the noise of my breathing and the blood pounding inside my head.

With strength and agility I didn't know I had, I climbed up the stacked chairs in one movement and was at the top of the pole almost before I thought of what I wanted to do. Then, I felt as though I hovered there for the briefest second, held up by nothing but my will. I loosened the case and its straps from its nail and was back on the ground. I glanced inside, and the glitters from the darkness there seemed to say *Go, go, go*.

And I went, Lord God how I went, at first pumping my legs through an air that felt thick and heavy like quicksand and then, as I built up speed again, an air that seemed almost buoyant. I felt that something was helping me along. Fear perhaps.

I didn't look back until I'd plunged into the brush on the ridge above and behind the house. I went in a little ways and then laid on the ground and tried to catch my breath and look back. The house was below me, and I had a fairly clear view of it. I kept expecting Rotbart or Helmut to come out the front door with guns and serious looks on their faces. But that didn't happen. What came from the house was silence. A bird chattered away above me in the trees, and in the distance a dog barked a few times and then quit.

I cautiously stood up. The pounding in my head had turned into a dull headache.

This wasn't right. In the movies the camera would sweep across just such a quiet prelude, and then, with little warning, the bandits would ride in, all hoof beats and gunshots.

But here, even the birds got quiet. It was simply another hot day in Louisiana.

Where were they? I had the gold and was on my way to warn everybody else, and still they hadn't sought me out.

I tried to flatten myself behind a tree so they couldn't find me. Something had to be wrong. I opened the bag, but no, the coins were there. To keep from dropping it as I ran, I strapped it on over my shirt.

I wanted to scream. Didn't they know their cues?

I began walking backwards again. I kept tripping over brush, but I kept walking. I tried to aim myself in the direction of the route the men had taken this morning.

I ended up walking at an angle to the main house and soon could see the Palladian window. Rotbart was there with his arms crossed. I tried to get deeper into the woods, but the going was slow. I tried to keep turned toward the house so they couldn't sneak up on me. As a result, I kept tripping over bushes and backing into trees. My arms and neck were getting scratched. Suddenly, Rotbart waved at me, and I knew it was hopeless.

And Helmut was there on the porch. He held his thumb up the way flyers going on a mission did. What chance did I have? It was their place and their show. I was just a bit player who'd gotten his parts confused. They didn't have to catch me. I would catch myself.

I started to cry. Huge tears washed down my face. I didn't want to die there. It was useless and pointless. I started running again, running toward where I thought the guys had gone. The exercise made the tears go away, and that was something.

I started running harder. I was going to try it. I didn't have much to offer. Hell, I was, after all, one of the losers, but I was going to try.

I ran as hard as I could, and soon all my thoughts went away.

# Twenty-Three

*THE WOODS ARE LOVELY DARK AND DEEP*, I said to myself as I ran through the trees. *The woods are lovely dark and deep.*

I ran. Oh how I ran. The coins in the case lifted up and clanked down with the rhythm of my stride.

I ran parallel to the road leading out of the compound, but negotiating past the brush and trees slowed me down. I finally stepped out onto the road. I stopped a moment, but I couldn't hear anyone following me. That was surprising. Didn't they care? I mean, I thought I had the money, but maybe the gold was gone, replaced by slugs. I looked again, and the coins looked very real to me. I couldn't figure it out. Why weren't they after me?

Then I walked on the road and studied the terrain. I tried to figure out where everyone had gone. It was just past noon, and I imagined that they had stopped for lunch someplace.

I suddenly realized that what I'd done had a larger impact than I'd planned on. Or hadn't planned on, really. Everyone was in danger now. It was all of us that had to get away. That thought made me start running again. I had to find the group before Rotbart and Helmut did.

I'd gone a mile or so and was sweating profusely when I saw the sign. It was crudely lettered script, as if someone had imitated an old-fashioned road sign. *Camp Fortitude,* it read, and a roughly drawn hand with a pointing finger indicated a narrow roadway that curved off into the woods. And sure enough, I could see fresh tire tracks in the sandy soil. That was it. They were eating lunch at camp, the way we did most days. I started running again.

When I passed the last of the bushes and stepped into the clearing of the meadow, I felt the pure sensation of victory. This must be, I thought, what it feels like to win a great race. I had a chance to escape. No, we all had a chance to escape.

The station wagon was parked beneath the tree. I could see Junior Junior's boots sticking out of the open hatch of the back window. He was probably asleep, and his boots rocked slowly back and forth.

Howard was standing near the car as if looking for something he'd lost. I could make out the shapes of the other men lying beneath the bushes at the far edge of the meadow. The black cook was the only person in the sun, and she was bent over, very slowly packing up the lunch gear. Perfect. All I had to do was get the car and get the men in.

"Howard!" I began yelling as I ran into the clearing. "Howard!"

True to instincts, Howard stepped backward when he heard my voice.

"Howard! Get the station wagon. It's a con job. There's no South America. We've got to get out of here." At the edge of my sight I could see the other men coming out of the bushes. The black cook had stopped her work. She had stood up and cupped her hand over her eyes to see what was going on.

"Rotbart and Helmut!" I was gasping. I could hardly breathe. "They'll kill us. Get the car. Get the car, Howard! It's our only chance."

Then everything went into slow motion, as if I was living my life frame by frozen frame.

In a Jeep I hadn't seen before, Rotbart and Helmut came skidding into the meadow from the other side. They were both screaming at us, but their speed left most of the sound behind them.

Howard saw them too and in one almost ballet-like movement he stepped to the back of the station wagon and slammed the hatch down on Junior Junior's feet. It was such a direct move I could hardly believe it.

But I didn't have any trouble believing Rotbart and Helmut coming toward us. Helmut had the passenger door of the Jeep open and was trying to steady himself in a standing position on the running board. He had the machine pistol.

I caught the end of what Junior Junior was saying as I ran up beside the station wagon.

". . . . the fuck," he stammered from inside, and then he began screaming. Both of his boots were twisted too far to the side, and there were irregular little spasms in his calf muscles that shook his feet as if trying, unsuccessfully, to get things back into their proper order.

"The fuck, the fuck, the fuck," he whined.

"The keys, Howard? Where are the keys?"

Howard gestured toward the front seat.

I was surprised at how easily I pulled Junior Junior from the station wagon after I dropped the lower part of the back door open.

"No, no, no, no," he said softly when I grabbed him by the ankles and jerked him to the ground. He felt light and broken, like a small hurt animal. I vaguely remember wanting to say I was sorry, but I didn't have time.

"Come on, Howard. Get in." I said as I slammed the back door closed. "There's no South America. There's just this gold and us, and if we've got our good sense, we'd better get going."

The Jeep was about a hundred yards away. Helmut had the gun pressed against the frame of the passenger window, but the bouncing of the Jeep prevented a clear shot.

"Come on, Howard." I said again as I got behind the wheel. I slid down to make myself a smaller target. "Come on, man."

"I don't know, Owen," he started to say as the machine gun bullets went through his neck like dots of indecision. His tentative smile lingered a little longer than it should and then the sounds of the shots caught up with us.

"No," I said, and then "Nooooo" drawn out like a keening. "No oh no no no no no."

I crouched farther down then and started the car and began driving it. The terrain slammed me up and down in the seat, the steering wheel rocking back and forth with each new rut. The passenger door was banging as well, still open from leaving Howard to die.

"Oh no no no no," I heard a voice like my own and hot tears on my face.

At first I went careening straight toward the Jeep, subconsciously taking Rotbart's great advice. He was so shocked he swerved to avoid me and almost tipped the Jeep over.

I drove toward the other men now, but Rotbart was soon behind me.

I tried to crouch so that my head was just barely above the dashboard. I heard a tinkle and then a scratching sound and looked up in the rear-view mirror to see the spider webs of broken glass in the back window.

155

The men were on my right. Rotbart seemed to have guessed that I would pick them up. He passed me on my right. Luckily, Helmut and that deadly gun were on the other side from me.

I jerked the wheel to the left, the rear of the car spinning out. I felt a thump; my back fender must've hit the Jeep. My car paused a moment as if checking itself for wounds, and then lunged ahead and up. A moment later it crashed back down, shoving me against the roof. I had a splitting headache.

I circled back around, but I was too late. Helmut had done his business. Tony LaCosta still managed to stand in the middle of the bodies. His last gesture was to wave me on before he collapsed.

And that was it. Of the ten local losers on the St. Louis franchise, I was the only one left.

I didn't have time to cry anymore. I looked over my left shoulder and saw that Rotbart was circling around behind me. This time, Helmut would be on my side.

I put my foot down on the accelerator of that car as if I were stepping into salvation. I hoped—and oh how hard I hoped— that the car wouldn't break as it rocked over the bumps in that meadow and onto the road through the woods. Oh, oh, oh.

Then, my God, I was in the woods and free. I had to glance out of the side window to see behind me since the back window looked frosted over, but nothing was behind me but dust. The passenger door, still open, clattered back and forth. Branches of the trees and brush along the road slapped the sides of the car like fans congratulating a player who's just won the World Series as he heads into the locker room.

Then I was in the yard of the compound. I circled it twice before I found the road we'd come in on. As I bumped up onto the clean blacktop of a highway, I saw that the bus which brought us from the airport was parked just at the entrance to the drive. I stopped for a moment to slam the passenger door closed. The rear end of the car squealed when it hit the blacktop and rocked back and forth.

After a half hour of driving, I came to a stop sign. US 171 to the left was south and to the right was north. I went north. I had a car, a direction to go, and absolutely no idea of where I was. But I drove on.

# Twenty-Four

**I DROVE ON INTO THE AFTERNOON.** I passed Leesville and Anacoco, Florien, and Many. I went through Noble and Converse, Mansfield and Grand Cane. I saw Stonewall and Keithville and Bossier City and Shreveport. I went near Dixie and Belcher and passed the sign for Plain Dealing, but I stopped before I got to Hosston.

It was late in the afternoon. I was tired. Even though I'd read the signs, I didn't know where I was. Louisiana was no more familiar to me than India. The signs didn't tell me what I truly needed. They didn't say, *You'll make it home all right* or *Watch out, trouble there, my friend.*

I needed to think; I needed a plan. I realized that I'd simply been stumbling into things without much forethought, as if my life were a picaresque invented by whoever ran the adventures I stumbled into. I needed to get control of things. I needed to figure out what I should do next. Moreover, I was scared. I was terrified of arriving somewhere and finding Rotbart waiting there for me. I assumed that he could out think me and had, in all likelihood, already figured roughly where I'd gone. I imagined him a few miles behind me, guessing each of my turns, as able to outmaneuver me as a master chess player outmaneuvers a novice.

I was sad, too. They were all gone, weren't they? All of them. This wasn't a television show where the dead came back on another episode. No, this was life, where some mediocre folks got erased as if they'd never been there. I thought about each of them by name, and I got sadder, because I would never know what a mother knew about Howard and Lucky Beal and Tony LaCosta and Murphy and Artie Hokum and Stanley Smith and Tyrone Butler and Merle Peppernow and Haskel Fortune. In fact, it didn't seem possible that someone named Haskel Fortune could die.

I wanted to think about all this and suddenly drove the car off US 171 onto an unnamed side road. As I went farther down the blacktop road, it became gravel, and then it turned into dirt. I came to a dead end in a sea of dry grass at the base of a hill. The road simply ended, as if there had been a failure of will to go on. Or perhaps the money had simply run out.

I drove into the grass and parked the car. I got out into the hum and rattle of insects and small animals. The noises stopped when I slammed the door shut. A few moments later, as if unseen eyes had checked me out and found me harmless, they started up again.

The grass was waist high and looked as though you could lie down in it and pull the earth around you like a blanket. I started to think over where I'd been and plan what I was going to do next, but my life had become so preposterous I didn't know what I could do but go on in some direction Rotbart wouldn't figure out. I guessed I'd been heading north, an entirely predictable choice. I was probably taking the main route back to St. Louis. My God, Rotbart would easily guess that.

But I couldn't let him find me. My escape had cost too much. I was probably the only survivor of our brave little group. If I'd had the time, I would've cried. All those lost souls, trying to be heroes with the insufficient stuff of their lives, were gone. I hoped God or somebody would remember them. I hardly knew them well enough to even recall their faces. I had to do something with their gold. It was my duty, but I didn't know what to do about the duty. At the very least, I had to escape Rotbart. I just had to. I hit the front fender with my fist and heard the tinkle of glass falling out of the rear window.

I got back in the car and turned the key. I had just under a quarter of a tank. I undid the straps from the leather case holding the gold coins and put it under the driver's seat. The thought of that $30,000 cheered me up a little.

*You should be traveling south,* I told myself. *Rotbart would never guess that. Nor would he guess that you'd pass him while he's coming north after you.*

Heading back south felt like a plan, and what's more it made me feel almost happy. I'd go south to a major city like Baton Rouge or New Orleans, ditch the car, and take the train north. Rotbart would never think of that. He'd figure I'd drive straight to St. Louis.

I put the car in gear and did a slow u-turn in the grass. It parted in front of me and closed behind like water. I told myself I was a bush-league Moses. As I drove back toward the dirt road, I tried to laugh at my stupid joke.

# Twenty-Five

**IT WAS GETTING NEAR EVENING** as I drove back out toward what I thought was US 171, but things just didn't look the same. When I found what appeared to be a main highway and turned onto it, I didn't see any traffic. Even stranger, there weren't any highway signs or businesses along the road. There weren't any signs for Plain Dealing or, in fact, any towns at all. I drove and drove, but what I found was myself and myself alone on a road going through the twilight-darkened woods of Louisiana.

After fifty miles or so of what I thought was a southerly direction, I finally came to a sign. It was a faded red in the beams of my headlights, and its top appeared to have been ripped off. *Four Miles Ahead* it advised, as if no further information were needed. I carefully checked my odometer and drove what I thought were exactly four miles and found nothing but woods along the road and more road. There wasn't anything, not even an abandoned building or a worn place that might indicate where something had been.

I was lost, and I certainly should've been driving to find my way out of where I was, but I was so taken by the idea of a sign that had outlived what it directed people to that I drove back to the sign again to make sure that I'd done nothing wrong. I carefully checked the odometer again and drove what I thought was exactly four miles. Nothing was there but a few low bushes with woods behind. I parked the car on the steep shoulder and got out. I couldn't even find the remnants of a side road.

The sun was going down, and half the sky was burnt orange becoming purple. If nothing else, Louisiana had the most magnificent sunrises and sunsets I'd ever seen. I tried to orient myself. Toward the descending sun was west, I told myself. But wait, didn't these directions change with the seasons? Wasn't the summer sun more in the north than the west? Or was that the winter sun? I tried to remember what I'd learned about these matters in a high-school science course, but unfortunately all I could remember of that was the shape of Donna O'Gorman's chest.

I started the car and drove toward the sunset, hoping that the obvious choice was the correct one, hoping as well to make a left-hand turn onto a major highway going south.

It got dark quite suddenly, and the dark made me realize how exhausted I was. I began to think about motels and restaurants, about getting back to civilization. Those thoughts, however, also reminded me that I didn't have any real spending money, that my gold was about as useless to me in the twentieth century as believing that the sun was a chariot of the gods driven across the sky by fiery horses. If I handed one of those coins to a night clerk at a Holiday Inn, he'd think I was crazy or perhaps a Russian. He'd probably call the police.

"Yessir, I knowed right off he was up to no good," I heard him say as I was led off by two burly county sheriff's deputies.

Great. Here I was, richer than I'd ever even dreamed of being, and the wealth was essentially worthless. What was the phrase? Rich as Croesus. Shit, I might as well be walking around in flowing hair, robes, and a crown.

As I began to worry and feel sorry for myself, I came to the next sign.

*Turn around,* it said, *and turn pink.*

It went on:

> *You've missed the Flamingo Island Motel*
> *Nothing like it anywheres*
> *Twenty miles back.*

Of course I went back. I mean, what would you have done? And of course twenty miles brought me back to nothing. Another four miles returned me to the first sign. I went back to the spot the two signs seemed so intent on. I got out of the car and looked carefully along both sides of the road for a sign of the Flamingo Island Motel. Surely no one would go to so much trouble for a hoax.

I was finally so tired of riddling out the signs and of the tension from my escape that I decided to sleep in the car. I guessed I was safe. I hadn't seen another car. I figured things might seem clearer in the morning. I figured I must've taken a wrong turn back in that field. I meant to go back there in the morning and get on the right road. For now, though, I figured I was lost but safe. I checked to make sure the gold was still beneath the driver's seat. Then the tension closed my

160

eyes like a mother. As I fell asleep, I thought it appropriate that a man with mythical money was sleeping at a mythical motel.

# Twenty-Six

**I HEARD HER BEFORE I SAW HER.**

I heard a soft rubbing noise first, the kind of sound a cat makes sliding along a nubby piece of furniture.

The car rocked ever so gently. I'd slept late. Even from my slouched position, I could see the sun overhead. I guessed it was ten in the morning.

I was curled up on the front seat, my head against the passenger arm rest. I could see that the driver's door was unlocked. I couldn't tell about my side from where I lay and was afraid to move. Whatever was shaking the car—it was just behind my head. I wanted to sit up far enough to peek out. I suddenly remembered Junior Junior's gun and wished I had taken it.

I heard a noise that sounded like a low moan at first, the kind of sound an animal makes before attacking. Then I realized it was singing, or a cross between singing and humming. That's when I figured out it was a woman.

This realization was so startling that I sat up and found myself staring into the face of a white-haired old lady who must've been at least eighty years old. Even in that first glance I could see her beauty. She looked like a young woman wearing the make-up and costume of an old woman. She smiled as if she'd been expecting me.

She said something that the window turned into murmurs.

I rolled it down. "What did you say?" I asked.

"Why, we don't get many visitors these days." Her voice had a lovely alto rise and lilt. She smiled at the end of her sentences.

"Nosir. Not since DuWayne edited the signs. But you must've figured us out. 'Between the twenty and the four is what Sylvie and I are living for,' is how DuWayne used to put it.

"Right," I said, realizing that the sign had kept its promise of *Nothing Like It Anywheres.*

"Did you have a reservation?" she asked. Her face seemed to change when she asked this question into someone harder.

The question was so improbable I simply answered it.

"Why no. I was hoping you might find room for me."

"I just don't know. We're just awful busy this time of year." The face looked implacable, as if she just realized that the place was full up. Perhaps she had decided not to trust me.

"I suppose you are," I went on. "What with all the tourists here and such."

I got out of the car. There was just the heat and the wilderness and, of course, me and this old lady.

"Ma'am," I said. "I don't mean to be rude. God knows I don't. But I've got to say this. There isn't anything here I could have a reservation for. I mean, do we sign up someplace for the hot air or for the woods or for this blacktop road? I mean really."

I thought that was some pretty tough talk.

"Or maybe the train for heaven starts up here," I went on, "or maybe it's the handcarts to hell. Is that it?"

"Sir, I just don't like no smart talk," she said. "No I don't. None at all is the best with me. And with DuWayne. I mean DuWayne, if he were here, but God rest his soul he isn't just now, though he said he might be coming back after he died.

"'Sylvie Mae,' he told me once, 'I'll die and be back in my green chair before you know I'm gone, and that'll be the plain fact of things.'

"That's why I got rid of that green chair because it spooked me to see it empty and that's why I talk sometimes like I do; I mean I talk in this rough way as if the resort is full up and that kind of thing. You see, I just don't know who to trust, so I tell them I'm full until I make them out. You seem to be all right in a pompous sort of way, though if you're not, I'd like to know.

"I don't know if I believe that, do you? I mean, about his coming back from the dead. Do you really think he could move all that dirt away from his grave? That would be hard for a live man, but for a dead one, why it must be close to just impossible. Perhaps, sir, you have some scientific understanding of things that might help a lady out. I mean, do dead men have any strength at all?"

Her eyes were wide as she asked me this. The hard face was gone, and the face of the young woman inside the old lady's visage was back. As she finished her question, she tugged on my sleeve.

163

"I'll just be goddamned if I know, ma'am. I just don't know at all."

I looked back and forth along the road, but there wasn't a clue about where she came from. I began to wonder if she floated in from someplace.

"Ma'am." I started up again, "Where is this resort you keep talking about?"

She stepped back from me as if she were astonished.

"Why, sir, you really can't see it? Is that what you're telling me? I thought it must be pretty obvious when you got up close like this."

"Ma'am, I don't mean any disrespect, but all I see is road and woods and sky. I don't see a resort at all."

"Why, it's in there. Where else would it be?" She swept her arm across the air before her as if her resort took in the entire world. I had a fleeting sense of her weaving a spell. I almost expected the air to change colors and a city to appear.

I then saw that she was pointing to a place in the woods about a hundred yards from where we stood. I squinted and tried to see what she meant.

"I'm sorry, ma'am, but I just don't see anything."

"Course you don't." She gave me a little poke in the side as she said this. "I've been testing you out. DuWayne hid things pretty well when it all went bad. He didn't want no one in there."

"But how about the signs?" I asked. "Why do you have the signs if you don't want anyone to know where you are?" I kept squinting at the woods. I felt like someone trying to find the key to the connect-the-dot picture.

"I did the signs," the woman said. "I got me some of those Walter Foster art books and painted those signs and a few things around here as well. DuWayne used to say that I was as creative as Disneyland in what I did, but that was a lie to make me feel good. DuWayne did all the designing. He was the genius in his own way. I wanted to tear the signs down when we quit but DuWayne said to let them be, because no one would ever find us anyway. Come with me."

She walked across the road toward the woods. I followed her, though before I did, I looked both ways up and down the highway. In that hard sunlight I felt vulnerable. I wondered where Rotbart was. I also worried briefly about the gold, but I also didn't want to draw her attention to it. I figured I would be safe leaving it in the car for a few minutes.

She walked toward a space in the trees along the road, a space that I simply hadn't seen before. It was almost like magic. I wondered how I could have missed it. When I caught up with her, I could see the twin depressions of worn ruts going up to some brush and a squat tree. It was unmistakably an old road. To the right of the old roadway was a tall metal pole that had, I guess, once supported a sign.

"It's in here," she said. "DuWayne planted the tree and bushes to keep folks out. He didn't even want them to find the road."

"But you still haven't told me why you went to all the trouble of advertising the place with those highway signs if you didn't want people to find you."

She looked at me curiously, as if I were a freak or a retarded person.

"Come on," Sylvie Mae said. "I'm taking you in now. You can ask questions later."

Beyond the tree and the brush, the road turned ever so slightly to the left through heavier growths of trees and bushes. The depressions of the old ruts barely remained; the scene was close to going. It was like an image of how fragile our hold is here. In a few years, the last bare spots in the ruts would be gone, and grass would turn into bush, and the bush to trees.

The road jogged to the right and back to the left and then it came into an opening. Judging from the halo of trees in the distance, I guessed the open space to be several acres in size. We crossed a wooden bridge that spanned a muddy creek. At the beginning of the bridge was an overhead sign, but I was too far past it to read what it said.

"Wait here," she ordered me and walked away to one of several cracked and collapsing stucco buildings. They all were colored a kind of off white. Then I realized they were simply faded pink.

She went into a building at the center of the complex and returned a few minutes later with an axe and a small, bowed saw.

"These'll get you in. No sense leaving your car on the road."

She handed me the tools, grabbed my arm, and started walking me back toward the road. I forgot to turn around for the sign until we were around the first curve in the road.

I chopped and I sawed and I chopped some more until the lane seemed wide enough for a car. Then I got the station wagon and drove it off the highway and onto the old road. It was slow going, but it worked. The remaining brush and grass pounded on the bottom of the car.

The gateway was visible above the surrounding forest, like a clear thought over a lot of doubt. It was made of very elaborate wrought iron that had begun to rust. The thing was quite high, maybe twenty feet or more. I backed the car away from it to get a better look. It was shaped like, of all things, a heart. A sign hung from the middle read *Your Welcome Is Straight from the Heart* and, sure enough, a *Welcome* sign was straight across the courtyard from the gate. Passing over the wooden bridge, the car made rumbling noises. I parked near the building the woman had earlier gone into.

I now stood opposite the heart-shaped entrance and had a better view of things. On the back of the welcome sign was: *You Gotta Have a Heart as Big as This.*

A moment or two later the old lady strode through the gate as if she were what the *This* referred to.

"Come in, Mister," Sylvie Mae waved to me as she passed and walked into one of the buildings. "Come in out of the heat of the day."

Inside the building was another era. This wasn't an environment that someone had collected, the way Rotbart had put together a combination of Plantation Owner and English Gentleman. Inside that building were the 1940s as they were in 1946.

It was hard to see at first. As my eyes adjusted from the harsh light of the Louisiana afternoon to the dim browns of the interior, I felt like someone on one of those carnival rides that disorients you by starting in the darkness.

I sat at the end of a couch in the living room. The furniture was fat and covered with a heavy, satin fabric. There were (and it took me a moment to remember the word) antimacassars on the arms and the backs of the sofa and upholstered chairs. There were doilies on the table tops. In fact every surface was covered with something—an ornate lamp, a photograph in a silver picture frame, a piece of China, or a little statue.

166

I could hear the woman in another room. A moment later she came into the living room with a silver tray. A piece of heavy linen was folded in the middle of the tray and on it were a cut-glass pitcher, two glasses, a silver container filled with ice, and a sugar bowl. Sprigs of mint were arranged in a small vase. She set the tray down on a low table in front of the couch. A lock of her gray hair fell across her forehead as she stood up. She brushed it back and stared at me.

"Mister, would you like a touch of sugar and mint in your tea? You should, you know, to fight back the days out here. They're hot and wearisome."

I nodded. The tea made me remember that I hadn't eaten since breakfast the day before. In fact, the last refreshment I had was iced tea in Rotbart's office. Everyone had been waiting for lunch when I tore their world apart. I was hungry. But I was so hungry I was into some kind of zone where things were calm and in slow motion.

"Ma'am, this is lovely." I took a sip of the tea, and its taste had a slightly mossy flavor. "Just lovely," I said as I finished it.

"Would you like some lunch to go with that, young man? It's almost noon, and DuWayne always said that our guests are entitled to two meals a day. They paid for them."

"Right. Yes, I would. Very much." The idea of food was now making me a little weak. I stood up, hoping to shake the weakness away by moving. "Do you mind if I look around while you fix lunch? This is quite a place you've got here."

"Why, make yourself to home. You're our guest here."

I stepped outside, into the noon sun, and light seemed to come down in sheets. It brought tears to my eyes. I could just barely see the station wagon and stumbled towards it. I cupped my hand over my eyes and looked inside. I could see one of the leather straps from the pouch of gold. I thought about hiding the gold someplace else and then decided not to. Moving it would be like telegraphing where my valuables were hidden, like patting a wallet in front of the pickpockets.

I wondered if the woman or someone else were watching me. For the sake of an explanation to the eyes that might be looking, I opened the door, got Junior Junior's sunglasses from the dashboard, closed the door, and walked away from the station wagon like a tourist intent on the next sight. I put the sunglasses on, stuffed my hands in my pockets, and began to whistle "It Ain't Me, Babe."

And, indeed, it wasn't me. It wasn't the sort of place I—or most of the people I knew—would put together. The old woman's comparison with Disneyland wasn't entirely off base. I could see four one-story stucco buildings behind the one in front. Behind them were two or three larger buildings. All these structures faced the heart-shaped entrance and the stream or the moat or whatever the wooden bridge crossed. I glanced into a couple of the buildings. The main doors opened onto hallways with more doors that led, I suspected, into the rooms of the motel. One of the buildings was a garage and housed a rusted-out pick-up truck and, beneath some old cotton sheets, a pink Edsel in just about show-room condition.

"Lunch is ready," Sylvie Mae called.

A pink Edsel, I thought. That, here, made a perfect kind of sense, or it did until I realized that the right lens from Junior Junior's sunglasses was missing.

"Lunch," Sylvie Mae called again. "Lunch is ready."

It certainly was, and the meal was delightful. We sat facing each across the long ends of an eight- or ten-foot dining room table. We had cucumber soup, tuna in puff pastry, fresh tomatoes on Bermuda onions that were covered with an oil and vinegar dressing, chilled white wine, and lime sherbet with a sauce made from Kiwi fruit for dessert. When we finished the meal, I thought to myself how well I felt. Never had I felt more alive. I was on the edge, I thought, living moment to moment, making it up as I went along. I briefly wondered how she'd learn to cook such things.

"You belong somewhere else, my young friend." The woman raised her wine glass to me as she said this and emptied it. I smiled and drank mine down.

"You're right. Righter than you know, but you can't help me."

"You'd be surprised what I can and cannot do. Look around. Is this the kind of place a helpless person would run?" Her voice sounded firmer than the one I'd heard on the highway.

"No, I guess not. But I'm in . . . ." I paused before going into this. But then, what did I have to lose? "I'm in terrible trouble."

"I gathered that, my boy. I could see that when I saw you on the road. Even from a distance you didn't look like the sort of redneck who usually hangs around the edge of my life. You certainly looked different, that's for sure. I figured you were all right in a serious sort of way."

"I'm being followed. I'm being followed by people who'd just as soon kill us as look at us." I didn't really know if this was true or not, but I figured it would make my point.

"Oh no," she said, "They won't be killing me. No. It's not a death by killing I'll be having. It's death by fire. Those things are in the cards so clear you can't get around them. DuWayne played the Tarot out for me. For you, why I don't know. You'll die the way you're going to die. Maybe you've got the rumor of your death from another source. But me, I'm for fire."

"Right, ma'am. But I'd just as soon make sure those killers aren't coming up the road. Do you mind if I check around outside? Kind of get the lay of things?"

"Why, not at all."

Walking back out into the light was even harder than before. The sheets of light seemed to have grown sharp edges. Outside the door I stood rubbing my eyes, trying to get tears to wash the harshness away.

By the time I went back through the gate my sight had returned. The roadway into the motel looked pretty abandoned. I walked back to the highway. The only signs of recent life were the two slight indentions in the grass from my car tires. It wasn't hard to kick them back and forth into standing grass. I studied the road from the highway again. No, you couldn't tell much of anything. To go up that road, you'd have to know exactly where it was, an unlikely thing for Rotbart to figure out.

"Ma'am, I just wanted to check the road," I said when I got back. "I think we're OK here."

"OK? That's what you think? Just OK? I mean, we're more than initials here. We're a sentence or two, maybe a paragraph, perhaps a page."

"I just mean there's no one on the road to gun us down."

"Pishwah. There's always someone on the road to gun you down. It might be God, staring down the barrel of your number's up. I sometimes see it that way. Like waiting in line at the butcher shop, you know, where they have those little cards with numbers on them. The way your number does come up, just like it says. What if it's like that, in the hereafter? Someone walking across a room with a number that he puts on a hook. The number's just up there. And it must be pretty high after all these years and all these folks. I mean, you and me would have to be a billion some odd million. Do you think someone is keeping track of all this?"

I didn't know how to answer her question. I kept looking around to see if someone else was there, to see if DuWayne or whoever might come strolling around a corner. I just couldn't believe that she kept the place by herself.

We had somehow ended up close together as she spoke. We were at the side of the parlor, standing in an almost amber light, as if we were being preserved in a dusky liquid. She had pulled out an album of old photographs.

"That's how I was," she said and pointed to a statuesque woman who stood smiling languidly out of the photograph.

"I was in show business. I was a dancer. Oh God, how I could dance. You've seen those chorus lines of girls, all legs? Well, that's how I was. I was just spectacular. I'd walk out of the hotel where I lived in New York City and just stand for a moment on the stoop, and people would stop and look at me. That's how it was, but it's all gone now. I'm just the wreck of what I was.

"Back then, though, we had the loveliest of days. I grew up in a town just over the hill from here. Or there was a town. The town for me's here in my head, because I haven't seen it now for years. I hardly leave Flamingo Island anymore. Everything I need is here. The boy delivers the groceries on the road out there and comes two days a week to help me with the work. I haven't had any mail since 1962. I don't need any mail. What's the government ever done for me, except send me tax returns? My friends are dead or disappeared. I had a television for a while, but I got rid of it. I don't want someone else's view of things. I want my own.

"This town that's over the hill had six streets, three running north

170

and south, and three running east and west. The Illinois Central used to water its engines there. My grandfather settled the place. He was in the hardware business.

"I grew up there running around like a wild girl. The town was on a hill, and we had the highest place in town. My room had a tower room at the corner. The house had a turret. I thought if you stood in the middle of that round room and spun around it was like magic. I could see everywhere. I can remember spinning around and seeing China. I mean I really thought I could.

"I saved money. I sold eggs and raised lambs. I cared for children. When I graduated from high school, I had a $100—a huge sum in those days. You're probably a highwayman and have all kinds of money hidden in your car and think that a $100 is nothing. Well, then it was big, I can tell you that.

"I had my $100 and I knew how to dance. I learned how at Miss Vickerey's School. I still have one of her flyers. She was a skinny, long-necked goofy old broad. I probably look like her now. She came from the east, everybody said. Everybody came from the east then. The ones who went west didn't come back, or if they did, they'd gone broke or had some bad business up their sleeves.

"Miss Vickerey just showed up in town one day and went from house to house with her leaflets. She'd rented the floor above the grocery store. It was a big loft with tall windows at each end.

"That used to happen before the Second War. People would arrive in town and start doing something. It really was the Land of Opportunity, the good old USA was. Alice, that's the town, though it hardly exists anymore. It hardly existed back then. We had two or three hundred people, but we figured out things to do with each other, just like life in the big city. But there can't be much left now. The whole business of Alice was taking care of the trains.

"Yes, people would just come to town, and the rest of us would take a chance. That's how the world worked then. If Horace Greeley went west today, he'd need a license and letters of recommendation."

"I live in that kind of a world," I said.

She turned and looked at me as if she'd just noticed me there.

"Yes," she said, as if she were trying to get her bearings. She paused

171

and then went on. "Yes, people like you. That's what's wrong with everything."

Her voice drifted off, and then mumbled away like a line cast out for the deeper fish. Then her voice came back as if she were reeling it in.

"I got a job in New York. I savor this sentence. *I got a job in New York.* Those words were printed bold inside my head and in my heart. *I got a job in New York.* It was incredible. No. I was incredible. Do you have any idea of what that meant, to get a job in New York? Someone like me, from a town like Alice? Think about it, for God's sake."

Her voice rose as she said all this. I thought for a second she was speaking to ghosts that were hard of hearing. Indeed, she was facing one of the photographs on the parlor wall.

"It was 1919, and I had this floppy velvet hat I ordered from a shop in New Orleans. The bodice of my dress was cinched, tight, just below my breasts, and I can tell you I looked like something, even in New York.

"I went right to the Garrick Theatre because that's the one Miss Vickerey had told me about. Even her flyer, the one for Miss Vickerey's School of Theatre and Dance, said her 'young women were as joyful to behold as the ladies on the stage of the famous Garrick Theatre in New York City.'

"I didn't know what I was doing when I got to New York. That must be what saved me. But I'd taken Miss Vickerey at her word that I was as good as those girls in New York, and there I was— walking up that street in New York, the sunlight glittering off the shop windows, the shouts of peddlers, the clatter of horses, the chugging of the first automobiles. There I was—the best dancer from Alice, Louisiana, seeking her fame and fortune.

"Great God they took me. The stage manager looked at me and said I was hired. Just like that. I figured people were so good in New York that they could see into what you were. It never occurred to me that he might've seen something else. Five dollars a week he gave me and board and room. They put me up at the Sweetheart's Home.

"The Sweetheart's Home was five stories of dancers. Five stories of the most beautiful women you ever saw. That's what all of us were like. The hearts we could break, the memories we could become. I'd never seen anything like it, all of us in our dresses, some of us in outrageous hats, all of us so beautiful Michelangelo would've ached to draw us. We came together every morning like some flock of birds at the trolley stop, and then we disappeared as each of us went her separate way into this car or that and on to this show or that.

"A few men had figured this out, and they'd be there in the morning in their suits, doffing their hats as we went by, but they were just overwhelmed by all of us. They wouldn't have known where to begin making passes. I remember, they just stood there and slid their hats back on their foreheads and smiled.

"Do you have any idea of how hard it is being beautiful? You've got to think about it, the way some folks think about money or about painting the world's great picture. What's worse, you've got to think about beauty as the beauty is going away. I mean, it just goes, no matter what you do. You put yourself together after a bath. A little make-up here, a little pat there. You do all this, but then you look in the mirror one morning, and a small corner of an eye has slipped a bit and formed this little wrinkle. It's not much, this tiny corner of an eye. It's nothing average folks would think about. But if you're beautiful—and God I was beautiful, you see something like that as the beginning of the end. It's the beginning of the goingness of it all. Pretty soon you end up like this."

She got up from her chair and bent over in front of me.

"What do you think? Should I have worried about the wrinkle?"

It took a moment for my eyes to focus on her. Beneath her wrinkles she still had the look of a young woman. I had the sense that she was playing hide and seek in there. It was as if I only had to call her out.

"My dear," I found myself saying, "you're really not that bad at all."

She snorted at me the way a thoroughbred horse might, and then she walked back into the dining room. I heard her start picking up our lunch dishes.

"I've had a wonderful life here," Sylvie said when she came back. "A wonderful life. I couldn't really be a dancer in New York, though God knows I got very close. I guess that's what I really wanted to be, though DuWayne helped me on that one.

"'Sylvie Mae,' he wrote me in a letter while I was staying at the Sweetheart's Home, 'you can dance anywhere. You can dance in New York and you can dance in Alice, Louisiana, but you might just have the best audience right here in Alice. Think about it, Sylvie Mae.'

"Well, he was right, because the audiences got worse and worse. As I said, I started at the Garrick and went to the Stanford and after that came the Variety, but then I noticed how each place was just a little seedier than the last. I noticed that each theatre had fewer people in it, and the laughs got rougher. Soon, (too soon) I was standing on the stage of the Belle with about fifteen other girls. We'd been rehearsing this fast number with an out-of-tune little band. After our break, the director had us all come downstage to talk about how to get our tops off for the finale. I hardly even heard what he said because I was still going over steps in my mind.

"Pretty soon I realized that what he's talking about is taking off our clothes, and then I happened to notice this group of men kind of hanging around the way the men about to look at naked women hang around, and then I saw that the stage manager had all these little packets of money wrapped in ribbons for us.

"It came to me in a flash then that my career in New York was over. Oh, I wouldn't have minded strutting around naked, I guess. When you're beautiful, there's nothing in God's great world like having somebody stare at you like you're the only one on earth. That's why dancers dance, and I don't care if you're a ballerina or a tumbler or a stripper. It's all the same thing. It's a sweet feeling living in the middle of those loving eyes. The trouble comes afterwards. I looked down at the men hanging around. I looked at one especially who had this thin little moustache and blotches all over his face. Suddenly I could imagine him kissing on my neck, and right then and there I wanted out like I'd never wanted out of anything before.

"'Excuse me, excuse me,' I said to other girls when I walked across the stage. 'Excuse me, excuse me,' I said to the stage hands and costume fitters waiting around backstage.

"'Cindy, come back,' the producer yelled. 'Cindy, you're missing a real opportunity. You could be somebody's fancy girl. Think about it.'

"It didn't bother me that he couldn't remember my name. At least he came close. Most of them call you Girl in Red or Tall One in the Third Row. No, that didn't bother me. It was the fancy girl stuff. That crystallized something. It meant being used. I hated that.

"I just walked out of there and back up the street to the Sweetheart Hotel. I got the little that was left of my money and my peau de soie bag, and I left. I was so irritated I didn't even pay my last week's bill. That bothers me to this very day. I don't think it's a fair thing, leaving unpaid debts behind. But I was done with strutting, I'd decided. And I needed my money to go home.

"Well, I took my money—I had $27.00 left, I remember that. I took my money and bought a train ticket to New Orleans. The trains huffed and puffed and got stuck here and there over cows and weather and coal shortages, but four days later we pulled into New Orleans. I was covered with soot and sorry to be coming home with my tail between my legs, but I was happy to have my tail, if you get my drift.

"I'd sent my Daddy a telegram, and he met me there in his new Overland automobile, a name that was a misnomer because that car had a harder time going overland than I did. I mean, we could've walked back to Alice with less trouble. With the help of three different farmers and their wagons, we finally got back home."

She looked at me for a moment.

"You. Why you must be having an adventure of your own, aren't you?"

"I guess you could say that."

"Didn't you tell me the outlaws were after you? Or are you an outlaw after somebody else? I've lost track."

"It's a long story, ma'am."

"I'm not sure I want to hear any long stories. I suppose you saw my pink car out there."

"As a matter of fact I did. It's lovely. It looks like new."

"It should. Why, the care I've given that car. It's my tribute to DuWayne."

She cried a little as she said that. And she even looked beautiful while she cried, with her head resting on her bent hand. The last of the afternoon light came through the window on her like a little spotlight of tragedy. The light was filtered by the screen on the window and subdued by the dull browns and ochres of the interior until it looked like old yellow linen.

"I'm sorry, Sylvie Mae. I'm really sorry."

That was the first time I'd said her name, and the moment seemed intimate somehow.

"DuWayne just loved that car," she said between sobs. "Loved it. I sometimes wondered if he loved it better than he loved me.

"He put that car away almost as soon as he bought it. He had somebody put The Pink Flamingo on the doors in gold lettering. He did that right away after he left the dealer. Then he brought it here. Parked it just about where you see it. Oh, he had great plans, he did. The weekend after he got the car, he had me work on those highway signs. The place by then looked pretty much like what you see today. He'd worked so hard. He designed the buildings and supervised all the construction. Everyone around here thought he was crazy. And I guess he was. I guess he really was, to pour his heart and his money into this little lost city in the middle of nowhere. He had a small inheritance from his father, who'd been President of the local bank. There might have been fifty or sixty thousand dollars. He had the money and the land. He'd dreamed about this compound since he was a boy.

"You know, DuWayne is like all the unknown artists. In a way, he was a great man. I think that's what consoled him in the end.

"But first, he just got bad news. At some point he figured out that no one would come here, that there never would be a tour bus full of people from Chicago.

"After he hid us, he used to say that Flamingo Island could be like Atlantis. I mean, you really had to be something to lose on a scale like that. The Lost Motel was what he wanted to call it. Flamingo Island, the Lost Motel. He even wanted me to work up a sign like that, but I didn't have the Walter Foster art books on scenes. I couldn't do it then, though he told me exactly what it ought to look like. He even drew me a little sketch. It would be the view from up the road with the heart-shaped entrance and the pink buildings behind.

"You sit right here and have another glass of iced tea, and I'll find you that sketch. Someday I may do that sign. He'll have two legacies then. The car and the sign."

I stood up and stretched when she walked out of the room. This time, I studied the pictures on the wall more closely. In a silver frame was a group of workmen kneeling in front of the unfinished construction that would eventually become the stucco house I was standing in. In another photo, you could see the cleared-out circle of the entire compound. Or heart rather. "Something isn't it?" Sylvie Mae said from behind me. I hadn't heard her come back. "It was all first class. That's the way DuWayne wanted us to go. 'No need to go down no old used-up roads. No, we'll build something they'll build roads to.'

"He was right, I think. Here. I couldn't find the sketch of the Lost Motel, but I found these. See for your own self."

She had some old brochures. They were beautiful, done up in turquoise with red trim. They looked like Formica and Corvettes and Wurlitzers. They were the kind of thing Elvis would've loved. In fact, I could imagine him staying here.

"When DuWayne got done, the place looked beautiful. The stucco was bright and pink and new. The heart-shaped sign stood out clearly as you got to the end of our road, and even the road was beautiful. It was all covered in new white gravel.

"Well, we waited and we waited and we waited. We waited a week, and no one came. DuWayne got so he didn't say much after awhile. He'd get up in the morning, eat his breakfast, and pace around the grounds pulling weeds.

"After five weeks of this, he got in the Edsel and sat up by one of the signs on the road. It was just sad.

"'You know, Sylvie Mae,' DuWayne said, 'I've heard it said that if you build a better mousetrap people will come right to your doorstep. I always took that as a really true statement, but maybe it only applies to mousetraps. Or maybe you have to build the road and drive the people here. I don't understand it. I thought I was in the motel business and not in the waiting business. It's just not coming clear.'

"I admired him. I did. We went two months. We changed the linens once a week just like *The Motel Owner's Guide* told us. The book said it would keep the place smelling fresh and sweet, but finally it all got to DuWayne.

"He got up earlier than usual one morning. For some reason I got worried and followed him. That's when he planted those bushes and trees in the road. I guess he'd dug up a bunch the night before. When he got done with those, he came back for lunch, and I tried to talk with him. But he waved me off.

"'Not now,' he said.

"The way he talked then, I thought I was in some lost chapter of *Little House on the Prairie*.

"After lunch, he got out his chainsaw. He left then. I tried to go with him, but he waved me off again

"I was plenty worried I can tell you that. You know, I could've had smarter men than DuWayne, but I loved the stupid son of a bitch because he was delightful. He had more ideas in ten minutes than most people have in ten years. I mean, think about it. He created a whole world where only flies and swamps and mosquitoes had been.

"I've been polishing on that car of his ever since he died I changed the oil just the way he told me to. Every two thousand miles or two months, whichever comes first. Of course, I never get to the two-thousand-mile part. I have a boy come out from the Sinclair station every two months. He brings oil and gas and sometimes he carries along spark plugs as well. In September and February we start her up just to make sure nothing's gone wrong inside.

"The motel—well, DuWayne closed it down. He took the chainsaw and cut down all the signs beside the drive out there. I can still hear the high whine of the saw as our entrance signs went down. He left the signs farther out on the road as a joke, I guess. He figured that no one would find us.

"He opened up the Pink Flamingo for about two months altogether. And then he closed it down.

"'If no one wants me, honey, then no one gets me.'

"I tried to talk him out of it. I was always the optimist. I always figured if you gave a thing enough time and care it would work.

"'No, my love, it won't be the same then,' he said 'It'll be impure. We'll beg the people and mess with the place until it will be like spring water in the city—all full of dust and grease. It's beautiful this way. At least we've got it perfect. It won't ever be better than this, and no one can get in here now. We've gone private. No one can get to us.'

"He meant that, too. Or he meant that no one could ever get to him again. I found him the next morning dead in the front seat of the pink Edsel. I think he died of carbon monoxide poisoning from letting the motor run. He was sitting there holding on to one of his pink flamingo statues."

Sylvie Mae's voice caught on the word *died,* and she sobbed a bit. I came over and sat on the arm of her chair and tried to put my arm around her.

"It doesn't do any good—the touch of one person to another, does it?" she asked me. "But, oh, how good it makes you feel. I've been alone out here ever since DuWayne went."

The daylight seemed to be receding from the room. It was a strange feeling, as though the circle of light around us grew slightly smaller all the time, sending the corners and edges into a brown darkness.

"You can't stay here," Sylvie Mae said abruptly. "I'd like you to, I really would, but you've got to get going. There's something lovely here, but there's something cursed as well."

"I suppose you're right," I said.

"This place isn't going to do you any good. I like you. I think you're delightful, but you've got to leave here. This is all sinking away. This is no place for a young man. Look. You can have the pink car. I love it, but it isn't going to bring DuWayne or my youth back. Take it. Drive on out of here like you're going to pick up the guests for the Pink Flamingo."

"That's awfully nice of you," I said. "But you don't have to give me your car."

"Right, my friend. I mean, do you really think you'll get very far driving that station wagon with the shot-out rear window? I may be an old lady, but even I know that such things attract attention. Take the Edsel, drive it to New Orleans, park the car somewhere, and get you a train home. DuWayne will love how I took care of the only guest we ever had. And no one will hurt an old car like that.

"Come here, my fine young friend. Come here."

I followed her into a small room off the dining room. There were stacks of old and yellowing papers bound up by purple ribbons on a table. There were books with crumbling leather bindings. She shoved these to one side and brought out a green metal box that had been underneath the papers.

"Here," she said and produced a cracked leather fob with two keys. A ceramic emblem on the fob read Edsel. "I think DuWayne would want you to have it. I think you're his kind of man. Try it and see."

Outside, the day had lost its hard edge and was changing into the soft blues and oranges of evening. A cool and steady breeze was blowing in from the north.

I took the soft cotton cover off the car and slid in behind the steering wheel. The Edsel had the smell of old plastic and mold. There were dials and knobs and chrome covering all the empty spaces. The car started instantly. When I slipped it into gear, it moved as if it had been waiting to leave. In fact, I had trouble getting it back into Park.

"Are you sure you want me to do this?" I asked Sylvie Mae after I'd stopped the car in front of her door. I got out of the car. "This is a collector's item, and you may never see it again. I can't make any promises."

"Promises," she said, "What good are promises? Most of them turn out to be lies. Think of all the promises we gave the Indians. I'm not interested in promises. I'm interested in lives lived out the best that they can be."

"That sounds good," I said, "but what do you get out of this? You may end up losing this car you've taken such good care of, you know."

"Come in here," she said, as she held the door of the stucco building open. I followed her inside. This time she walked through the dining room, around a corner, and up some narrow stairs. The stairs led to a small bedroom.

"My life is shrinking. Pretty soon this will be all of my space. The world is too large and difficult for me. I think that's what DuWayne saw at his final end.

"We all need to be loved and noticed, but my time for that is going. I want to live in somebody's memory.

"Look at me," she went on. She grabbed my face. "Look at me."

Then she stood back and began doing a slow dance around the small room. She closed her eyes and hummed to herself. In a moment I realized that she was slowly dancing to "Diamonds Are a Girl's Best

Friend."

As she moved, her stiffness seemed to go away, and I sat down on the bed to enjoy her performance. Even after all these years, she danced well, almost like a professional.

I don't think I was really surprised when she began taking her clothes off. She did this delicately, as if she'd been thinking for years about how she might transform being a fancy girl into something lovely. And lovely in her way she was. Her body was strangely unwrinkled.

"Just hold me," she said and sat in my lap like a child. "Just hold me a small moment."

We sat there awhile, her nude on my lap, in that small room in the middle of nowhere, all the dreams fading faster than the pink on the stucco walls.

"Now go," she whispered harshly. "Get free of those men and find your own place. If the car survives, bring it back here. I'll miss it almost as much as I miss DuWayne. Now go."

And go I did. I laid her gently in the bed and covered her up. I kissed her on the cheek and walked slowly down the stairs and out of the building.

I got the pouch of gold out of the station wagon. When I slammed its door shut, the glass in the back window finally came to pieces. Its shattering sounded like applause.

It was just beginning to get dark when I drove out DuWayne's road, first curving to the left and then to the right. The car bounced out on the highway. I backed it up a bit to see if my tracks were noticeable, but already the green of the grass and bushes was straightening itself, and my traces were beginning to disappear.

I patted the case of gold and, following Sylvie Mae's directions, drove toward New Orleans.

# Twenty-Seven

"THAT'S REALLY SOMETHING," Maybellene said. "That's beautiful, or she is, or was."

She paused and went on, "Well, what happened then? What did you do?"

"From there it was quite simple. Her directions to the highway were accurate, and I drove straight on to New Orleans. I got there in about three hours. She'd even left me fifty dollars on the dashboard so I could eat along the way. She knew what I needed. I sometimes wondered if she'd searched the station wagon and knew about the gold. As I said before, that gold would have been completely worthless along the average roads in Louisiana. I might as well have been carrying my rock collection from third grade. She must've known that ahead of time. She even wrote *License Applied For* on two pieces of cardboard and fastened them to the bumpers.

"The hardest part of all this was finding the railroad yard in New Orleans. As it happens, it was near the French Quarter. I drove there and left the car beside a warehouse for Fletcher's Plumbing Supplies. I had to leave that lovely car somewhere, and the business looked respectable enough. I figured that the owners and the workers would be the kind of people who protected private property.

"I left the Edsel about midnight. I put the keys inside the front left hubcap. I don't know why I did that, but the car seemed precious, too precious to leave without its keys. I figured if someone really coveted that car, he or she would find the keys. It was too beautiful a thing for ordinary stealing. Then I carried the pouch of gold off into the dark, took off my shirt, and strapped the bag of gold against my chest. With my shirt tails hanging out, you could hardly notice the bulge.

As I walked away into the cross tracks of the train yard, I looked back once. That pink car seemed to glow there underneath the mercury vapor light at the corner of the building. The car glowed there as if it contained some sweet knowledge. I silently said goodbye to it and to Sylvie Mae.

"I walked across train tracks for a long time. I didn't know much about trains, but I knew that I wanted one to take me and my gold north to St. Louis. I mean, that's the only city I really knew about. But then I remembered Rotbart. He'd look for me in St. Louis. No, I had to do something unpredictable. Chicago, I thought finally. Chicago would be the place. He wouldn't think of that.

So I just wandered around hoping that I would run into someone who could direct me to the Chicago tracks. And, sure enough, in this story of one improbability after another, a man in a top hat was sitting by one of the tracks. He had a brightly burning Coleman lantern and one of those European-styled portable camping stoves and was cooking something. The whole scene had an eerie greenish yellow glow to it, as if the man had been beamed there from someplace else.

"'Do you have any olive oil?' he asked as I came near. He had a vaguely English accent. 'I'd prefer the extra virgin kind. I find that the ordinary olive oil is a little harsh, rather like mineral oil and just won't do for fresh fish. It just thickens things up when you're looking for a touch of subtlety. I've got some soft-shell crabs here that need just the lightest touch of oil.'

"'Well, why not?' I thought. 'There are gourmets everywhere these days. Why not one among the bums?'

"'Olive oil,' I told him, 'is something I don't have. I'm just trying to get to Chicago. Can you help me?'

"'Directions,' he said, 'is that all you're looking for? You should set your life on finer terms, my man, so that you're looking for reservations at the Four Seasons or a Pulitzer Prize or something important, but directions? Directions are quite ordinary, you know. Anyone can have directions.'

"'But since you've asked so politely . . . . Say, you sound like an educated man. One of the problems in this mode of living is finding those who care about the better things of life. You'll notice, since I can see that you're a man who appreciates distinctions, that I don't speak of the finest things. No, I'm merely interested in the better. The Buick over the Chevrolet; the California Cabernet over the Mogan David; the Omega over the Timex. That kind of thing. I don't care about the Ferrari or the Château Margaux or the Audemars Piaget.'

"'Listen, Estophe, do you have any money? That's very important around here. I would prefer an emphasis on matters spiritual, but, alas, matters spiritual around here tend to be matters of spiriting away a fifth or two of the more severe beverages. No, money is what we're after here. Of course, if you don't have any money, then we're interested in what can be turned into money. Do you see?'

"I tried to answer his question, but I didn't quite know how.

"'Look,' I said, 'I'm just trying to get to Chicago. That seems simple enough. I'd just like to know where the trains to Chicago are.'

"'I'd like to help you out,' he said, 'I really would. You're a nice-looking young fellow. You're tall and thin. You have the nicest hair I've seen in years. In fact, have you thought of being an actor? Me, I'm just a character beside the road. I'd like some olive oil, and I'd like a Russian cigarette. You know, the ones with the black paper and the heavy-smelling tobacco.'

"'You mean,' I said, 'that I should tell you where my money is. That's it, right?'

"'Ah, you're a lovely man. You are indeed. Yes, your money. We can't say, 'Your money or your life.' No, we can't say that anymore. No one would believe us.'

"Well of course, Maybellene, I should've known. I mean really. He wasn't just chatting me up for fun. No, he was trying to get a bearing on me. He pulled out a pistol from beneath a stack of old clothes sitting by him.

"'Are you serious?' I asked. It was an inane question, but I couldn't think of anything better.

"'Serious? Of course I'm serious, my lad. Why shouldn't I be? Good gravy, man, I'm impoverished. I'm a government statistic on what's wrong with the American socio-economic system. I'm trouble in River City. And you, my friend? Why, you must have more than your share of the world's goods. You certainly have more hair. I'd like a bit of the goods at least. You see, I'm a better income redistribution system than the government. I'm the Robin Hood of things, taking from the rich and giving to me, the poor. Hand it over, bub. I figure you've got a chance to earn some more, but me—ah, I'm afraid the middle-class world won't have much to do with me.'

"I don't know what made me do it, but I made a run for him."

Maybellene and I were sitting at the dining room table by now. She reached over and touched my arm.

"You didn't," she said.

"Yes, I just leapt. I leapt the way you see professional wrestlers leap. I had my hands around his throat as I heard the *click, click, click* of the gun's hammer hitting an empty chamber.

"'Why you son of a bitch,' I said. 'Which way is Chicago?'

"'There,' he squeaked out through my clenched hands. The tracks with the Illinois Central signs. 'There.'

"I hit him across the face with the gun then. I guess I shouldn't have done that, but he reminded me of me farther down on his luck, and that scared me enough to hurt him. I felt the cracks of bones as he fell away from me.

"Then I threw the gun into the brush and walked toward the tracks he'd pointed out."

# Twenty-Eight

**THERE WAS ONE TRAIN** on the Illinois Central tracks. I walked up and down its length a couple of times to check things out. I'm not sure what I was looking for. The only trains I had much experience with were either electric toys or the ones that charged through the small towns of my childhood.

What I saw was the rusted old metal on the sides of the cars, the splintered wood floors of the boxcars, the oiled and massive parts of the wheels and couplings, and the greasy bulk of the diesel engine. Seen up close, that train was a nasty, huge, powerful thing. It made me think of my fingers and how easy it would be to lose them in the slamming of so much metal. Then I began worrying about my toes. These were the thoughts that made me walk up and down the tracks, keeping my toes curled inside my shoes and my hands firmly inside my pockets, except for the times I patted the pouch of gold.

After two or three trips alongside the train, I finally stood in front of a dirty red boxcar. I looked inside the doorway, put both hands on the floor, and jumped up and inside. I paced around, the way you might look over an apartment you were about to rent. It was as empty as a dance floor on Sunday morning. I pulled on one of the doors, and it moved with surprising ease.

Excelsior was piled up beneath pieces of cardboard in one corner. I sat down behind the cardboard and pulled the excelsior up around me. It made a warm bed. I got back up and walked toward one of the doorways. I looked out onto the reds and greens of lights along the tracks and the flickering yellow lights of the New Orleans skyline.

I finally sat down in one of the doorways, my feet dangling in space. I tried to feel bad about the bum I'd beaten up in the railroad yard. I tried to feel bad about the nine men dead at Rotbart's, but what I felt bad about was Sylvie Mae.

I finally got tired of thinking about all these people, of trying to make moral distinctions. I got so tired that I walked back to the corner of the boxcar and covered myself up with the cardboard and the excelsior and fell asleep.

In the middle of the night, I woke up to hear the slow clunks and feel the jerks as the train started up. When I woke up again, I saw brave blue skies sliding by outside the door and felt the confident clicks of the train rattling along. I pushed the excelsior away, stood up, and yawned. I felt as though I was going to be all right.

Carefully, I walked over to the doorway and hung on to its edge. The train was rising away from a river, and fields were going by like cards laid out for a game.

I passed the day in that car sitting with my back against the wall at one end. I got hungry a few times and worried about my future, but the rattle and shake—and then the forward travel of that boxcar massaged those problems away from me. Sometimes the train would stop, and I could hear the sound of cars being coupled and uncoupled. The next morning I woke up just as the sun was coming up through layers of golden lights on the eastern horizon.

I wasn't quite awake and began having a reverie about the summer I turned eight.

Jack Carey was my best friend that year. We went everywhere together. Mornings, we stayed in his room and read the Hardy Boys mysteries. Our afternoons were spent hanging out at various grocery stores and gas stations, reading Little Lulu comics, and filling our nickel Cokes with peanuts. Sometimes we stood around the pool hall, at the edge of the halo of light that encircled one of the tables, while the balls in their beautiful colors shaped and unshaped patterns across the green baize.

After supper, we went to the edge of the Town of Myrtle and watched the evening train thunder by on its way to Kansas City and other places we couldn't even imagine. How we could dream when the dining car and its patrons in their dress clothes roared past! Afterwards, we walked down the middle of the tracks. The heat and the smell of the coal and the memory of the train's huge noise felt like adventure to us.

I remembered how Jack and I went down to Harry's Grocery Store, where we bought lemon Popsicles with our allowances. Then we walked to Dick Allen's Rexall and sat in front of the magazine counter reading Uncle Scrooge comics. We slurped chocolate malts at the soda fountain there and walked around to various sites in town, including the widow Cathy Mulligan's at the corner of Jackson Street and Pine. There was an ancient oak near the sidewalk, and we'd climb three quarters of the way up and sit in the branches not ten feet from her bedroom. There (when we were really lucky) we got to watch her parade around in her slip if she'd forgotten to pull down the shade.

I hadn't seen Jack Carey for almost twenty years. Yet, for all those twenty years, I had dreamed of having an adventure, of jumping on board that train, of stepping out of my average life into one of those boyhood adventure stories of Frank and Joe Hardy. I wanted to chase after the German spy in my high-powered speedboat.

With $30,000 worth of Krugerrands, I guess I'd finally done it: I was having the adventure of a lifetime, but it had almost killed me. I was dirty and scared and tired. I was so weary, I was probably hallucinating. Unlike the stories of Frank and Joe Hardy, my little tale didn't yet have the security of a happy ending. Unless you counted the few sentences in my notebook, there was no text with its plot and numbered pages that said, comfortingly, how far I was from a happy ending where the speedboat finally caught up with the German spy.

My parents moved from the Town of Myrtle, and I went to high school in the suburbs, where the stories were supposed to have happy endings. I wasn't supposed to be riding the rails with thirty big ones dangling from my neck.

I was half asleep with hunger and exhaustion and worry about my future when the train slowed down. I heard voices and, I thought, the sound of someone climbing in the car with me.

That's when I saw a bearded man coming toward me. That's when he dragged me across the boxcar on my chest.

# Twenty-Nine

**I TOLD MAYBELLENE THE REST OF THE STORY** then, about the way McCoo had thrown me from the boxcar and brought me to Mary Lynn. I told her about that and our trip to St. Louis, where I'd finally escaped into her arms.

"Whew," she said, "that's really something. I didn't think that things like that happened to people in real life."

I got up from the dining room table and went to the refrigerator.

"That really *is* something," she repeated. "But the question for me has nothing to do with money. The question is, as it always was, is you is or is you ain't my baby?"

She was smiling when I got back to the table with two apples.

"Well, I guess I is," I said and gave her one.

"You seem a little tentative," she said, "as if you're not quite sure." We looked at each other over the apples we were eating.

Finally, I got the Krugerrands out of my shoe.

"It doesn't seem that important somehow," she said. "I mean, all those men gone. This terrific fuss of Mary Lynn and Elwin—I mean, it just doesn't seem that important, does it?"

"Well, I thought it was. I started out with a hundred coins. Mary Lynn and Elwin have one, and we have the rest. Let's see what the ninety nine are worth."

I whistled when I read the *Post-Dispatch*.

"My God, gold is worth almost $350 an ounce. It's gone up $50 in a few weeks. Isn't that something?"

"You mean we could be paid for lying around here and making love?" Maybellene asked. "You know, I like that. Rolling in my sweet baby's arms for dough. The slide in and out along the walls of love for money. I think that's where America went wrong."

"I don't follow you," I said. "I don't see what you're getting at."

"I think we'd be better off if we were in it for the fucking instead of the power or the greed, don't you? I think that's why Washington and Jackson and Lincoln and Roosevelt and Eisenhower all ended up wrong somehow. Instead of making love they were making ready for history. You can't sleep with a history book, and you can't make love to a bank account.

"Besides, I'm sad about the guys. All those unloved people gone. That was Howard's trouble. He really died for lack of love. If he'd had a lover, he never would have signed up for such foolishness. You, too, my friend and the others, too."

She was right, of course. If I'd had someone to love, I never would've gone.

Well, this time I had someone to love, and love we did.

What I remember of that time was the green, enveloping branches of the trees outside her window behind us as we threw each other this way and that in all tanglings of love.

"Oh, God, where have you been?" we asked each other as we finished up this time and that. "Oh where oh where have you been?"

We hardly went out, except for trips to the grocery store. And even then it seemed that the lights of the supermarket were too bright. We were used to the dim lights of love. We made so much love it was like being on drugs. I don't think we were in the world very much after a few days of that.

That's why I really wasn't sure that I saw Pee Pole in the Produce Department.

"It was the strangest thing," I told Maybellene when I got back to the apartment after a trip for groceries. "He was standing there like he owned the place. He had the bandanna over his head, the armless T-shirt, the low-slung jeans, and the chain from his belt to his wallet. He was standing there flipping a head of iceberg lettuce up and down. It was scary."

"Are you sure it was him?"

"Well, no, to tell the truth. I thought I was hallucinating, so I thought I would go around one of the aisles and come back. I went on by him and turned left and came back through the cleaning supplies and the paper goods. When I came around, he was gone."

"Good. Maybe you just imagined him."

"I suppose, though when I left the store, I also thought I saw the backs of Mary Lynn's and McCoo's heads in a car in the parking lot."

"Come on."

"I'm not kidding."

"You didn't even get the right kind of meat," Maybellene said. I barely heard her.

"This is all the damndest thing. You know, maybe their leaving me was a trick. Maybe they figured I'd lead them back to the gold."

"You're making this up," she said. "They can't all be around here. Come on, Owen. Don't tease me like this. You're scaring me."

"I'm serious. They're all out there." I was gasping as I told her this. It was as if the three of them had reached inside of me and pulled my breath out.

"Did they see you come back here?" she asked.

"I don't know . . . no, they couldn't have . . . they weren't around when I turned down Kingsbury . . . I looked . . . I didn't see them. I don't know. What do you think?"

"I think," she said and looked very seriously at me, "that we should get our young asses out of town."

The air seemed to change when she said that. It changed the way it will when a threatened thunderstorm disappears.

Packing was simple.

A few days earlier I had bought two changes of clothes, and these fit nicely in a grocery bag. Maybellene set out three suitcases on the bed.

"What doesn't fit I'm leaving. I never cared all that much for my life here, and it would be clean just to walk on out of it. I'll send another month's rent in. If we're not rich by then, I'm going someplace else. Mr. Sheets can have my stuff."

"Mr. who?"

"He's the landlord. The day I moved in here he came around lifting this packing box and that book like he expected cock roaches or communists to crawl out from underneath. 'Don't want no foolishness,' he said as he left. 'I like it quiet. I like it when you pay the rent, and I don't like no foolishness.' The way he tried to pat my rear end when he left, I think he was the one interested in all the foolishness.

"There must be more to life than this," Maybellene went on. "You know, I'm another local loser like you. That just hit me. I'm like you and Howard and Lucky Beal and all the rest. Cruising along, expecting miracles, but I don't even get the ordinary stuff right. You know, I've

191

just remembered my Aunt Lou. She was always waiting on some news. She sang at church, and she expected the record companies to call. She danced in a little modern dance group called the Daughters of Isadora Duncan, and she figured the New York dance companies would come. Well, she got heavy, and then she got thin, and then she just shriveled up and died, and the only one that ever came for her was our loyal friend Mr. Death. Everyone else avoided her like the crazy lady she was. And I guess the message is, Go out and get the future you want before the future you don't want comes and gets you.

"The world belongs to the Mr. Sheets. They've figured the angles; they know the odds. You and I—why, we expect to get lucky, to hit the big jackpot on the slot machine, to catch the lottery when it's full. The Mr. Sheets and the Rotbarts know better. They know a lot better. They'd rather have the steady nickels than the lucky dollars.

"Let's you and I go back and get that dough, and then let's you and I vow to live for steady nickels instead of lucky dollars, OK?"

It sounded good to me. I stood next to the window and looked down onto the street where reality began. There were Chevrolets and Fords and a Buick or two. There was Maybellene's brown Honda. I didn't see any trucks, and I didn't see the faces of McCoo and Mary Lynn and Pee Pole.

"Do you think you can find the gold?" she asked.

"I think so. It won't be easy, though."

"What is? Let's get out of here," she said.

"OK," I said back. I guess it was a vow. "OK," I said again. "But I think we should leave when it gets dark. Leave by the back door just after the sun goes down. I think we should be careful. It's a lot harder to go for those steady nickels if we have to split our treasure too many ways."

Maybellene went to the bank and brought all her money back in cash. She had a hundred twenty-dollar bills.

"This ought to get us someplace green and nice," she said. "Green and nice like this loft of love."

We had a heavy meal of steaks and potatoes and salad. We finished up with ice cream. We drank tea and waited for the dark to come on.

The cicadas droned to us as we made love one more time. Then we packed our bags and tiptoed down the metal fire escape, walked around the building, and crept out onto Kingsbury.

We carried everything in that one trip, tossed our stuff in the back, got in the car, and drove away.

"Did you turn off the water in the bathtub?" I asked.

"Who cares? I mean, I don't give a shit if the whole place floats away. You and me are on our way to the heavy money."

She whistled when she started the car.

"But wait," she said and killed the engine. "There's one thing I don't want to forget. A shovel. I need a shovel."

That said, she got out of the car and ran behind the building. She must've been gone ten or fifteen minutes.

"Here," she said when she returned. She opened the passenger door and handed me a sheet covering something that dangled down. It scared me, and I tried to push it away.

"No," I started to say.

"Don't be silly, dear. It's a plant. It's my inheritance. It's the most valuable thing I have. Except for you."

And then I realized that I was holding the plant and limbs and blossoms of her grandmother's Clematis. Dark purple blossoms and dirt dribbled off the sheet onto my pants and the car seat.

"It's like a love child, right?" I asked.

"Right," she said as she closed the driver's side door. "Let's get us the hell out of here."

We drove around the block a couple of times with the headlights off just to be sure we weren't being followed. The neighborhood seemed peaceful enough, the golden light of domestic scenes here and there along the street as we went by. The people bathed in the gentle glow of that light would never suspect, I thought, what fierce energy our little car contained.

# Thirty

**IT WAS HER IDEA** to stay at the Paradise Motel for the rest of the night.

"They're never going to guess that one," she said and smiled. "Never in all the years you could number. We'll throw them off the trail. We'll get some sleep, and I can see where this all started out. I'd like to get the flavor of things."

She smiled and rubbed my crotch as if her hand were the most reasonable argument in the world.

But I didn't like the proposition very well. My instinct was to leave St. Louis. I had an Illinois map and had circled what I thought were likely areas to look for the gold. My plan was a version of what I'd done earlier—drive south on back roads to make sure we weren't being followed and then circle back north to Illinois. I also thought we should simply abandon Maybellene's car and buy another one. If Mary Lynn and Company had really discovered us, the Honda was too visible. We'd have better luck disappearing in a used Chevrolet.

"No way, Jose," she said when I proposed leaving the car behind. "When I got my divorce, I got six thousand bucks. Half of it went to this little baby right here. I ain't gonna do it. Besides, you already told me what you did with Sylvie Mae's car down in Louisiana. You can sure be a hot guy, but you're not reliable. No, I'll just keep this little foreign lady." She patted the dash.

The Paradise Motel certainly hadn't changed. It looked like bad luck going broke. The vandalized sign read *A Little Tit of Heaven Right Here on Earth.* This time, though, the parking lot in the middle of the horseshoe-shaped buildings was pretty much empty. A rusted-out Grand Prix sat there like a prize for a contest no one had entered.

"There'll be two of you then, sir?" the clerk asked when I went to check in.

"Right. Just the lady and me."

"Is that right, then? Then you're married to the lady?"

"Excuse me?"

"Why, married. You can understand my position. I only rent to a proper man and wife."

"A proper man and wife," I said. "Is that as opposed to an improper man and wife?"

"Sir, this isn't comedy here. This is a motel. This is a motel where proper things happen."

"I don't believe this. I mean, I really don't. There are people all over the country fucking their eyeballs out in motels like this. I mean there are people fucking like tomorrow won't come, if you'll pardon the pun, and you, why you, you're asking if we're a proper man and wife. I just can't believe this. We'd like a room, that's all. I've got real money."

I really didn't care if I insulted him. I didn't want to stay there.

"Go on now, sir. I don't like this sort of talk."

"I've got good dollars, my friend, and you've got bullshit. The last time I was here, I was lied to and cheated by a meeting that went on right out there. It almost killed me. You sponsor a thing like that, you haven't much right to ask for licenses. A room, sir. The lady and I are sleepy."

The talk of the meeting seemed to freeze his face in a permanent smile.

"Was this meeting you are referring to held in July?" he asked. "Two months ago, and was there a kraut in charge? He was a big guy, and there was a little guy too. And a lot of bums came. Was that the meeting? Because if it was, they owe me twenty dollars. That's what I charge for clean up. I was up half the night picking up styrofoam cups. If you were with that party, sir, I'd appreciate you saying so. I really would."

I could see Maybellene yawning in the car.

"Yes, I was. I tell you what. I'll make everything good if you don't mind taking a local check."

With a flourish I produced the check I kept hidden in the pocket of my Adventurer's Notebook.

"How much," I asked, "do we owe you for our room tonight and the clean up?"

I could see greed take over his face as he calculated.

"Ah, you were happy with the party? Is that correct?"

I nodded.

"Well, with the cleaning supplies I used, with everything it comes

195

to . . . let's see . . . $25.62. Yes. It's $25.62 exactly."

"And the room tonight," I said, "add that in. That's right, the room we'll take tonight."

"With the tax and the service, why that'll be another $10. But since you've been such a good customer of ours all these years, let's just round it off to $35. You'll hardly miss it, a prosperous man like you. I mean, $35 is hardly worth thinking about, don't you think?"

I didn't know what to say, but I wrote him a check with the biggest version of my signature I could manage.

"You know," I said, "I'd like to make this an even $40 if you don't mind. I think you've earned it, don't you?"

I could see him smiling when I lifted a suitcase out of the car. I guess real, genuine married people traveled with luggage.

I wanted to chuckle about the check, but—by some perverse coincidence—he gave us the same room Rotbart had used on the night of the meeting, and I lost my sense of humor.

"I really don't like this," I told her. "We're asking for trouble. This is the wrong kind of pattern. In fact, we're probably doing something Rotbart has already thought about. He could be out there waiting for all we know."

I turned off the lights and peeked out between the curtains. I studied the terrain outside for a long time, and there seemed to be nothing but the flickering blue of lights above a parking lot empty of everything but Maybellene's Honda and the ancient Grand Prix. I probably studied the scene too long, for after awhile the flickering pale blue light made it seem that we were all under water, slowly drowning in a sea of shabbiness.

When I turned around, Maybellene was asleep, her gentle snores and noises like somnolent jazz. I tried to join her in bed, but I was simply too worried. I got back up and sat by the window, looking out into the impossible blue.

It was hard to spot the sunrise, certainly much harder than it had been in Louisiana, but soon the blue lightened up, like depression giving way to cheerfulness, and the sky turned a very pale orange and then deepened into the day's blue as the lights above the parking lot went out.

I felt better then. I figured if we hadn't been attacked in the night, then we were all right for another day. I got back into bed with Maybellene. As I finally went sleep, the alarm said it was 5:30.

I dreamed. I remember that. It was the falling business all terrifying dreams have, and I fell and I fell and I fell. I remember that. I remember getting up, or I remember dreaming that I was getting up and looking out the window and seeing Rotbart, arms folded, standing in the center of the parking lot, looking toward our room and talking over his shoulder to Helmut, who relayed the message back to the two Juniors, who did the same back to Mary Lynn and McCoo. Soon, they were all pointing toward our room and laughing.

We got up into reality when we heard someone banging on the door. The sunlight formed a bright square around the shades, as if something hard and vivid were trying to get in. It was ten in the morning.

"Just a goddamned minute," I heard Maybellene say back to the noise. "I mean just a goddamned fucking minute. We're on our honeymoon."

That did it. The pounding stopped. I suppose there is something sacred about honeymoons, the way there is something sacred about childbirth and death and things that bring us here and take us back out again.

From someplace Maybellene was pulling on a plaid robe.

"OK, what you do want then?" she asked the door. "What's it all about?"

"Let me in," the voice from outside the door said. "Let me in, or you'll be hearing from the police."

I sat up in bed.

"Let him in," I said, as if I were in charge.

"Right," Maybellene said. "I can see that you know exactly what you're doing." Then she went and stood to the side of the door. "Who are you?" she yelled back. "What do you want?"

"Your check's no good. I called the bank. That account's closed."

Maybellene stared at me as if I were the dumbest thing on earth.

"Why . . . ?" she started to ask me.

"Because I didn't want to come here," I said, "because I hated what

197

happened here, because I'm tired of ducking other people's blows. Come on, Maybellene, he can't hurt us."

"What if he calls the police?"

"Then we'll pay him." To the door I yelled, "Just a minute. Let us get dressed, and we'll bring you the money."

"You're probably not even married," he yelled back, if a defeated voice can be said to yell. "I should've asked for the license."

We got back into yesterday's clothes and brushed our teeth. As I stood before the mirror, I realized that I was exhausted.

He kept his word. He was standing outside the door with his arms folded across his chest and a deep scowl on his face.

"No telling what went on in there," he said to no one in particular.

I steered Maybellene to the car. I suddenly saw a way to kill the proverbial two birds.

"Get in," I whispered to her. "Get in."

The man followed us to the car using odd little steps so he could keep his arms folded across his chest. I think he was afraid of us.

I opened the hatchback, set in our few things, and came around to the front of the car.

"My wallet's in the glove box." I tried to smile nonchalantly as I said this.

The rest was fast, a scene I'd practiced once before.

I had the key in the ignition and the car started before the tight smile faded from his mouth.

"Wait. You can't . . . ." was all I heard before we roared out of the parking lot.

We were several blocks away before Maybellene spoke.

"That was dumb. That was really dumb," she said.

"So was staying there."

"But that was my version of dumb, and that's OK. Kind of like Dumbo." She was smiling as she said this. "But your version of dumb is just plain stupid."

"Maybe, maybe not." I paused because she wasn't going to like the second bird I was about to kill. "Where do you want to leave this car?"

"What do you mean?" She put her hand to the base of her throat as if I'd threatened her physically.

"I'm sure he's called the police by now and given them your license number. Do you really want to get arrested?"

"Let me think about this."

"There's nothing to think about. I'm leaving this car. If you want to keep it, fine. You can explain things to the police, but I'm leaving. If you have any sense, you'll come with me."

I parked the car at the side of a residential block as if I lived there. I got out, picked up my sack of belongings from the trunk, and just walked away.

# Thirty-One

"IT'S NOT FAIR, YOU KNOW."

She was driving along the side of the street just behind me. We both stopped at the intersection.

"It really isn't. It's half of what I got from that awful marriage. I just can't leave it behind." Her head was crouched down so she could see me through the passenger window.

"I can't help it," I said as I started walking again. "There are too many people after that car. Leave it here, Maybellene. We're on our way to get enough money to buy all kinds of Hondas."

"I'm tired of taking money from men. It's not fair."

"All right, then we'll use your money. $1,000 will buy a decent car."

"And I'm tired of giving away my money to ten-watt losers. It just isn't fair."

I was so exasperated I threw the bag down, marched over to the car, and jerked the door open.

"Don't you understand that there are people who want to kill us? I know that's not fair. Nothing's fair. But you keep looking for fairness, and you're going to be fairly dead, my dear. I'd advise you to start walking with me. We've got a lot of figuring to do."

She followed me for a couple of blocks. When I didn't hear the whining noises of the car running in low gear, I turned around and saw that she had stopped and was carefully locking it up. She almost looked as though she wanted to kiss it goodbye. She walked slowly with her head down. She was carrying the Clematis bunched up in the sheet. Petals dragged on the ground behind her. When she got up close to me, I could see that she was crying.

"It's really not fair, Owen. Not at all."

"Aw, Maybellene," I said and hugged her close. "Where are your suitcases?"

"Left them. The only thing I really care about is this plant. If we're going for real, I want a clean break I've got a change of underwear and one more outfit in my purse"

As we walked, I briefly wondered if there were things that could identify us in the car, and then I figured that it didn't make any difference if people couldn't find us.

It's easier to buy a car with cash money and little identification than I would have guessed. When we looked under Automobile Dealers in the phone book, we found several on Kingshighway. Since that sounded a little like Kingsbury, Maybellene, the plant, and I took a bus there. As the air brakes of the bus hissed and the door flopped open, we stepped into the heat and humidity of the treeless spaces along Kingshighway. A moment later, in air conditioning that seemed a bit too cool, we were seated in the showroom of Bob Papini's Frontier Dodge. A man who could have been anywhere between thirty and fifty five ushered us into seats in front of a grey metal desk covered with pictures of his extensive family. On the wall of his little cubicle were awards from the Chrysler Corporation. On the desk facing us was an engraved sign that said Wm. P. Coyle, Salesman.

As we all sat down, he folded his hands together on the desk. He wore a pinky ring. He had on a short-sleeve shirt that had two front pockets with a plastic pen holder in each pocket.

"How may I help you folks?" he asked. "We have some wonderful cars here."

I noticed that he was wearing a wig.

"I want something outrageous," Maybellene told him. He was taking notes of what we said, as if a listing of all our words might transform themselves into a car. "I want something long and big and brutal. I want to spend this much. She set fifty twenties on the top of the gray metal desk."

The salesman tried not too look up. You could see him mentally thumbing through a book called *How To Close the Deal* for the right angle on this one. For a brief second, I thought how great it was for me to be there. I would help her out, make sure she got a good deal.

But when she looked into the salesman's eyes with that clear expression of hers, I realized that I was more nervous than she was.

"Long and big and brutal," he repeated slowly. "I think I've got exactly what you want. It'll work for the plant, too."

I thought he was being sarcastic, but it was hard to imagine how someone who wore a plastic pocket protector could be sarcastic.

Exactly What You Want turned out to be on another lot miles from Kingshighway. He ushered us into the back of a limousine that he drove while we sat in the back like rock stars. It had a passenger compartment that would've held five or six people separated from the front by a heavy glass window. We set the plant between us.

"Just relax," he said over a pa system. "We'll be at your car in twenty minutes."

The opening of "Strawberry Fields Forever" came on a scratchy radio, as if "Let me take you down" had been taken down a field of thistles by mistake.

"What have you got in mind?" I asked Maybellene.

"I'm not sure I'm talking to you. Hilary's been alone for almost two hours now."

"Hilary?"

"Of course. Hilary the Honda. She'll know something's wrong, being left on a strange avenue like that. In fact, I think she's in a No Parking Zone if you want to know the truth. I hate to think of what'll become of her. No one will change her oil every fifteen hundred miles like I did."

"You changed her oil every . . . ."

"Every thousand miles in cold weather, and I would've done it every five hundred if we'd had dust. That little lady was going to live a long, long time."

I started to tell her how careful Sylvie Mae had been with the Edsel, but the moment didn't seem right, and I kept my mouth shut.

Then we stopped, and Mr. Coyle opened the door for us, and we stepped out into a landscape that could've been the moon. As far as the eye could see were broken-down homes, each with its rotted porch and its engine block in the front yard, and empty lots filled with shards of broken glass that sparkled like the jewels of the poor.

In the middle of all this was a car lot, all right, the kind of a place that made you nervous, locked as it was behind a ten-foot-high barbed-wire fence with swirls of concertina wire at its top, concertina wire that looked as if it had been made from the blades of surgical knives.

"This is where we keep our specialty cars," Mr. Coyle told us.

As he bent over to unlock an enormous padlock, I could see the rivers of sweat running out from beneath the back of his toupee.

"There we go," he said as the gate swung open. "More cars than you could ever dream about. Ma'am, if there isn't a car for you in here, your car doesn't exist."

After we'd walked a few feet into the place we heard the clang of the gate shutting behind us.

"Can you believe this?" Maybellene asked as we walked along past Chevrolets and Mercuries and Pontiacs and Chryslers and the whole panoply of American cars.

"Do you have foreign cars here?" she asked Mr. Coyle.

"Foreign cars? Oh no, ma'am, you won't be wanting any foreign cars. They don't fit your description." He pulled out his notebook and stopped by a particularly fierce looking Chevrolet Camaro. Someone had chopped off the center of the top and made it into a convertible. There was duct tape along the places that had been cut.

"Ma'am, you said you wanted something—and here I'm quoting— 'long and big and brutal.' No foreigners make anything like that. Be patient. I've got exactly that car if I can just find it."

He pulled out a handkerchief. His toupee rocked back and forth as he wiped his brow. We spent another half an hour going up and down the aisles.

We saw Maybellene's car before Mr. Coyle pointed it out. He didn't have to. It was quite literally long and big and brutal.

"My God," Maybellene began. I couldn't tell if she was delighted or horrified.

"Really something, isn't it?" Mr. Coyle asked.

"It's a . . . ." I began. It's one of those cars everyone knows. The plant was getting heavy, and I switched it to the other hand.

"Yes, a 1959 Cadillac convertible. Really something."

"I especially like the steer horns on the hood. They give it quite a touch," Maybellene said. "Especially the way they lean to one side."

Mr. Coyle was beaming, a salesman who had made the perfect match. His toupee now seemed an inch off his head, as if it had done its own version of puffing out its chest.

"I don't know," I put in. "This is a very old car."

I began walking around it.

"I mean, this is a very old car with some serious rust problems."

The top was down, a curious state for a car on a lot. At first I guessed they'd prepped the car for us. When I opened the door and sat down, however, I realized that the top probably didn't work. The seat squished beneath me the way an over-ripe peach responds to a squeeze. A moment later I realized that the backs of my pants were soaked.

I was about to point out this deficiency to Maybellene, but when I looked at her, I could see the glazed expression that all buyers have. She was quite taken by the car.

"Move it on over, Owen," she said, "I want to feel this baby up."

As I stepped on the floorboard to slide myself into the passenger seat, I felt the metal give the way a rotted wooden floor does.

"Oh boy," I muttered. I think we'd both gone crazy.

"Oh boy is right," Maybellene added. "This is just the car for me."

"I knew it," Mr. Coyle said, beaming like a father watching over his children. "Let's just write it up."

"Wait a minute," I said, "we should check it out."

"Waste of time, Owen. Mr. Coyle, do you have key? If it starts and the price is right, you've sold yourself a car."

Mr. Coyle fumbled around in his pockets, producing key after key, but none fit. As if produced by telepathy, a short black man seemed to glide up to us out of nowhere.

"Angel," Mr. Coyle said, "Do you have a key for this?"

"Ain't no key," Angel said in a voice not much louder than a whisper. "Car almost starts by its own self. Like this a-ways."

He reached under the dash and pulled out a wire with a plug attached. He pushed the plug into the empty cigarette lighter socket, and the car coughed a bit and then started. After running for a few moments, it steadied itself into a throaty purr. I had to admit it sounded like a strong engine.

"If you'll take two hundred dollars, you've sold yourself a car," Maybellene said.

The muffled *voom va va va voom* sound the engine made was almost hypnotic. I began to forget that the backs of my pants were soaked and that the car's whole body was likely rusted beyond repair beneath its paint. I suspected that the top didn't work, that the car had, in fact, more problems than successes. Though when I clicked the radio on, it played, in fact played "Let me take you down" as if "Strawberry Fields Forever" were becoming my anthem. When Maybellene jerked the plug from the cigarette lighter, the engine stopped so abruptly and left such a silence that I missed its bass cadences.

"Oh, Miss, now $200 isn't enough to drive a dream. This isn't just a car. The way I see it, you ought to spend the $1,000 you were talking about. You should at least consider $500."

"I may be cute, Mr. Coyle, but I'm not dumb. If I give you half my money, then half my money will be gone. Did you think of that?"

Mr. Coyle looked puzzled.

"The way I figure it," she went on, "is that this car is probably worth about one more thousand-mile trip before she gives up the ghost or whatever it is old Cadillacs give up, and then—dream or not, she's scrap. I figure if I pay you about what a thousand-mile round trip ticket is I'm OK. Tell you what, I'll give you $160."

She got eight twenties from her purse and handed them to him.

"Miss, this isn't how things are supposed to go." Mr. Coyle was standing up against the driver's side of the car wiping his forehead and his toupee furiously back and forth. He was trying to smile. Suddenly I could see that his days were made up of just such encounters. He reminded me of Howard.

"OK, for you, I'll give you $240. That's twelve twenties. I just can't make it $250. I need the money, Mr. Coyle, I really do. It's all me and Buster here have." She pointed her thumb over her shoulder at me.

I kept my mouth shut. I wasn't any good at car deals. I would've paid the $1,000. To stay out of the way, I studied the windshield wipers, wondering if they worked. I thought to turn them on, and then I realized that they were probably vacuum powered and would only work with the engine running, and then I realized that windshield wipers were meaningless if the top didn't work.

To close the deal, we walked to stairs at the side of a fabricated metal garage. The stairs took us up two flights and ended at a room like a control tower where a very heavy man sat before an enormous desk that faced a long window, a window that must've been fifteen feet long and six feet high. He could see every car and every face on the huge parking lot of cars. The man had on a baseball cap with gold braiding on its bill and the word *Commander* embroidered on its peak. He must've weighed five or six hundred pounds, and his flesh hung in globs over the sides of his chair. He was puffing on a cigarette and didn't see us come in. He was, in fact, puffing so hard on the cigarette that he appeared to be making the kind of noise children produce by striking their open palms against their pursed lips.

"Mr. Hazelton," Coyle yelled, "the Cadillac. I sold the Cadillac."

Maybellene was smiling almost as much as Mr. Coyle. They both seemed to feel that they'd consummated an historic transaction.

"Money," Mr. Hazelton said between puffs on his cigarette. "Has she got money?"

"$240 cash," Mr. Coyle said.

"Has she got more money?" the fat man asked.

"All totaled, a thousand, maybe."

"Let's take that then. With a car like that Cadillac, you don't need money anymore. With a car like that, you've got no place else to go. What more could you want?"

"But we've already made a deal," Coyle said.

"Jesus fucking Christ, you've never made a good deal in your life. You know that? You're useless. You're a waste of time. You're an ice cream cone at the end of a hot summer's day."

"Come on, Dean, give me a break. They're the first luck we've had in weeks. Take their money and give them the car."

Angel appeared out of nowhere and grabbed Maybellene's purse. He emptied its contents out on the large desk. Coins, a wallet, a compact, a tube of lipstick, a sanitary tampon, clothes wadded into a clear plastic bag, and a copy of *How To Win Friends and Influence People* fell out.

Hazelton looked down his nose at these items as if he didn't want to dirty his hands with these details.

"You can't do it," Maybellene said. "It's all the money I've got in God's great world. It's not fair. You're a big tough businessman, and I'm just a little lady. Take $500 and give me the car. That's more than fair."

Hazelton lit another cigarette.

I let out a low whistle. It was half of what I would have paid.

What's your problem, son?" he asked me and then turned back to Maybellene.

"OK," he continued. "I'll do it just this once. You got identification?" He spoke between puffs on his cigarette.

"Driver's license," Maybellene answered.

"Sign these papers and get the hell out of here. Angel will get you started."

The *voom va va va voom* sounded reassuring as we drove out of the lot.

# Thirty-Two

**IT WAS ABOUT THREE** in the afternoon when we finally got on Interstate 55 heading north. Maybellene was driving, and I was yelling out directions over the roar the old convertible made going down the road at sixty miles an hour. The clematis, which was beginning to look a bit wilted, was on the back seat, its blossoms shaking in the wind.

It was one of those sharp, dry days at the end of summer when the sky has that hard blue ache that implies the world is lovely, though just enough dried and dying leaves were falling, reminding you of what's coming and making you want to hold on to everything before the world goes to the chill of autumn and the hard luck of winter.

I'd heard it said of cars that they seemed to own the road, but the Cadillac possessed it, and possessed it grandly. People waved at us, and once someone tried to pass, but when he got alongside, he seemed to think better of it, and backed away. In spite of its age, the car ran well. We stopped at a hardware store and bought a sheet of plastic to put on the seats so our bottoms were dry. At that same stop, we went to a small grocery store and bought the makings for tuna-salad sandwiches, bags of potato chips, and cans of soda. As we drove along, the wind tousled our hair as if to say we were good little children after all.

"Owen," Maybellene yelled at me. I could barely hear her over the roar of the road.

"What?"

"Owen, do you still love me?"

"Maybellene, how could I help but love you?" I yelled back over the sound of the world pouring over, under, around, and through us. "I mean, I've got a girl who owns a car with steer horns on the hood. She's got cold cash money. I've got to be the happiest man alive."

I lifted up the cheap sunglasses I'd bought along with our lunch, leaned over, and gave her a kiss.

Central Illinois is more beautiful than most people think. It has this rolling green quality, a matter of huge cornfields interrupted by stands of woods and then corn again. Once in a while, there are these towns of white clapboard houses and grain elevators and train depots. I studied each of the grain elevators we passed, but none had the angles I remembered.

It's amazing how varied grain elevators can be when you really look at them. I suppose they're like anything else. To the outsider one sports car looks like another, but tell the driver of a Testarossa that he's got a nice Corvette and see how he reacts.

Some of the grain elevators were big rectangles stacked on top of one another, their shapes culminating in something like a cupola so the whole thing looked like a galvanized version of a cathedral. Others were round like giant bottles of shortie beers. We stopped at a Dairy Queen for an afternoon snack. When the woman opened the service window to help us, the cool air coming from inside was almost chilling, like a message from the Great Beyond or even farther.

"Help you folks?" she asked.

"Air conditioning is a wonderful thing," Maybellene said. "Wonderful. I'd forgotten it could be this cool, even though it's just hitting my face."

"We have ice cream in every form you might just want and a few you wouldn't. Honey, you just look over our list out there and choose."

With that she slammed the inside glass of the service window closed.

"You know, don't you know, there's air conditioning in the Cadillac," a voice behind us said.

The voice seemed to come out of the atmosphere, as if we had an owner's manual in the air. I halfway expected to turn around and see Frank Morgan of *The Wizard of Oz* cranking away at his machinery and explaining how the Cadillac worked.

But no, it was the short black man who called himself Angel.

"Hi there," he said and looked at the ground, where the open toe of his dirty tennis shoes drew diagrams. "Car has a lot of features. The air conditioner would like to ice you out, but with the top down it's a standstill. Half your body's cool and half's still hot."

"I'll have a small strawberry sundae," I said because I couldn't think of what else to say.

"Well, I'd like to know where he came from," Maybellene said.

"As for me," Angel said, "I'll have the french fries and the hamburger and the several kinds of ice cream. I ain't had no food since God knows when, and man can't certainly live by Cadillacs alone."

Maybellene's money on the scale of Dairy Queens and ancient Cadillacs and black car jockeys and broken-down adventurers seemed endless. She pulled this huge wad out of her pocket. It was held together by a rubber band.

I have never seen anyone eat the way Angel did. He sat by himself at one of the several picnic tables next to the Dairy Queen. After he sat down, he pulled the bags and cups of food near him as if they alone were his friends in a hostile world. For a moment he looked suspiciously around him for those who might take his food and his friends. I briefly wondered where he'd been hiding in the car, but that seemed like too ordinary a problem.

"What are we going to do?" Maybellene whispered to me as she began licking on a giant cone.

"Beats me," I said.

"No wonder you keep getting pushed around. You don't know what you're doing, do you?"

I guess I didn't. I still was taking things as they came, but even if I wanted to plan things out, what would I do? I mean, what was the next step?

"No, I don't," I said aloud. "I really don't know what I'm going to do next. I mean, I'm going to search for the gold I left along the railroad. I'm going to do that, and I'm going to hope that you'll help me. I'm even hoping that Angel will help us, too. For some reason I like him. He's like a lucky charm."

Angel seemed to have heard that and looked up and smiled, crumbs of food dropping from his lips. He had, I noticed, a large gold-framed tooth.

"You can count on me, Mr. Cadillac," Angel said to me. "I'm the surest merchandise you'll ever own. Let's get up and go for that gold you've been speaking of."

And get up he did. When I looked over at Maybellene, she seemed a little tense. I don't think Maybellene liked this turn of events much.

"My man," I said to Angel, conjuring up an accent I imagined was hip. "I'm pleased to have you here. I think you're lucky."

210

"You know, my other man," Angel said back, picking up my accent perfectly, "you're right, and I want you to be lucky with me."

His hair looked a little like rusted steel wool, and for some reason I couldn't resist rubbing it a couple of times.

"Well," Angel said, "what do you think? Is we lucky, or is we not? That's the question, is it not?"

"God, good luck and rhymes. Maybe you know where the gold is, too," Maybellene said.

"You're not happy?" I asked.

"I don't know. I hadn't planned on things going quite this way."

Welcome to the club, I thought. Welcome to the damned club. We were all Senior Picaro stumbling through our lives, but at least I knew it. I thought of trying to explain that to Maybellene, but I figured we ought to get going. The sooner we got that gold the better off we'd all be.

Angel was right. The car had air conditioning, and it worked. With the top down, it took the edge off things. After awhile, Maybellene got tired of the wind in her hair, so we stopped and tried to get the top up. Though an electric motor somewhere whined and groaned, the top stayed resolutely down. Finally Angel looked at her and asked, "How can anyone get tired of the wind in their hair? That, lady, is what it's all about. Don't you have any romance left?"

Maybellene didn't say anything, but you could tell she was taking things under advisement.

A moment later, eight or nine motorcycles roared past us. In the middle of the group, one of the bikers raised his fist up to us as if in celebration of, I guess, old Cadillacs.

I suppose such a tribute was appropriate. The bikes looked old. A couple even had antique license plates on their front fenders.

The bikers, though, didn't look particularly old. They had beards and bandannas and leather vests over hairy and naked chests. They looked mean, very mean. One of the last in the group was driving a bike with a sidecar. A crudely lettered placard across the back of the sidecar read *The Antique Indians from Hell.*

"What do you think?" I asked Angel. "What's that all about?"

"More than you and I want to think about, man. They're off the ranch. Let's just have a peaceful good time and stay away from folks like that. You know, I take it as a rule that a honkie with a motorcycle you stay a long ways away from."

# Thirty-Three

That's what the sign said, and I admit it sounded attractive. We'd been on the road about five hours, and we were tired. It wouldn't normally have taken five hours to drive the two hundred miles between St. Louis and Rosedale, Illinois, but we stopped at every grain elevator and at every Old Timer's Pigfeed sign.

"Whoa," Angel said at one point, "stopping again. You white folks figure that if you find the right elevator, you won't have to bother with church or good works. With the right elevator you'll go right to heaven. Is that it? Is that what we're doing?"

"In a way," I said. I liked Angel and couldn't help but answer him.

Maybellene looked at me as though I were crazy.

In fact, she grabbed me as we walked away from the car together, on the way to check out what I considered a promising sight for the buried gold.

"Look, asshole," she said through clenched teeth, "let's drop Angel, all right? I don't want to cut this deal any more ways than two. As I told you when we got together, I've met too many losers and lost too much of my life going after them."

"I think Angel's brought us luck," I said. "I mean, he popped up after about the first lucky break we've had. You almost did us in, you know, going back to that motel. I'm still not convinced we weren't seen by Rotbart. That motel is where I'd come back to look for stragglers like me. No, I say we keep Angel with us. I'll pay him if he needs to be paid, but he may not want money. He ought to be pretty grateful. I mean, in a way we saved his life."

I looked back toward the car. Angel was sitting on the deck behind the back seat. From someplace he had produced a boom box and was rocking back and forth to some music we couldn't hear. He had on a pair of white-framed sunglasses that seemed the perfect match for the car.

"I say we keep him," I repeated, like a man trying to convince himself.

"Another of life's local losers," Maybellene muttered as we walked beside me back toward the car. "I won't even ask about the gold."

"It's farther on." For some reason I was beginning to feel chipper. "But not to worry. There are lots of grain elevators and many miles of railroad tracks to cover. Or maybe you have something else to do with your time?"

"I used to like you," Maybellene said, "Now I'm not so sure."

I stopped. I was a little scared. I didn't want things to go quite this way.

"What do you mean?" I asked. "This whole story is full of characters just popping up and going away. I've gotten sort of relaxed about it. Look, until we find the gold, we're fighting over what we don't have, and finding the gold could take awhile.

"You know," I went on, "I think we could all use some relaxation. Why don't we plan on spending the night at Rosedale and go to the fair? Who knows, it might take our minds off our troubles. Besides, maybe we can enter your plant in the wilted flora contest."

She smiled then.

"That's my boy," she said. "That's why I fell for you."

Angel was still sitting on the back deck of the car singing along with a radio station he'd found.

"Right back in his arms again, so satisfied," he and the woman on the radio sang.

As Angel's tunes played away, Maybellene and I leaned up against the car. I put my arm around her and nuzzled her neck.

"Mmm, this is very nice," she said and pushed me away, "but this is a little public even for me. Let's go to the fair. Maybe they have a Tunnel of Love."

Just as the three of us were about to get going, one of the bikers we'd been seeing for the last several days drove up. His motorcycle sputtered and popped, and flames came out of the exhaust. He appeared like a god from bad planet.

"Hi, folks," he said as walked up to us. "I don't mean to scare you. Folks always think we were extras in the *Wild One,* but we try to be

214

good citizens. We're even incorporated. Here's my card."

It sure seemed improbable to be receiving a business card from a biker, but—well—why not? What else made sense?

J. D. McClatchry, it read, Outlaw Indian from Hell, Inc.

"I apologize for the tough sound of our name," he said. "We don't mean things quite the way these cards sound, but we're trying to create a reputation, you see, and this is how we were advised to do it."

He smiled as he said this. His top teeth were dark brown. He turned around to get something from the saddlebags on his black cycle, and I read the crude lettering on the back of his leather jacket.

*Outlaw Indians* arced across the top of the jacket. Below these words and a drawing, the inscription said in a more cramped writing style *The Cavalry Won't Save You This Time.* The figure in the middle was, improbably enough, somebody like George Custer with blonde curls floating out behind a snarling face on a poorly drawn motorcycle. He reminded me vaguely of Pee Pole.

"Well, friend," I said for lack of anything else to say, "we're happy to have you stop. What can we do for you?"

"You can't help me. No, I'm beyond help. I've got some money for your car in here somewhere."

"Our car doesn't need any money," I said. "Our car needs a new top."

Maybellene almost tripped me as she pushed me out of the way.

"God, but you're dumb," I heard her mutter as she stepped toward the biker.

"Hi there," she said in what I thought was a voice just a little too soft. "You have some money for my car?"

"Yeah," the biker said without looking up. "We took up a collection. It's the kind of a car we need to take on our caravans.

"Here it is," he said after a pause. "Ma'am, here it is. We'd like to buy your car."

"On your caravans?" Maybellene asked. I could see that she was trying to count the money in his hand without being too obvious. "What are your caravans?"

"What, you writing a book? Caravans are caravans. We take these trips, and we want a car that's appropriate. Chevies don't do much for the guys. Look, here's the money. Count it and give me the car keys."

He handed her the money. He seemed almost shy about it, "There's only $200 here," Maybellene said after she finished counting. "This car is a special collector's model. It'll cost you at least $1,500."

"Lady, you don't get the picture, do you? I'm a guy from a motorcycle gang. People do what I say, or they're in for big trouble. Give me the fucking car keys."

Is this how things like this happen? I wondered. I could imagine the news stories. Three innocent people killed by rogue motorcycle gang.

"I don't think she wants to sell the car, motherfucker."

This voice and the edge in it were surprising, especially when we noticed that they were coming from such a compact frame.

"Look, asshole," Angel went on as he walked toward the biker, "the lady paid over $2,000 for this car. This car used to belong to Muhammad Ali. Owning this car would be like owning the Lincoln Continental Kennedy was shot in. This car goes beyond cars. $2,500 takes it. If you haven't got $2,500, you might as well forget about it, fuckface."

By the time he finished saying all this, Angel was right in front of the biker. If he'd been taller, his pose suggested he would have grabbed the biker by the front of his shirt. As it was, his compact size almost made him seem more menacing while he rocked back and forth with his hands on his hips. Rotbart had taught us that there is something extremely menacing about an aggressive short person.

The biker's hands went fluttering in the air in front of him as if he didn't know what to do with them.

"Well, right," he said. "I can see your point on this one. But I'm a biker, and the guys told me to come back with the car keys. They won't like it if I come back empty handed. No, they won't like it all. How's $400 sound?"

"I told you the lady paid over $2,000. You don't want her to lose money, do you?"

"Angel," Maybellene said, "you're being too hard on the man. As I said, I'd let it go for $1,500."

"I don't have it, ma'am. I just don't have it."

"Look," I put in, "why don't you go back and talk it over with your

216

buddies? We can all meet at the Rosedale Fair and talk it over. I'll bet you can find more money. And I'll bet the lady would take $750 in cash, though we've got to be careful of the short guy. He's killed people for less. I wouldn't underestimate him."

"Now that was real dumb, Owen. Real dumb," Maybellene said after the biker quite literally roared away. The smell of gasoline and exhaust fumes hung in the air as if evil had become an odor. "Why did you tell them where we're going? How can we have any fun with them hanging around?"

"Maybellene, dear, do you really think we can just drive off and leave them? They're all over the place. What's more, they're not going to steal your car in a public place. No, think about it. We just might sell this baby for a profit."

"Oh, I suppose," she said wearily. "Don't you ever get tired of all these angles? I mean, wouldn't you like just to go straight for something?"

I glanced in the rear-view mirror as we pulled back on the highway and headed toward Rosedale. Angel, in his stark white sunglasses, was nodding his head and singing to something on the boom box, which he now held against his left ear. I couldn't hear the words.

Straight for something, I thought. Right. *A message straight from the heart.* I wondered how Sylvie Mae was doing. She certainly was right to stay out of the world. It would have overcome her.

"Sometimes," I said to Maybellene, "I think angles are all there are."

# Thirty-Four

**THE ROSEDALE COUNTY FAIR** was arrayed behind a root-beer stand like a gleaming corona of lights and faded colors.

We drove the Cadillac into a field to the left of the root-beer stand. It was a rough field, and the Cadillac bounced up toward the starry sky and then down toward the grassy earth. A boy with an orange flag directed us to a parking place.

Has anyone since Wordsworth written about breezes? Someone should. They are marvelous things, these breezes. It was hot when we parked the car. As we walked across the soft grass of the field in what was left of the evening's light, a breeze came up, carrying a little section of cool, as if a bit of the far north had traveled all the way to where we were. The breeze seemed to circle around us a few times and then go away.

The ticket booth at the entrance was a simple affair. It didn't need to be very complicated or advertise much of anything. No, the lights of the carnival rides behind were all the advertising anybody needed.

We bought tickets for two adults and one child. No one questioned Angel's age. And then we were in. All three of us held hands as if we were on a school trip and walked into the spinning red and yellow and blue lights of the carnival.

"Step right up," someone was calling across the midway, and Maybellene smiled at me.

"You were right," she said, squeezing my hand. "We'll have us a good time."

There were shades of Mary Lynn in that comment, but that was a connection I didn't want to make.

The midway had two lanes about three blocks long. On either side of each lane were rows of games and rides. The Tilt-a-Whirl came first on one side, followed by Ducky Ducks and Sky King's Sky Chairs and Hell's Hot Rods and Dunk the Dumbo. Along the other lane were the Ferris Wheel and the Round About and the Merry-Go-Round. A tent show called Fatimas, Freaks, and Fat Ladies was near the end of this row right next to a large wooden cylinder called the Wall of Death.

I suggested walking around the midway once to get our bearings.

"Owen, you're so cautious," Maybellene said.

"Getting cautious, dear. I don't want any more adventure stories to tell my grandchildren. I've got enough already."

Angel walked ahead of us, almost the way our child would've. And there certainly was something childlike in the way he stared back and forth at the various rides and games and carnies.

"Come on in here, little fellow. I'm just waiting to give you this teddy bear. Just knock over the milk bottles. You did it all the time when you was a baby. Three shots for a quarter."

The carnie held three rubber baseballs out to Angel. His arm was so heavily tattooed, it looked like it had some kind of disease.

Angel began going through his pockets for a moment before he realized that he didn't have any money. He then turned around rather sheepishly to me.

"Son, I can't help you out. The lady's got it all."

And the lady didn't look very pleased as she looked back and forth between us.

"Owen, I want to have a good time, but this isn't fair. I shouldn't have to carry the two of you. It's like I've got to give everyone an allowance."

I laughed. "I suppose this is annoying, dear, but we're too far in to quit. Believe me, I'd go back to my miserable acting career in two seconds if I could undo this summer. I wish I hadn't read the want ad, but wishing isn't going to get us out of here. Who knows, maybe we can keep trading cars and get rich as we roll into Chicago."

"Are you giving up on the, ah, you know?" Maybellene asked. She didn't want Angel to hear the word *gold*.

Angel was rocking back and forth waiting for a quarter.

"No," I said. "But you can't take all this so seriously. Betty Crocker recipes just don't apply to outlaws, and I think that's the world we're in now. Give him ten bucks."

"Did it ever occur to you that I'm tired of taking orders from losers? My grandmother always said that if you give a man an inch, he'll order you to give him two more."

"I agree," I said. "If I were you, I'd be angry. Hell, I used to specialize

219

in anger. Nothing ever went the way I imagined. I set out to play Hamlet, and I didn't even get the chance to play Rosencrantz or Guildenstern If I was lucky, I got to put on someone else's makeup I know it's hard, but as Willy the Shake told us, we've all got to play our assigned roles, and yours right now is to hand out money. You can quit if you want. But if you want to go with Angel and me to find that gold, you've got to pay. After what I've seen, I'm not letting go of any good men. And you—you can quit if you want. I don't care. I just want to get on with things. In a way, I don't care about the money. I just want to see where things will lead."

I guess I said too much, but that's what I believed.

She gave him ten bucks. A moment later, Angel was heaving those baseballs, at the milk bottles as though he were born to pitch.

I don't know why, but there were tears in my eyes when I looked at her.

"Thank you," I said. And then, I went on, "God bless you. I love you. You're better than you know."

I began studying the carnival, because I couldn't understand the feelings I'd let lose.

I've always thought that carnivals were fun for a while. We strolled the midway a couple of times and watched the people. If you tried real hard, you could pretend that the carnival was a metaphor for life, that the give and take of the midway was how life worked, but what I really kept seeing was how people kidded themselves. I saw the teenage girls and boys who covered up their longings and their loneliness with these hard-looking clothes and hair styles. The carnies, who seemed exotic and interesting from a distance, up close looked merely worn out and dirty.

It didn't help my outlook to go on the rides.

The Merry-Go-Round wasn't bad, though when you got on, you realized that the recorded calliope music was out of tune and that paint was chipping from the horses. The Tilt-a-Whirl riled up my stomach, and Sky King's Sky Chairs finally did me in. As we swung out from the ground, I began to get dizzy and got dizzier as we swung up from the ground and down again. I began to notice that the reflectors on the chairs in front of me were broken and that the metal holding the chairs in place was badly rusted. I tried to remember if I'd ever heard of someone dying on a carnival ride, but the up and down finally got to my stomach. When we finally stepped off the ride, the ground seemed to be going up and down and up again, as if the terra wasn't very firma any more.

We walked under some stark fluorescent bulbs into Blimpy's Burgers. It was set up to resemble a lunchroom counter and had these lunchroom stools mounted on some two-by-four's. On the counter were the round things that held pies and behind the counter were milk shake mixers and Coke signs, but the whole was somehow wrong, as if Archie had been taken on the road without enough sleep. I halfway expected Veronica to show up in a tight dress.

We had tired hamburgers and Cokes without any fizz.

A heavy woman sat across from us and ate three or four hamburgers. In the hard light of those fluorescent lamps, her skin looked blue and mottled.

"This is America," she said. "This is 'The Star Spangled Banner' with ketchup and mustard."

A moment later, still spinning from hamburgers lying inside a stomach, which was itself still spinning from Sky King's Sky Chairs, I was standing in front of Dunk the Dumbo.

"Ah-huh, ah-huh, ah-huh," a crudely amplified and disembodied voice laughed out into the night. A clown sat in a caged dunk tank to the side of a roughly painted bull's eye. If you hit the bull's eye, the clown dropped into the water at the bottom of his cage.

"I'm high and dry, and all of you are stupid enough to be here thinking how you can knock me down. If you were smart, you'd be home with your families. Ah-huh, ah-huh, ah-huh. But since you're here, let's see your stuff. Three shots for a quarter. If you think you're man enough, pocket change sends me out of here. Ah-huh, ah-huh, ah-huh."

The woman taking tickets for the Wall of Death was so thin that she looked like an aging adolescent boy.

"Step up right here, and see the man who invites his death. Yessir, Yes ma'am, right here, right now, he rides his killer motorcycle to his death. See it all, see it here. Your money back if it isn't what we say.

221

Yessir, Yes ma'am, the Wall of Death right here, right now. The Wall of Death and The Great Beyond. Step up and see."

I wasn't really in the mood to see anyone confront The Great Beyond, but Maybellene was. She paid the woman a dollar for each of us, and the woman lifted a frazzled hemp rope. Then we walked up a rough set of wooden stairs to a rickety walkway that went around the wooden cylinder. Once we got to the walkway, we could look down into the cylinder. A black-framed motorcycle leaned against a pole in the center. A wooden floor was set at an angle to the walls of the cylinder. After half an hour or so, twenty people were standing on the walkway, waiting for the show to begin.

"Ladies and gentlemen," a rough voice said. "You are at the wall of death. Look down. This is where you see the man who will risk everything for you. This is your Man for the Hour of Death. This is the man who looks death in the eye and lives."

The woman who'd been taking tickets opened a door in the side of the cylinder and stepped into the ring.

"Eddy Beaudry is the man who'll ride the Wall for you. Let's hear some applause."

After we'd clapped for a while, a young man stepped out of the door, bringing a young girl with him. The two of them joined hands and then held up their joined hands and walked around the angled floor of the tub.

He had a leather coat hanging over his shoulders, and she plucked it off, as if this were the cape of a bullfighter. She plucked it off and held it up for our approval.

We applauded again, and he walked around the bottom of the cylinder with each hand clasped into the other above his head.

"This," the lady announcer said, "is your man for the Wall of Death, but now he must face it all alone."

With that, the young girl and the woman walked out. One of them slammed the door shut a couple of times as if checking for its fit. A moment later, the young man got on the motorcycle and, with a couple of kicks, started it.

The bike in that closed environment seemed ferocious. It was like an animal, except this animal belched blue flames occasionally.

A moment later, he was circling the bottom of the cylinder, occasionally going up on the sides. Soon, he was roaring around the bottom end of the sides, the power of his coming and going making the stakes of the wooden cylinder go in and out with his motion. Then he was arcing up and down the sides.

This all felt cleansing and powerful as his circling generated its own wind. For some reason, I felt clean and happy, and Maybellene and I were smiling at each other.

Yes, this was all very exciting and pleasant until I happened to look across the top of the Wall of Death and see Mary Lynn standing there and watching me back. Just a trace of smile was on her face.

Just what I needed, I thought and looked again to see McCoo a few feet away. He was smiling.

And of course, not three feet from McCoo and Mary Lynn was— who else?—Pee Pole wearing the jacket of the Indians from Hell.

As I saw all this, the bike was roaring around the cylinder, filling it with smoke and engine fumes.

"Maybellene," I tried to yell over the engine noise, "you're not going to believe this, but . . . ."

When I turned and began to finish my sentence, I discovered that she was gone. That frightened me, but I got even more scared as I figured out how they must've found me. That's why she was so insistent on staying at the Paradise Motel, why she was so reluctant to abandon her car. She was leaving a trail to follow. No wonder Maybellene had been resentful of Angel. He would've figured out that Maybellene must've been working with Mary Lynn. He would've protected me. No wonder she hated the little guy.

No wonder, indeed, I thought to myself as I saw Pee Pole coming one way around the cylinder walkway for me, and Elwin coming the other.

As I straddled the canvas-covered railing at the outside edge of the walkway, I caught a glimpse of Mary Lynn. She had that same tight little smile.

Everything repeats itself, I thought and then went over the edge into, I guess, my own version of The Wall of Death.

# Thirty-Five

PIECES OF CANVAS were joined where I went over the edge. Luckily for me, rope laces between the sections made footholds for my descent, though I think those footholds were more for my head than my feet. I don't remember so much climbing down as just falling and then landing on the midway dirt in a puff of dust.

I ran toward the car. I thought of looking back, but I remembered some advice of Rotbart's that explained how looking backward only slows you down and calls attention to your dilemma. What I also remembered was that I should get behind McCoo and Mary Lynn and Pee Pole, get where they wouldn't think to look.

I did just that. I cut over into the next lane of the carnival and walked rapidly back the way I'd come. I stopped when I got to Dunk the Dumbo, which was just across from the Wall of Death.

A large crowd had gathered there to watch a muscular farm boy in a white T-shirt with a pack of cigarettes rolled up in one sleeve try to sink that noisy clown.

"Ah-huh, ah-huh, ah-huh, my dumb young friend," the clown said over his scratchy p.a. system. "I may be the Dumbo, but you've spent all the money, and high and dry I am. Ah-huh, ah-huh, ah-huh."

I got into the middle of the crowd so I could appear caught up in the fuss about the clown while I looked around. I didn't see anybody. Mary Lynn and McCoo and Pee Pole just weren't there. I hoped that they were running toward the exit. I wondered where Maybellene was, but then I wondered if I really cared. She's the only one who could have given us away.

"High and dry. No one has touched me yet. Ah-huh, ah-huh, ah-huh."

Unfortunately, I had lost Angel as well, and I guess secretly I had begun to count on him. I could imagine him getting us out of this.

I was so busy thinking about my problems and backing into the crowd as hooked around for my enemies that I wasn't looking where I was going.

"Careful, you dumb son of a bitch. Careful."

I had stumbled against the barker, who was collecting money for those who wanted to dump Dumbo.

"Sorry," I said over my shoulder. I kept looking in the direction Elwin and Mary Lynn and Pee Pole had gone, but I still couldn't see them. All I saw were farmers arriving at the main entrance and going on rides and playing the shining and noisy games.

I guessed Mary Lynn and the others were standing around the Cadillac by now waiting for me to show up. I wished that we had picked out a less conspicuous car. It would have been a lot easier to escape this little scene in a Pinto or a Chevrolet than in a white Cadillac with steer horns on the hood.

In the distance I heard the shriek of a siren and briefly hoped that the three of them were being arrested. What an easy way to get them out of my life.

"Ah-huh, ah-huh, ah-huh, I'm high and dry and drying out, you Tinker Bells in the brain department. I mean, if you people were any stupider, you probably wouldn't know how to get home from here. Ah-huh, ah-huh, ah-huh. Three shots for just a quarter. Ah-huh, ah-huh, ah-huh."

It wasn't the insults that bothered me, it was the false tone of the laugh.

"Here," I heard myself saying to the man I'd bumped into. "Here's your quarter."

"Ah-huh, ah-huh, ah-huh," Dumbo went on from the booth. "You're right about that, fluff head: now it's my quarter. Let's see what you can do."

My three shots didn't even come close.

"Ah-huh, ah-huh, ah-huh. Another man who didn't do it. Another failure. Dumbo goes high and dry and on his way. Ah-huh, ah-huh, ah-huh."

That stiff version of Goofy's laugh was certainly annoying.

"Ah-huh, ah-huh, ah-huh, yes, another of life's local losers has paid his fee for losing, but this one has some property of mine, some property I'd certainly like back. Ah-huh, ah-huh, ah huh."

My God, it couldn't be. No, it just couldn't be.

"Ah-huh, ah-huh, ah-huh. You want to try again, Owen? Ah-huh, ah-huh, ah-huh. You're such a pal of ours, I'll give you three shots for nothing. Ah-huh, ah-huh, ah-huh."

I looked more closely at the barker. I really hadn't paid attention to him. It was Junior Senior, who held out a set of three rubber balls to me.

"Hey, this is it, big guy. Your chance to sink Mr. Rotbart. Go for it."

Just as I was looking around for a way to run, I felt a hard grip on my shoulder.

"You better just throw the balls, laddie pup," Junior Senior said. "It'll be your last chance to have fun before I kill you for what you did to my brother."

I really thought this was a bad dream. How had they gotten to Illinois? It was more than I could take in. It was like being presented with a list of all your sins.

"Excuse me. Excuse me." I heard a rough voice in the distance saying. "Excuse me. Excuse me." It came closer and closer.

"Out of the way, please," the voice said as it came up to us.

"Oh, shit," Junior Senior said and let go of my shoulder. "It's the cavalry."

And indeed it was. Policemen were standing around me as though I were something precious.

Four of them had circled me, and through the circle came the lady who ran the Wall of Death.

"That's him. That's the man who hurt my Eddie. That's him all right."

She folded her arms across her chest and looked at me fiercely.

I could feel Junior Senior backing away from me.

"She's right," I said. "I'm the criminal. I've got an arrest record that'll make your hair stand on end. Take me out of here before I hurt somebody."

The four policeman paused and looked at each other as if they were voting on who had the courage to arrest me.

"You might as well know," I said in my best pompous actor's voice, "that there's a bounty on me. The man who gets me will get the entire reward."

The policemen bumped into each other like characters from an old cinema comedy, and one stepped forward, his gun held shakily out.

"You come with us, you, you," he sputtered.

"I don't know," I said and held my arms away from him. Then I backed up as though I were truly a desperado, but someone kicked me from behind. I thought about that kick for a moment, and then I went down.

"Come on, sucker, get up. Get up and take what you deserve."

It was the woman from the Wall of Death.

"Do you know," she went on, "what you did to Eddie? Do you know? He was riding around that wood like it was money in the bank when you decided to leave. He was halfway up, the way he always got when I started talking in the microphone about how difficult it was. And then you and your friends ran away. Do you know what that did? You popped him off of the wall like he was a ping-pong ball. That you did. When you jumped off the edge, Eddy flew out the other way. I was watching the whole thing. He was unconscious when the ambulance took him away. He could be dead by now. I think you deserve having the shit kicked out of you."

She kicked me in the side a couple times, and then the policemen picked me up and escorted me to a waiting squad car.

I didn't see Mary Lynn or McCoo or Pee Pole or Maybellene as they hauled me out. I didn't even get another glance at Junior Senior and Rotbart. I briefly wondered if Helmut had come to Illinois with them.

# Thirty-Six

**AT THE ROSEDALE COUNTY SHERIFF'S OFFICE** being booked was quite a literal matter. My four arresting officers, followed by the lady who ran The Wall of Death, surrounded me as I stood before a desk on a raised platform. A thin, ashen-faced deputy sat behind the desk. His shirt seemed about three sizes too large. As a result, his badge was barely above his waist. Before him on the desk was a huge book. Closed, the book would've been six or seven inches thick. Open, it resembled an ancient family Bible. As I stood before the desk, my hands manacled behind me, my eyes were just level with the book. For a second, I thought he was going to read me something. He looked like the sort of character you might encounter after dying. He would be the person who reviewed the history of your life before routing you on to heaven or hell.

"You're charged with assaulting Edward P. J. Beaudry. Do you have anything to say for yourself?"

I wondered how a biker got two middle initials.

"It was an accident, officer," I said. "Some friends and I were just leaving the show. We didn't mean to hurt the man. I think the wooden cylinder was poorly constructed. I don't want to be rude, but I think Eddie did himself in."

"That means you plead Not Guilty to the charges, son." The deputy's voice was surprisingly deep and resonant.

"Name?" he continued, and I answered in the soberest voice I had. His hand seemed to hover above the great book, pausing as if to prepare itself for the descent into the serious facts such a great text required.

"Address?" he went on.

"Louisiana," I heard myself saying. Then: "Louisiana," I repeated with more conviction. "It's not a regular address. You just write me care of Sylvie Mae, Alice, Louisiana. It'll get there."

"This Mae person," the ashen policeman said as he bent over his great text, "is she a Miss or a Mrs.?"

"Mrs.," I said.

Getting booked into that hefty volume required about twenty

minutes. Then they took away my pocket change, my belt, and my shoe laces.

"For such a heavy criminal you sure don't own very much," the deputy collecting my things said.

He ushered me through a heavy metal door and down a long hall with dirty translucent windows on one side and jail cells on the other. The light coming through those windows was a sickly green color. The place smelled of cigarettes and urine and machine oil.

"Here you go, Stud," the deputy said to me when we got to the last cell. "You can keep Herbert company. He gets lonely sometimes."

Then the deputy laughed this huge and hearty belly laugh.

"Lonely. Oh, I like that. Here, Stud," he said to somebody in the cell. "Here's a college boy to keep you company." I guess he called everybody Stud.

He laughed again as he pushed me into the cell.

"Just give me a moment," Herbert said from the darkness of the corner of the cell. "Give me a moment, sport, and I'll be fine."

I stood a moment by the cell door until my eyes adjusted to the dark.

On each side of the cell were two metal platforms with thin mattresses on them. Between them was a stained sink and an even more stained toilet without a seat. If I could see those stains in the semi dark, I shuddered to think of how they would look in the light.

Herbert sat at the edge of one bed. He cupped his head in one hand and held the other up as if in greeting or to warn others off.

"I'm Owen Hill," I said and held my hand out.

"Be all right in just a second, old sport. Just give me a moment."

I stood before him waiting for him to look up, but he stayed in that position.

"Are you sure you're OK?" I asked.

I got the same answer back. Tired of worrying about another lost soul when I had my own to find, I sat down on the other bed. When I rested my hand on the mattress, I could feel hard bugs scurry over it.

Sitting in that dim, green light of the jail cell, I felt about as lost as I've ever felt. While I didn't want to think about staying in jail, I also knew that all my greedy acquaintances would be waiting for me if they turned me loose. My situation was beginning to resemble that old puzzle where you have to figure out how to get someone out of a room without exits. It was like trying to solve a puzzle all right, except I was both the puzzle and the player—and likely the solution as well.

I slept off and on. Herbert woke me up a couple of times with his usual assertion, "Yes, old sport, I'll be all right in a moment."

A deputy got us up about seven in the morning and took us into a large room where we sat around a scratched-up ping pong table with several other deputies eating cold scrambled eggs and greasy bacon. The room was, a deputy explained, the recreation area.

Herbert and I were each ceremoniously given a cigarette by one of the deputies, who seemed hurt to discover that neither of us smoked. The deputies did, however, and Herbert and I sat around watching them smoke, play ping pong, and shoot dice. It seemed an odd way to begin the day, but I guess watching these activities was supposed to be our recreation. An hour later, one of the deputies marched us back to our cell. After the door clanked shut, and Herbert and I were both seated on our respective bunks, he held up a hand and said (of course), "Don't think anything of it, old sport, I'll be fine in a moment."

I began to feel that I was living in a bad movie, a bad movie that kept repeating itself.

I think that's why I was very happy to see Maybellene when she came to visit me the next afternoon. By then I was desperate for company from the normal world, even for company that may have gotten me into this mess.

I tried to be aloof as the deputy led me to what he called the visitor's center, which turned out to be the same old recreation room. He put us at each end of the ping pong table. He sat in a corner chair reading a magazine and smoking a cigarette.

"I don't know why we're going through all this baloney about visitors," Maybellene said. "You're free. The Wall-of-Death lady didn't file any formal charges. She got some free publicity. It turned out that nothing happened to her Eddie. They got a couple of newspaper stories and had the most popular show at the midway. Now they've left. The cops can't hold you anymore."

While I was secretly happy about this news, I was a little scared as well.

"Does this mean I go now?" I asked. "I mean I'm not so sure I want to leave just yet. I've been talking over current events with Herbert, and we haven't covered today's news."

"Are you serious?" she said. "Let's get out of this rat hole."

"Why?" I asked and took a breath before I went on. "So you can have me take you and your friends to the gold? Is that the game? No thanks. I'd rather stay right here with Herbert. I'll confess to something."

"What are you talking about?" Maybellene looked astonished. "Let's get out of here."

"Deputy," I yelled across the room. "Take me back to my cell."

"Owen, cut it out. You're free. The charges have been dropped."

The deputy, I noticed, was asleep. His hands were folded beneath his pot belly, and he blew little bits of phlegm into the air as he breathed.

"Maybellene, I love you. I really do. But I don't trust you. Something doesn't make sense. McCoo and Mary Lynn and Pee Pole and Rotbart and Junior Senior all show up at the same county fair. Can that really be a coincidence? Can that really be an accident? I suppose you're going to tell me they were all driving along in their little groups and decided, 'Hey, what a fun thing. Let's stop at this cheesy little fair.'

"No, I just don't believe it," I went on. "Someone told them where to go, and I think that someone is you, my sweet little dear."

She looked gorgeous as she stood there at the other end of the ping pong table. She was dressed in a pair of tight, fawn-colored corduroys and a top of hunter's red. I loved the doubtful little turn her mouth had and the way her hair seemed to curl off to the right. I wanted to jump her right then and there.

The deputy slept on, oblivious to us, dreaming of a love, I suppose, like the one I could walk out of that courthouse and have.

"It's not fair, Maybellene. Goddamnit, but it's not fair at all. We were it. We were the Top of the Ritz and our own table at 21. We even had a meaningful car instead of some seriously practical piece of engineered tin from Japan. We were all this, and you fucked it up. You went for the money, and you did us in, my love. You did us in when we could have done it on and on. We were better than rock and roll, my sweet."

She was crying. Angry as I was, I could see that. She was still standing there. From a distance, she had the pose of someone telling me off, someone about to go. She looked strong. But up close, her face was smeared and out of focus.

"Owen," she said between sobs. "Owen, you don't mean it. I didn't do it. I really didn't. I came with you because I loved you. You were the man for me. If you want to know the truth, I even called my Mama about you. The rest of this . . . ."

She swept her arm around the room, as if *this* included everything.

"The rest of this—I just don't know. I didn't bring them here. Owen, come on, I didn't start this. Don't you remember? I didn't find you. You found me. Or we found each other. I was a waitress in a bar when you walked in with that psychopath chained to you. I didn't have anything to do with that. Come on, baby. Think about it."

She was pleading with me, her hands scratching at the air before her as to make the reality I'd described go away.

"Don't you see," she said. "I was there when you walked in. You mean, you think I was a plant? Come on, sweet baby. We're in a world that wants to do us in. We're in a world that means us harm. What we've got is love to take us out of this, and now you want to take our love away. Owen, let's get out of here."

I looked at the guard. He slept on, his hands still locked beneath his gut.

"I don't know, Maybellene. Something's wrong here. How are you going to explain Mary Lynn and McCoo and Rotbart and Junior Senior all showing up in the middle of downstate Illinois? And what about you at The Wall of Death? I see all these villains coming after me, and you're gone. Come on. Get real. Someone brought them here. You know, I'd even take McCoo and Mary Lynn as an accident, but not Rotbart. No. Someone spread the word, and that someone had to be you. I figure you did it when we stopped at the Paradise Motel in St. Louis."

"You're paranoid, Owen. How would I spread the word? I mean, I couldn't even get a few punctuation marks out, my friend. If you'll recall, we were sound asleep at the old Paradise Motel. Come on, Owen, can't you just believe they were following us? The way I figure, it's not much more than that. They just watched where we went.

"Owen, please. I beg you. Let's get out of here."

"You might have been sleeping," I said. "But I wasn't. No. I stayed up the whole night staring out into the parking lot for trouble."

"Well, there you are," she said and came over to me. She put her hand on my cheek. "I couldn't have called, Owen. And, Owen, I didn't call. I didn't get in touch with them. And the reason you didn't see me at The Wall of Death is so simple. I went to the damn bathroom. That's all. Look, Angel's back. He's with me. He's waiting outside. He was the one who brought me here. He saw the police take you away. He saw them chase you off the Wall of Death. He's living up to his name, the little guy is. He protects you like a guardian angel. He's got a gun now. It's almost as big as he is. He's even been taking care of the clematis. He's got it in a bucket of dirt, and I think it's going to live. You know, until I ran into him on the midway, I thought you'd run off to get the gold for yourself. I mean, I came back from the bathroom, and you were gone.

"That's what usually happens to me, you know." She was kneeling beside me now, her head on my leg. "I fall in love, and I get left. I've paid my way to so many losses that I thought you were just another one."

I put my arm around her shoulder.

"Owen, I don't want the money. I'm not interested in getting rich. I want to be in love. Do you understand that?"

Now I really was afraid to look down at her, for fear that I would believe her. I was more scared than I was when I hid the gold. Being in love was a lot more frightening than avoiding bizarre enemies.

"I don't know, Maybellene. I don't know. This wasn't how things were supposed to work. I wanted a *Treasure Island* adventure, you know something with a happy ending, not something out of Beckett with no ending other than *to be continued in the next book*. I wanted to fight off the bad guys and come back with the treasure. Right now, I'm not even sure who all the bad guys are. But what can I do? I surely don't want to stay locked up with a faded preppie who's being held for repeating himself."

I avoided her eyes.

"Does that mean you're coming, then?" she asked.

By way of answer I stood up and shouted at the deputy, "I'm going.

233

Is that all right?"

He stirred once in his nap and tightened his grip on his paunch.

I held her hand as we walked out past the booking desk. The ashen-faced sergeant was still behind it, as if contemplating all the crimes of man. He looked very serious up there.

He handed me a sack of things.

"Try to stay clear of the law, Prisoner 87,316," he said. "Try to mend your days and ways."

He then bent over his book and ceremoniously put a mark beside, I guessed, my entry.

The bag was stenciled with the number 87,316, and I emptied out its contents. The only items of real value it contained were my shoelaces.

A moment later, we were standing in the fresh sunshine of a fall day. Angel was waiting for us, standing beside the 1959 Cadillac with the steer horns on the hood.

"Well here we are," I said to reassure myself as much as anything. "Here we are," I repeated, as though the repetition would make the way clear.

"Where is that, my man?" Angel asked. "You know where we're going, man? Because if you do, I want you to say it out loud so we all can hear We've been hanging around here far too long as far as I'm concerned."

It was delightful to have Angel back. His only vested interest in all this was survival.

"I think," I said, "that we should ditch the Cadillac. As much as I love having it around, it gives us away. I think we should leave it here and find ourselves another car."

"You're fabulous, you know that," Maybellene said. "You've made me get rid of more cars than I used to even think about owning. I come and get you out of the tank, and you tell me I've got to get rid of my car. You know, ditching the Honda didn't do us a bit of good. I'm not so sure I trust you. Why was I crying in there? You're the unreliable one. For all I know, you're working for some car dealer. Maybe that's how you get paid."

She was only partly kidding.

"My lady and my man," Angel put in, "we haven't time for these disputes. I agree with both of you. We can leave the car. In a town like this, no one will steal it. It'll just get a few parking tickets. We'll come back after it later. For the time, though, the bad actor is right. These steer horns will just shout at where we are. You must remember that one of my great skills is picking up cars. I'll have something appropriate in an hour or so. Why don't you folks relax in the park across the way."

The park across the way was one of those small-town squares where old men sit and chew tobacco and talk over the weather. This time, though, Maybellene and I sat there drinking some coffee I got from a nearby restaurant. We sat there drinking coffee from styrofoam cups and eating crullers. We drank and ate and talked ourselves back into love. I guess it wasn't all that hard. We were still suspicious—she because she'd been left so many times—and I because I still wondered if she'd given us away. But we wanted to be near each other.

"Owen, have you ever thought about the word *longing*. As in the sentence *I'm longing for you, baby.*"

"Well, no," I said and looked at the way her eyes looked up at me from beneath her lashes. "No, but I'd agree."

"It seems like it means I'd get long so I'd be next to you. I'm stretching myself out for you."

"Baby," I laughed, "that's more for me to say than you. I'm getting long for you even as we speak."

I could have gone on like this for hours, but a rusty, dark-blue car pulled up beside us.

"This may not be the limousine you had in mind, but it should whisk us out of here," Angel said. He was wearing the largest pair of tear-dropped shaped aviator glasses I'd ever seen. He was also wearing a blue cap that read USS Constitution in gold letters across the peak. "I did an even trade—the Cadillac for this."

I meant to ask him where he got his sunglasses and his cap, just as I meant to ask him how he kept showing up at the right time with the right stuff, but I was afraid to break our luck by talking about it.

"Beautiful," I said instead. "Just the kind of car we need right now. Something ordinary and dirty."

"That worries me," Maybellene put in. "You haven't been right about cars yet."

The car was a Ford. When I got inside, it smelled of cigarettes. Dotted across the dashboard were black burn marks, and the ashtray was filled to overflowing with cigarette butts. There were so many beer cars on the floor that it was hard to put our feet down. The back seat was covered with old and yellowing newspapers. But the key was in the dash, and the motor purred.

"You drive, boss," Angel said. He got in the back seat. To my ears, his imitation of Jack Benny's Rochester was perfect, though he'd be living the Jack Benny part by riding. By driving, I became Rochester. We lived in confusing times.

"Where did you learn to do Rochester?" I asked.

"Rochester?" Maybellene asked as she got in the passenger seat. "Isn't Rochester the guy who wrote all the dirty poems in the eighteenth century?"

"Whatever," I said as I pulled away from the Rosedale County Courthouse and drove down Main Street toward the highway. "Everybody always knows more than me. Rochester this and Rochester that. What we need is some gold."

"Gold," Angel said. "Oh boy, is that what's been going on here? Oh boy. Gold. I'm paying attention now. Boss, I'll do all the Rochester imitations you want if you're really talking about gold."

"Right," I said into the rear-view mirror. I then noticed that Angel was sitting with his arm around the clematis, and a purple blossom hung down over his shoulder.

# Thirty-Seven

**THE EDGE OF ROSEDALE** wasn't much, just the A & W root beer stand and the remains of the carnival and, as it happened, our Cadillac all alone in the parking lot.

"It's kind of sad," Maybellene said, "that beautiful car all by herself. She had real character. You don't find that in cars today."

I wanted to change the subject.

"I can understand Mary Lynn and McCoo and Pee Pole, but Rotbart—how did Rotbart and Junior Senior get here?" I asked. I wanted to know who'd found me out. Until I got those questions answered, I wasn't interested in any romance about old cars.

Angel responded to both of us.

"You're both such white people. You really believe what those advertisements tell you? Figure it out. Cadillacs are nothing more than Buicks some designer overworked. As far as the characters from Mr. Actor's bad script of life—why not believe they just showed up? Hey, it happens, doesn't it? I mean, bad stuff shows up with the good. The lady didn't do it, man. I can tell you that. I mean, when she found out you were gone, she came crying to me like there was no end to sadness. I was standing there, trying to knock over some milk bottles, and she almost knocks me over. She was running around that hard trying to get you back. No, the lady didn't do it."

As he said this, Maybellene put her hand on my leg.

"He's right," she said softly.

Tears came up in my eyes in spite of myself. I had promised myself that I would stay tough. I had promised myself that I wouldn't play the love game until I had things figured out. As I said all these good ideas to myself, what I heard was "Don't worry, old sport, I'll be all right in just a moment."

"What are we after, folks?" Angel asked after a discrete few minutes to let me finish up my crying. "What's going on?"

I gave him the short form of my history. Even with a few embellishments, the story only took about five minutes. I was surprised that I and my now dead friends didn't amount to more. "Gold along the railroad tracks," Angel said by way of summary. "That shouldn't be so hard. We need to find just the right sort of grain elevator and an Old Timer's Pig Feed, and then we're there. Is that it?"

"That's it, old sport. That's it exactly."

Well, of course Angel found the spot. I was beginning to wonder if Mary Lynn and the rest were on our trail, but no one seemed to be following us.

"There," he yelled as we drove along, "There it is. Just what you described."

Indeed. Indeed it was. I stopped so fast that I almost turned that smelly Ford over. When I hit the brakes, it paused as if thinking things over and then careened to the right and onto the shoulder. Fortunately, the car stopped completely before those erratic brakes took us into the ditch beside the road.

"By God," I said, "I think you're right."

I don't know how Angel happened to see the Old Timer's Pig Feed sign; it faced toward the tracks that ran along the right side of the highway and the fields beyond, but there it was, and there, too, was the grain elevator I remembered.

I was shaking when I got out of the car. After all this, I thought, it might turn out to be true. I was finally coming to the climax. It was hard to take. I had spent so much time with nonsense, I didn't know if I could believe the real thing.

Maybellene, like my own true love, could read my mind.

"It doesn't seem possible," she said as she came up behind me, "that so much money could be hidden here in such ordinary surroundings. It's like a fairy tale, gold amid the corn."

"Yes," I said, "but this is it. This is where the real search begins."

I felt suddenly lighter-hearted about Maybellene. Mary Lynn, McCoo, and Pee Pole were at the fair because this was their county. Of course. Though I still hadn't figured out Rotbart and Helmut.

"What's the plan, boss?"

"Yes, folks," I said, "this is it. If we don't screw this one up, we'll get us a nice round sum of money."

We walked down into the ditch beside the road and back up the other side and into the brush and trees along the road. It's strange how quickly the world gets hostile. That brush, seen from a car passing by, appears benign, like a decoration in the scene beside our happy lives. But up close, that brush scratches faces and hands as if it were made from thousands of tiny wooden spears to keep us out.

The three of us were puffing as we came through the brush and stood beside the five or six-foot embankment leading up to the railroad tracks.

I looked up and down the sides of that embankment, but I didn't see any signs of an upside-down twig or a brass belt buckle. In fact, I got nervous as I even thought of them. It still didn't seem possible that I might find them. A moment or two later, Maybellene and Angel caught up with me.

"Not here," I said and scrambled up the embankment and onto the loose gravel of the roadbed. I stepped onto the tracks, and I felt as though I were entering a dream. I began walking toward the Old Timer's Pig Feed sign and the grain elevator. I did this for a tie or two and then, for the briefest second, I thought I saw twin points of light.

I've come all this way to die, I thought. McCoo's been waiting for me. I froze there for several moments until I realized that my eyes had played a trick on me.

"What is it, my man?" Angel asked behind me.

"Nothing. Just glimmers of my former life."

"Does that mean you've located the gold?" Maybellene asked.

"No," I said and started walking again, but I still couldn't see any signs of my gold. I stopped suddenly and felt Angel bump into me and then Maybellene bump into him. We must've made quite a sight. The Three Stooges go looking for the loot.

"We's here, boss."

"Great," I said. "I know you're nervous. I am too. But I need some space if I'm to find the pay-off. Stand back a bit, OK? I won't run off with the gold, I promise. If we blow this part of the story, it's all been a waste of time, and I'm sure Howard wouldn't approve. He wouldn't approve at all, to come all this way and not get the hero's kiss."

"What are you talking about?" Maybellene asked. "I don't get it."

"Never mind," I said. "I'm running on. Look, we've got to figure out a system. I mean, I know we're in the right area, but we've got to double-

239

check the terrain. I've just realized that finding the gold is only going to be slightly easier than locating that proverbial needle in the haystack. Compared to all of nature that we see, my markers are pretty small."

I told them I'd buried the gold along the left side of the track as you faced the Old Timer's Pig Feed sign, but I also felt that we were too close to the grain elevator.

"We need to walk back south and get some distance, but I'd like to check things out as we go along. Let's do a version of leapfrog. I mean, you and Maybellene stand there," I said to Angel. "I'll start out, and you stand there until I stop, and then Angel comes along looking things over and goes on beyond me and stops. Maybellene passes both of us and goes another distance out. Then I go past her. You see what I mean?"

I looked at both of them, and they nodded.

"This way, we'll triple-check the terrain. We're bound to find the gold."

We certainly were optimistic when we began. It seemed impossible to miss the gold, but we leapfrogged over each other for three hours, and we didn't find anything except frustration.

The sun was almost exactly overhead when we stopped for a break. While the day was cool when we left the courthouse square at ten, it felt as though the whole summer's warmth had been stored up in the embankment beneath the tracks. Waves of heat kept rising up when the wind died down. All three of us were sweating profusely.

"Are you sure this is the area, Owen?" Maybellene asked. I could hear the weariness and the exasperation in her voice.

I looked up and down the tracks. It seemed to be exactly what I remembered. But as my glance went back and forth over the brush and the tracks and the graveled embankment and the grain elevator and the pig feed sign and the sharp blue of the sky—as I looked, I felt less sure. And I began to have another, more worrisome vision—what if someone had already found the gold and taken it? I put that thought out of my mind

"I think so, Maybellene. I think so."

"Boss, now let's not get vague about it. Is this it, or is this ain't? It's one or the other."

"Look," I said, "let's go back once more. I'm just sure this is the place."

We walked together this time. Angel suggested the three of us stand close together and look up and down each side of the tracks. When we finished one section, we crossed the tracks to the other side and repeated our performance there.

Do you have any idea of how long it took us to move along at this rate? By late afternoon, we still weren't half-way back to our starting point. We were getting edgy and tired. Maybellene pushed Angel to the ground after he accidentally stepped on her foot, and out of no particular context, Angel said, "If we don't find the gold, you call me *Boss*, OK?" I just looked at him.

We could feel the hum and rumble in the tracks before we saw the train. We ran from the tracks to the brush as it arrived. The very earth seemed to vibrate. First my feet and then my legs and then my whole body was trembling with that train. It was fun to watch at first, the way the yellow locomotive came upon us. It was a huge piece of machinery, like something from another planet until the engineer waved to us, as if to suggest that all this power was guided by this very ordinary guy with a striped cap.

That train made us feel better, because it diverted us from our failures at hand. As the empty boxcars came clattering behind the locomotive, I remembered my arrival in Illinois. I still couldn't believe I'd lived through being thrown from the train.

We were probably watching the very train that had brought me here. As the open boxcars rattled past, I could hear the squeal of metal grinding on metal; the train was braking.

Then it occurred to me that I'd survived being thrown from the train because it was moving very slowly. If I had jumped from the train now going past, I probably would've broken several bones. No, I'd been tossed someplace farther north. This realization meant that the gold was even farther on.

I'd heard the first squeal five minutes ago, and the train was still braking.

"Let's take a walk," I said. "I think we're at the wrong spot. There must be another Old Timer's Pig Feed Sign."

241

It was close to four when we passed the grain elevator. We were walking along the embankment on the left side. The train wasn't moving much faster than we were. I was thankful for the rattle and clatter of the cars. It kept me from thinking. I didn't even want to consider not finding the gold.

After we went on by the grain elevator, the tracks seemed to rise, and we couldn't see very far ahead. It was almost as if the tracks were pointed toward the heavens.

"Should we get the car and drive?" Maybellene shouted over the noise of the train.

"No," I said and shook my head to emphasize the point. "I want to cover all this ground. Let's keep looking."

I was pretty sure the gold was not hidden near the ground we were now covering, but I liked the idea of practicing, of sharpening our looking skills. We had, I figured, no more than about three good hours of light. I was glad that we were moving to another area. It felt good to have a slightly distant goal in front of us.

At the top of the small rise, the tracks headed down again, and there—in all its glory—was another grain elevator with another Old Timer's Pig Feed sign in the far distance. It must have been a good two miles away. While the train had pulled away from us, it was crawling past the grain elevator. It couldn't have been going more than two or three miles an hour. If we walked at a rapid pace, we could easily catch up with it. I walked back up to the top of the embankment and stood in the middle of the tracks. I could feel the dissipating heat of the train. I crouched down and picked up two pieces of gravel, shook them in my hand, and tossed them out like dice.

"This is it," I said as much to myself as to Angel and Maybellene. "I can just feel it."

I began walking down the center of the tracks. After about ten minutes, I picked out the withered leaves of my branch. I was glad we'd practiced looking; the branch wasn't all that obvious. My heart pounded, and I felt dizzy as I ran toward the twig.

Sure enough, the belt led right to the branch. I briefly worried about giving away the location of the gold. I guess I still wasn't sure if I could trust either Maybellene or Angel. I'd have more money if I kept

242

it all. But you can't always live for greed, I thought. That's what Rotbart and Helmut did, and look where greed had gotten them. I pulled the branch out of the ground and began digging. Yes, I thought when I lifted out the pouch with its straps. It was just that simple, as if I only had to reach and wealth was there.

Heavier than I remembered, the coins jingled their little melody inside.

"So that's what all the fuss is about," Angel said when he saw the bag that I held up.

"That's it?" Maybellene asked as she caught up to us. She seemed astonished. "All those people dead over just that little bit of things."

As I held up the pouch against the green of the brush, as I thought about the gold against the sky, against what we'd all been through, Maybellene was right; it didn't seem like very much money at all. I mean, a few weeks ago, I'd been walking down the railroad tracks singing about $30,000 as if that were the Abraham Lincoln of money come to set the slaves of my little life free.

I pulled the leather straps between my thumb and forefinger several times to get the dirt off. I removed my shirt and then I put one strap around my neck and felt the satisfying thump as the bag hit my chest. I pulled the other strap tight and put my shirt back on. I cautiously stood up.

"I mean, after all our trouble," Maybellene said again, "that's it? It hardly seems worth it. Split three ways, that's not much over ten grand apiece. Honest work would be a better route to money than this. I'm not even sure this gold will pay expenses. I'm several thousand in the hole for cars alone."

I heard Maybellene, but I really wasn't listening. As if out of nowhere, the wind had picked up and was blowing over us. I stood up and wondered briefly where the wind, in fact, came from. The wind was a great mystery. I patted the bag of gold partly for luck and partly because I was thinking of Howard and the other guys. I had to do something remarkable with the money.

"Can desperadoes go to the bathroom, boss?"

"Sure, Angel, why not? We're not in a hurry any more. It's over."

I heard him crash into the brush, probably near the place where

243

McCoo had shot me. That seemed like years ago.

The wind was doing things to me, lifting me up and out of the ordinariness of it all. I thought about the unmarked place where I'd been shot and then continued on to think of all the unmarked places where good and bad things happened to man and beast.

I walked back up on the embankment and the tracks. A chill was coming in behind the gentle September wind, and evening was arriving.

I had done it, I supposed. I had captured the golden fleece. In this era, that had to count for something. Even though the fleece had turned out to be only a few gold coins, that gold had certainly ruled my life. I wonder what the original Jason would have thought. Our treasure probably wasn't worth a quest. It was merely a trip or two.

Maybellene was right. Our portions hardly covered expenses. I thought briefly of how it would have been without my two partners, but even having all the coins wouldn't have amounted to all that much. $30,000 just wasn't very much money.

I picked up some pieces of gravel along the track and was tossing them out into the brush to punctuate my thoughts when I saw the first shape moving along the tracks in the distance. It was hunched over, like an oversized raccoon. Then another one came up behind it. This time, I wasn't surprised.

"How's it going in there?" I yelled to Angel.

"Great. I'm having the first dump I've had in days. I'll be awhile. Why don't you and the lady just kiss a bit? I don't know about you, but some things are more demanding than dough."

Maybellene was walking along the bottom of the embankment. I could see the third shape out of the corner of my eye. The shapes were certainly still interested in the money. I kept throwing pieces of gravel in the woods. This time, however, I tried to hit Angel. I hoped that he still carried his gun.

"Maybellene," I whispered as loudly as I could, "Maybellene" She seemed to be studying the ground intently, as if she expected to find more gold.

The three shapes were humping along toward us, one behind the other. Maybellene was still looking at the ground. For a moment, I suspected her again of giving us away, but then I realized that she couldn't have. Unless she carried a secret radio transmitter in her shoe, she was just another innocent bystander.

It was amazing how fast those humping shadows came toward us. They stayed low and on their hands and knees, but they covered several hundred yards.

I felt oddly calm as they moved our way. I'd been through so many little events like this, I wasn't that worried, though it occurred to me that by now our enemies probably had both weapons and a serious purpose. I glanced down at the sack of gold. I doubted that anyone could see it under the folds of my shirt.

I could, I thought, throw the gold into the brush here. They'd certainly never find it, and maybe I wouldn't either, and we could all go on back to the usual evils of regular lives instead of having these contests over what really was a small amount of money.

The air was bright and clear. It was a September twilight with that hint of colder weather. We had, I guessed, a couple of hours until sunset.

I could have just run into the brush and headed north. I thought I had a fair chance of making it. After all, I'd practiced Dodge the Villain in the Bushes at the beginning of my adventure. If I escaped from here, I could have gone off to Chicago and resurrected my minor acting career.

What kept me there was, I guess, curiosity. I wanted to see what happened to us all. And love, too. When I glanced over at Maybellene, I felt warm. I didn't want anything bad happening to her.

While I crouched there tossing stones toward Angel and watching the three dark shapes coming toward us, I heard two sharp cracks, and everything seemed to stop. The shapes no longer moved. I held my breath. The evening breezes quit bringing in their taste of winter.

Two of the lumps stood up and began pointing toward the woods across the tracks from them. The third lump didn't move.

"Owen," Maybellene said as she came up beside me and crouched down, "what's going on?"

"Either Angel has a gun and is going after them or someone new is shooting up our friends."

245

We heard two more shots. The shapes dropped down and became lumps again.

We lay flat and edged our way backward down the embankment and into the brush and crawled inside far enough so that we were covered by the leaves. As soon as we were covered, I realized we'd made a terrible mistake. We were on the wrong side of the tracks. To get back to the car, we'd have to go back up and over the tracks.

We sat there for what seemed like hours. I pressed the flat of my hand so hard against the bag under my shirt that my hand fell asleep. On my knees, hand against my chest, I must've looked like someone who was simultaneously praying and pledging his allegiance.

"Now what?" Maybellene whispered. "We can't stay like this forever."

"I don't know, but I'd rather not stand up and ask any questions. I think we're trapped. Our car's on the other side of the tracks, and I don't want to risk going over those tracks, at least not in daylight. We'll have to see what happens. I wish Angel were here. He'd know what to do."

As I spoke that last sentence, I realized that I sounded like Howard. I supposed that's what really happens as we get older. We keep learning so much more until the world seems a confusing place where facts contradict each other with glee. No wonder religious people believe that a child will lead us. Children aren't so full of useless information.

Mary Lynn was past us before I heard the steps, which were barely a rattle of gravel as they went by above us. I recognized her from the back. The next set of footsteps was heavier and more tentative. We heard them coming ten yards away. They ran at first, crunching the gravel. Then they stopped and ran down to the bushes to check things out.

I looked behind us from my crouched position to see if we could move deeper into the brush. As I did, I twisted myself and fell over. Maybellene was helping me up when I saw the legs before me and then the gun. I didn't want to look any higher. I didn't want to know what came next.

The gun was aimed exactly at the middle of my chest when he yelled.

246

"Ja, here, in the bush he is, the one that took the gold, with the woman he is here, Rotbart."

My chest lifted and fell with each stuttering burst of the gun, and I waited for the end of it all. But my life didn't pass before my eyes. No, I heard the rattle of the bullets coming back to earth and felt the hot sting as one singed the back of my hand. It left a mark like a little red comet's tail. He had fired the gun above us into the air.

"So this is it," Maybellene said three or four times. I guess what had been a story was coming true for her. "I don't believe it. I really don't. I'm not going to die in the middle of nowhere for nothing."

"You might, you know." I tried to be funny when I said this, but I was pretty worried myself.

Helmut now stood with his back to us as he scanned the tracks for Rotbart. I patted my chest once for luck. The gold was still underneath my shirt. Then Rotbart was standing before us, with his jodhpurs, swagger stick, and grin. As usual, I had the urge to stand and salute, but Helmut didn't like the move I made to stand up and kicked my legs out from under me. I fell backwards again.

"Owen, I'm just delighted to see you. Yes, I am. It's been— what?— a month now since you left my estate. We've missed you. Yes, we have."

He held out a hand to help me. I was suspicious at first, but Helmut nudged me, and I grabbed his hand and stood up. My hamstrings began little spasms and threatened to topple me, but Helmut put a hammerlock under my arms and held me up. As he did so, the bag of gold swung out of my shirt.

Jokes weren't going to help Maybellene and me out of this. It really was possible that we might die in nowhere for nothing. Who'd ever find our bodies here?

Rotbart flicked the leather pouch with his swagger stick.

"Ah, but that's an old friend. You know, I've missed it. I was disappointed when we lost it and you, dear Owen. I had great plans for you. I really did. I wanted to make you a partner.

"We have another group of trainees at my estate now. Unfortunately we had to leave them while Mut and I went off to chase down this little bad debt of ours, dear friend. But they've come with their deposits, just as so many have come. We have another forty or fifty thousand

247

hanging from a pole in a leather bag. It happens over and over. You know, we haven't even started. There are so many cities we haven't even thought of. Owen, you would have done a wonderful job in our endeavors. You really would have, Owen. But now . . . ."

He shrugged, put the swagger stick in his belt, and lifted the pouch of gold from around my neck.

While Helmut pointed the gun at Maybellene and me, Rotbart set the bag on the ground and counted out the gold.

"We're missing some coins. Not bad. I hardly expected to get anything back, my dear Owen," he said as he looked up from his counting. "We've lost three coins, and I think that rather sharp-tongued young lady has walked out of here. I don't think that's so bad. Now let's take these folks back to the other bodies. If we're going to have a batch of dead ones, we should keep them together, don't you think?"

Helmut first shoved me and then Maybellene up the embankment.

"You know, my young friend," Rotbart said when we were all standing on the tracks, "you made quite a fool of me. Helmut was dead set against my telling you anything. He said you were a spy. He certainly was right. Come. Let's get going."

Helmut waved the gun at us and marched us back in the direction the shots had come from.

"I have a moral lesson for us all," Rotbart said.

The hardest part was seeing the ravens pecking away at the faces of McCoo and Pee Pole. Their eyes were gone, as if the gelatin of their sight had only been an appetizer. Their cheeks were full of holes.

Maybellene began gagging and then thought better of it. She took a deep breath and looked up at the last of the daylight.

"Will you just answer one question?" I asked. "If I'm going to die, I want to know how you came back here. Who sent you to the Rosedale Fair?"

"I thought you'd be surprised, Owen," Rotbart said. "I wish I had a picture of your expression when you realized that I was the clown at Dunk the Dumbo. Ah-huh, ah-huh, ah-huh.

"After you left Camp Fortitude, Owen, we went after you, but then we gave up on you and the money. I figured you'd never say anything to the police. Who'd believe such a story? So Mut and I and some of my faithful helpers went on to Milwaukee and collected our dues there. We had fifteen hands this time, loyal and true. Unfortunately, none of them died on the hike up to the house; the weather was cooler. We were working on this wonderful food poisoning that tastes like chocolate when the phone rang. It was some woman asking about gold. I thought it was a crank call, but she kept asking questions about me by name and South America. So I listened. I asked her how she got my number. This part will just slay you, Owen.

"She studied the map, she told me, and figured that I must be near one of about four towns. So she called up Information. It was just that simple. Louisiana only has one Area Code. She called the goddamned operator and got my number. I guess I was the only Jason Rotbart in all those towns.

"Anyway, she asked if I took a group of men to the Amazon for gold. I tried to figure what the call was about. She could've been someone from the police or the wife of someone in the group. I tried to make her talk, and finally she did. I think she was frustrated. She told how she'd found you and about the gold you claimed you'd hidden in Louisiana. She said she'd finally let you go in St. Louis, figuring you'd lead her back to the gold. She followed you. But instead of going to Louisiana, you went north to Illinois. She got impatient. She believed that I might know enough to make you talk, and she figured that half the gold is better than none, so she called me. She offered to split it with me if I would help her.

"As you know, Owen, I try not to be foolish, so I told her if we captured you, I could help her find the gold. We agreed to meet at the Fair. She told me that she would be the only dark-haired woman wearing a white hoop skirt walking around with a man from a motorcycle gang. Then, without saying goodbye, she just hung up. It was like getting a call from Mars, but I took her seriously. I've got some new assistants back at the estate, so I left them with my troops. We drove all night to get here. I wanted a little protection and a little theatre, so I rented the Dunk the Dumbo concession for $50 a day. I told its owner that I wanted to surprise a friend. Then I paid Pee Pole to check the highways for you and make sure you showed up at the Fair.

I think our Outlaw Indian friends did a good job, don't you? The surprise worked rather well, don't you think?"

He crossed his arms over his chest and smiled. The gesture was so familiar.

"So you're the famous Rotbart," Maybellene said. "The fabled Rotbart. Well, you can have the gold. I'm tired of it. It's cost too much money and too many lives, but now that you have the gold, why can't you go back to your estate and leave us alone? We can't hurt you anymore."

She started to walk down the embankment, in the direction of the car.

It was one of those moments. Rotbart let his arms fall; he appeared a little deflated. Helmut, who never seemed able to work without a script, looked anxiously at Rotbart for a clue about the next move. Maybellene stopped and turned around.

"Even your language has become ordinary," Maybellene said. "I expected grand ideas, not the greasy details of recovering thirty grand. All you are is the scout leader for a troop of losers. Bah," she said with finality and waved her hand as if dismissing him. "Come on, Owen, let's get out of here."

"Wait, you can't . . . ," Rotbart started to say as he bent over and picked up the sack of gold.

"Angel is standing right over there with a gun. He's a very accurate shot," Maybellene said.

We all looked across the tracks at the place she pointed to and studied the brush for a moment or two. I, for one, began to see him there.

"Bluffing our call, she is," Helmut said.

Rotbart looked closely, first at the gold, and then at Maybellene and me.

"I don't care," he said. "We have the gold. Let them go. They can't do us any harm, though, Owen, I must say I'm disappointed. You really would have made a marvelous partner in my little enterprise."

Maybellene flipped them both the bird and turned away. I stood there for a moment and felt just a little sad. Rotbart had the gold that Howard and I and Lucky and all the rest had put up along with our pathetic dreams. In some perverted way, though, he'd earned it. He was the clever and merciless one who gave a shape to our desire of becoming rich beyond our wildest dreams. He was the one who promised to take us into the jungle as paupers and brings us back as kings. Even though the promise was a lie, even though the dreamer only killed, I couldn't quite forget the dreams that newspaper ad had given me.

I was just about to turn away when the shot went through Helmut's chest.

Time seemed to slow up radically, as if everything had been chilled.

First I saw the shot. It was a white burst of light from the brush across the tracks. Then I heard it. It made a humming noise that stopped suddenly. Helmut looked surprised, the way you'd be if someone hit you sharply in the stomach. A brief part of a second later, I could see shreds of cloth being ripped away from his back, as if something were tearing its way out of him. He dropped his gun and flapped his hands above the entry wound in his chest as if he were trying to cool it off. While he did this, he looked down in astonishment.

His whole body began to shake as first a fine mist and then larger and larger pieces of his flesh spewed out of his back. He collapsed on top of his gun as if the wound had simply let the air out of his body.

While I was trying to figure all this out, Maybellene came from behind me, pushed me out of her way, kicked Helmut onto his side, and picked up his machine gun.

"How do you work this thing, Owen? How do you fire it?" She was yelling.

"Wait a minute," I said. My voice seemed to come from far away. "Hold it. Get the gold before you kill him."

I stood beside her and released what I thought was the safety on the gun. She fired a burst of rounds into the dirt beside Rotbart. The power of that gun surprised us. It looked like something from a toy factory, but the way it fired had real authority.

Maybellene took the gold from Rotbart and made him lay on the ground. She ran her hands over his body a couple of times and even squeezed him between his crotch.

"No gun, no nothing, Mr. Rotbart." She squeezed his testicles again, and he lurched upward but didn't say anything.

Angel was indeed our benefactor and came loping out of the brush and up the embankment.

"How about that, boss?" he asked. I almost expected him to bring out the gun and blow across the end of the barrel.

"Where'd you learn to shoot like that?" Maybellene asked.

"The same place that taught me how to trade cars."

The ravens had gathered in a large circle some ten feet from where we stood. They were patiently waiting to taste our friend Helmut. Keeping both guns pointed at Rotbart, we had him stand up and march down the embankment, through the brush and back onto the road.

Four cars were parked on the shoulder of the highway as if we all were a hunting party.

"Make sure that old Ford runs," Angel said to Maybellene. He seemed as if he knew what to do.

Maybellene started it up and drove it up the road a bit.

"Good," Angel said. "Very good. I hate to do this to perfectly good cars."

While I stood covering Rotbart with Angel's pistol, he went to the remaining three cars and, swinging the machine gun around like a hose, carefully shot up the tires, shattered the windshields, and filled the radiators full of holes. In a few moments, green and blue anti-freeze solutions began to run out from under three of the cars as if they suffered from the automotive equivalent of internal bleeding.

"Now what?" Maybellene asked as she came over to join us. "Shouldn't we kill Mr. Rotbart here?"

"No," I said, "I'm tired of the killing. Let him go. He can't hurt us anymore."

"Are you kidding?" Maybellene asked. "Are you kidding?" This time she shrieked the question. "Are you out of your mind? Letting him go would be like letting Nazis go. You can't do it. He'd a bad guy. He's got to be punished."

"The lady's right," Angel said. "He's got to pay, and it oughtn't to be any little payment. Death's too easy for him. We should get him tied up with the cops so his talk doesn't do him any good."

"That's a good idea," Maybellene said. "I like that."

"How about the woman?" Angel asked. "Shouldn't we go after her, too?"

"You're both right. We've got to do something about Rotbart. Otherwise he'll just go on with his game," I said. I felt very tired. The gold kept getting more and more expensive. "But we can't revenge all the evil of this story. If we did, we'd have to punish ourselves. No, forget about Mary Lynn. After all, she sort of saved my life once. And I have an idea about Rotbart."

I walked over to the Ford, took the key out of the ignition, and opened the trunk. Sure enough—along with two spare tires, various wires, and oily car parts—there were several feet of clothes line.

"Can you tie him up?" I asked Angel. "Maybellene can hold the gun."

I emptied the trunk while Angel tied up Rotbart's hands and feet. Then Angel and I held on to his arms as we made him hobble over to the Ford.

"In you go, my friend. In you go." He looked startled, as if he couldn't believe what I was saying. "I'm not kidding," I said as I grabbed his feet and heaved him into the trunk.

"You can't do this," he shouted as I closed the lid.

"What's your idea?" Maybellene asked.

"Let's take him back to Camp Fortitude in Louisiana and call the cops. Just what Angel said. I'm sure there are enough bodies buried on that property to keep the police busy for months."

"Can he breathe in there?" she wondered.

"With all the rust holes? Of course he can," I said. "Besides, would it be a great loss if he died?"

I put the sack of gold around my neck, and we drove away.

# Thirty-Eight

**WE RETURNED TO ST. LOUIS**, where we cashed in a few gold coins with Mr. Johnson. Since we had more money this time, his eyebrows went up and down furiously.

Then we drove to Louisiana. I wanted to take the back roads, but Angel figured that it didn't make any difference if we were caught.

"If we're stopped by the police," he said, "we just tell them the story. If we're found by friends of the guy in the trunk, we kill them. I vote for the fastest trip we can take. I want this over with."

We drove in shifts and got into Louisiana about fourteen hours later. We went to the area near Leesville, bought a county map, and tried to cover the roads that crossed US 171.

Eventually we found Camp Fortitude. The bus with the windows painted out sat beside an ordinary country lane. That bus looked evil to me.

I drove back to Leesville, so we could check the routes and give the police exact directions. Then we returned to that lane and drove up to Rotbart's estate. I was so apprehensive as we stopped in front of the main house that I felt as though my heart were drumming throughout my body.

The black cook was in the kitchen. I'm not sure that she remembered who I was, but she refused to tell me where the troops were. When I told her that the police would soon be coming, she moved with an agility I hadn't seen before.

Angel and I hauled Rotbart out of the trunk and left him tied up on the ground. Maybellene covered him with a gun while I went inside the house and called, first, the county police and, then, the FBI in New Orleans. I figured we had about twenty minutes to escape.

We went back to Leesville and, sure enough, met four sheriff cars headed toward Camp Fortitude. Just to be safe, I called the *Times-Picayune* from a pay phone in Leesville. I gave a reporter named Ralph Davenport directions to the place where we'd buried Merle.

# Thirty-Nine

**THERE ISN'T MUCH MORE TO TELL.**

We drove to New Orleans and found the pink Edsel where I'd left it. Improbably, the keys were still inside the hubcap. It started on the first crank. While crime might be everywhere, it certainly hadn't sought this car out.

Finding Sylvie Mae was tougher. I figured I owed her half my share of the gold. With Angel driving the Edsel and me and Maybellene leading in the old Ford, we went back north to Alice. It took hours of crisscrossing the area around there until I found her road, but I couldn't locate the signs. After driving up and down that road, I found what I thought was the entrance to the Pink Flamingo.

Soon as I stopped the car and got out, an awful suspicion hit me. The air smelled of wet, burnt wood. I walked up the old trail and found that Sylvie Mae's Tarot-card fortune had come true. The place had burned to the ground. The charred skeletons of the buildings and the greasy looking water in the moat were the sole remaining testimonies to the best dancer in Miss Vickerey's class and the man who designed a version of Atlantis.

I checked the odometer and looked for the signs, but they'd been torn down. As far as the world was concerned, Sylvie Mae and DuWayne had never existed. I was sure she was dead.

I was sad, but Angel, ever the realist, wondered if he could keep Sylvie Mae's car. He said it was the most beautiful car he'd ever seen.

Maybellene, also a realist, said that we ought to split everything up then and there. So we did.

We had two cars, ninety gold coins, and some cash. Angel said he'd be more than happy with ten coins and the car. He said he thought that was all the wealth he should have. He also told us to get on with the love stuff.

As he drove off, he yelled back, "It's been fun, boss."

It was quiet when Maybellene and I left the remains of the Pink Flamingo. We had our own thoughts, but I think we were separately thinking the same thoughts of Sylvie Mae.

And that's how we kept going in the real adventure most of us have, the one where two people try to stay in love.

We drove to Chicago, where Maybellene and I planned on starting over.

The story of Rotbart and Camp Fortitude made the front pages for a while. The authorities found thirty-five skeletons. Ralph Davenport, in stories that eventually won him a Pulitzer Prize, got most of the details right. Rotbart claimed to be a victim of an out-of-work actor named Owen Hill. At first, Rotbart was thought to be the sole survivor, but the police found the black cook, who got the bad guys in their proper roles. The last of Ralph Davenport's stories I saw was near the back of the *Chicago Tribune* one Saturday morning. Rotbart had received another stay of execution. There was no mention of Owen Hill.

Maybellene and I have been a couple now longer than I thought possible. Our children are Howard (3) and Sylvie Mae (5). One of Howard's friends tried to call him Howie, and the little guy got very upset.

I tried to be an actor, but I was so worried about becoming famous and attracting attention I gave it up. I sell real estate and Maybellene teaches English at the high school. While we thought about what to do with the gold, it went up to $800 an ounce and made us richer than we ever thought possible. We spent most of the gold on a down payment for our house and saved the rest for a rainy day. If we'd done anything too dramatic, word might have gotten out. Then gold dropped in value, so we didn't pay much attention any more. We gave up greed, the way people give up alcohol or cigarettes.

After all our work, though, we figured we had to do something special with the coins, so I finally had a man melt down four of them and use the gold to coat the bottom of a silver serving platter, the kind of thing you put the roast beef on for Sunday dinner. I had a jeweler engrave the names of Howard and Lucky and Tony and Murphy and Artie and Tyrone and Merle and Haskel and Stanley and me on the gold. When friends come for dinner, I tell them I'm the sole survivor of my unit. I guess that's true enough, and it makes me feel as though I've got me and my fellow adventurers in the loving circle of a family at long last.

Maybellene thinks I'm being sentimental, but then Maybellene uprooted that damned clematis plant every time we moved. She plants it by the light of the moon. I don't know what the neighbors think, but I think that old folk tale has something to it. That clematis gets bigger every year.